"I've studied your daddy résumé, and I've been thinking about it."

"And?" Jake slapped one slice of bread over the other. Placing the sandwich on a paper plate, he turned to her.

"Well, I really need to know you a lot better, to begin with." Harley paused. "And I've got two conditions that are absolutely nonnegotiable."

Jake swallowed hard and crossed the kitchen. "Okay, come and sit at the table and tell me what they are."

She followed him to the dining room, sinking into the chair he pulled out for her. Once he was seated, she nudged the sandwich, breaking off small pieces of the crust.

"Well?" he prompted.

"First, you marry me for the duration. You can divorce me later. I'll sign whatever prenuptial agreement you want, but I will not bring an illegitimate child into the world."

"I'll consider it. The second term?"

"No artificial insemination. We make this baby the old-fashioned way."

He was grateful she'd waited until he was sitting down.

Dear Reader,

I grew up in a house full of people who loved reading. Trips to the library and bookstore were frequent. There's something magical about a book, isn't there? You can go so many places and meet interesting people....

It's magical on this side of a book, too. And talk about dreams really coming true? You're holding my dream in your hand right now. I hope you enjoy reading it as much as I did writing it.

Harley Emerson is a female mechanic with a criminal record and a deep desire to be somebody—somebody else. Jake Manning is an architect with a plan for a child of his own. But when he chooses Harley as the mother of his child, she throws a wrench or two into his plan—starting with a marriage of convenience and an old-fashioned conception. She insists on these terms to protect the child from society's sneers—something Harley knows too much about. What will happen when she realizes that this sham marriage and family is her real dream? Do dreams ever come true for someone like her?

This story takes place in my adopted hometown of Erie, Pennsylvania. My family and I have called Erie home for several years now and we love it. Even when it's dreary. Even when the winters seem to go on forever. Summers in Erie are wonderful, though. And if you ever get a chance to visit, don't forget to take in a sunset from the Peninsula. You'll see why Harley liked them so much.

I'd love to hear from you. Please visit me on the Web at www.susangable.com and e-mail me (Susan@susangable.com). Or write to me at P.O. Box 9313, Erie, PA 16505-8313.

Thanks for being part of my dream come true!

Susan Gable

The Baby Plan
Susan Gable

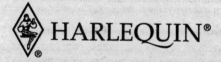

HARLEQUIN®

TORONTO • NEW YORK • LONDON
AMSTERDAM • PARIS • SYDNEY • HAMBURG
STOCKHOLM • ATHENS • TOKYO • MILAN • MADRID
PRAGUE • WARSAW • BUDAPEST • AUCKLAND

ISBN 0-373-71103-4

THE BABY PLAN

Copyright © 2002 by Susan Guadagno.

Visit us at www.eHarlequin.com

Printed in U.S.A.

To my parents, Allen and Bettylou Ackerson,
for raising me with a love of books and the knowledge
that I can do anything I set my mind to.

To my husband, Tom, and son, TJ, for tolerating life with a
writer. Thanks for your support and faith. I love you guys!

So many people helped educate and support me in my
writing. Without them, this book would not be. So I'd like to
thank Carolyn Greene, Marge Smith, Holly Jacobs, all the
Ditzy Chix, the Cata-rommers and Pennwriters.

Sus Harmon, for catching all those little things.

My cps, Lisa Childs, Kimberly Duffy
and especially Jen McLean, who was there from
the conception of this book to the delivery.

Rick Prokop, Chair of Dahlkemper School of Business
at Gannon University, Erie, PA, for helping me learn
exactly what a business degree requires. Harley attends
a fictional university, so her complaints about her classes
are figments of my imagination and no reflection
on Gannon's fine faculty.

CHAPTER ONE

"YOU HAVEN'T SAID A WORD since you got in the truck. What's bugging you?"

Jake Manning turned from watching the small, closely packed houses slip past the window to stare at his younger brother. "Just wondering about the car."

"Bull."

"Is that a cop's intuition?"

"No, a brother's," Dusty said as he lowered the visor to block the afternoon sun.

Jake ended up studying the photo of Dusty's very pregnant wife, Kate. Beside it was a laminated sonogram picture of their soon-to-be-born son. Perfect. Just what he needed right now. "I got a call from my lawyer today."

"It wasn't good news, huh?"

"No. The birth mother decided she really didn't like the idea of a single man adopting her baby. She wondered if I was gay or something."

Dusty choked off a short burst of laughter. "Sorry. I know it's not funny, but the idea of you being gay... I'm sorry about the adoption." He cursed under his breath. "That's the second one. Damn, that bites."

The house just wasn't the same without a child in it. He'd practically raised Dusty and Mel, his younger half siblings, from the time they were born—and taken on even more responsibility after their mother had left them to "find herself." He'd become their legal guardian when their father died. With Mel and Dusty both adults and on their own, Jake was at loose ends. He missed having someone in his life who needed him.

Of course, he'd foolishly assumed his marriage would take care of that. After the divorce, he'd enrolled in the Big Brother program and found great satisfaction in it.

The first adoption attempt had involved a four-year-old boy. Jake had met Austin's social worker through Big Brothers. He'd spent time with the boy every weekend for three months. It had damn near broken both their hearts when the social worker decided to place him in a home with both a mother and a father. After that, he'd investigated private adoption—and now that had turned out to be a bust as well.

His lawyer had offered him two new words of advice: surrogate mother. At least that way, Jake would have some rights as the child's biological father. He wasn't sure about it, though; he had a whole lot of thinking to do before he could make that decision.

Lifting one hand from the wheel of the truck, Dusty slugged Jake on the shoulder. "Hey, I've said all along you don't need another kid. You've still got me."

Jake arched an eyebrow at the man ten years his junior. Hard to believe his little brother was all grown up and expecting a baby of his own. "That's supposed to comfort me?"

"What? You didn't have enough headaches raising me and Melanie? You need a few more?" Dusty eased the truck into the garage's parking lot.

It wasn't the headaches of raising a family Jake missed, though God knows that becoming sole custodian of his two half siblings when he'd been only twenty-two himself had brought on plenty of them. It was the hugs he missed, the companionship, having someone to teach. He'd taken Austin to the zoo and the Erie Children's Museum, to a SeaWolves baseball game. "You and Mel are all grown up and moved out now, Dusty. Mel's got Peter and the twins. You've got Kate and my nephew-to-be."

"And you've got a bad case of empty nest syndrome. I didn't think men—especially thirty-five-year-old men—got that."

Jake slid from the pickup, slammed the door, then turned to lean in the open window, shaking his head. A cool breeze stirred the dirt around his feet, swirling it into the air. Off in the distance, Lake Erie shimmered beneath a perfect end-of-May sky, blue with puffy white clouds—the kind of day that made the long winters bearable. "I should've let you raise yourselves. Or maybe handed you over to a pack of wolves. Wait here for a few minutes, huh, Dust? Just in case the car's not ready."

"Sure."

"And be careful out there tonight." His brother loved his job on the police force, but Jake frequently wished he'd chosen a less-dangerous career. Though Erie, Pennsylvania, ranked as one of the safer small cities for cops, one of Dusty's co-workers had taken a bullet last week—fortunately, not fatally.

"Always am."

Jake tapped the side of the truck, then sauntered away, heading for the office. The open front door led to a small, dingy room divided by a long counter. A teenage girl with a round, pimply face perched on a stool behind it, chubby legs propped on the windowsill. She clutched a magazine sporting the latest hot boys' band on the cover; her jaws cracked a piece of gum.

"I'm Jake Manning. I'm here about my Mustang. It's supposed to be ready."

The magazine slipped from her fingers and her feet dropped off the sill as she gave him a wide-eyed once-over. "The M-M-Mustang? Uh, oh, yeah, it's in the bay. Harley'll explain it to ya." She disappeared below the counter, presumably to retrieve her magazine, ending their conversation.

"Thanks so much," he muttered, crossing the threshold from the office into the actual garage. He passed a sign warning No Customers Beyond This Point. Nice to know they took their safety measures so seriously.

The odor of grease and exhaust fumes lingered in the air, despite the open overhead doors. His old Mustang occupied the first bay, and Jake paused to run a loving hand along its white hood. The car had been a gift from his stepfather, whom everybody called Bud, for high school graduation, and he had every intention of keeping it forever. If only he had someone to pass it down to. He sighed and glanced at the remaining two bays but saw no sign of the mechanic, only a Stingray in the next slot.

"Harley?" he called.

"Under here" came a muffled voice from the direction of the cherry-red sports car.

Jake crossed behind the Mustang to discover a pair of work boots protruding from beneath the 'Vette. The boots twitched in time to the music drifting from a classic rock station. Billy Joel crooned about his uptown girl and Jake's mouth tightened. Uptown girls—or at least uptown girl wannabes, like his ex-wife, Stacy—were better forgotten.

He bent over and rapped lightly on the car's side. "Harley? I'm here for my Mustang. What was wrong with it?"

"I replaced the starter and a worn fan belt, and gave her a tune-up. She should run fine for you now."

The mechanic's sultry voice jolted him, and he glanced at the feet again. Their small size confirmed his suspicion—a woman lay beneath the car, a woman with a decidedly sexy voice. Jake waited, but no further conversation emerged. He wanted to hear that provocative voice again. "Is there anything else? Who do I pay? The charming young woman in the front office?"

"No, Ned's in the back. Move that 'Stang out first,

'cause I've got another car that needs to go in that bay.''

"No problem. Thanks.'' He straightened.

"You're welcome.''

She certainly had a way with words. The brevity of the conversation heightened the impact of her delivery. He shrugged, annoyed at his own reaction. Women were generally more trouble than anything else, but he still had an appreciation for them, especially a woman with a voice like that.

Jake wandered back to his car, opened the door, then eased himself into the black vinyl bucket seat. He turned the key and grinned when the engine caught right away. Cocking his head, he basked in the idle purr. She hadn't sounded this good in years.

He threw the car into reverse, waving his brother off before parking in the lot behind the pumps. The interior of the car sparkled, and the engine's rumble pleased him as much as the mechanic's lovely voice.

She deserved a tip. Jake pulled his wallet from his pocket, then riffled through the bill compartment. The twenty he wanted eluded him, so he stretched across the seat to pop open the glove box.

He retrieved the small black binder he used to organize the Mustang's receipts and jammed his fingers into the back pouch. Empty.

Jake peered inside. The twenty-five bucks in five-dollar bills he kept as an emergency stash were no longer there. He did a quick search of the rest of the binder, though he knew with absolute certainty where the money should have been.

His spare cell phone was also missing.

Jake leaped from the car and stalked across the parking lot. He circumvented a large patch of sawdust on the floor of the last bay and hammered on the office door. What was the guy's name again? Oh, right, the owner of the garage. "Ned!"

"Keep your pants on. Come in before ya bust my door down."

Jake shoved open the office door. Stale air laced with the smell of cheap cigars and even cheaper booze permeated the room. The small desktop fan served only to spread the stench.

Ned folded his hands behind his head and leaned backward, causing the chair he occupied to squeak in protest. His shirt buttons strained to keep the dingy white garment closed across an enormous beer belly. "What can I do for ya?"

"I'm Jake Manning. That's my Mustang your mechanic just repaired."

"Yeah, the one towed in a few days ago." The man swiveled on his chair, then dug into a lopsided pile of papers on a shelf behind his desk. When he turned his attention back to Jake, he clutched an invoice. "Here it is."

Jake accepted the document. Teeth clenched, he scanned the bill, certain a shop that robbed clients' cars would also steal from them in more devious ways. "This seems reasonable," he murmured.

"Of course. This shop ain't into rape and pillage of its customers, mister."

Jake glared at him over the invoice. "But theft from vehicles is standard procedure?"

"What?" The man's face grew pale and he slammed a fist on the desktop, scattering papers. "Damn it to hell! What's missing?"

"Twenty-five bucks in cash and a cell phone."

The owner muttered a few choice curses and lurched to his feet, brushing past Jake to stand in the doorway. "Harley! Get your butt in here now."

Jake grimaced. *Women. Can't trust 'em with your car—or your heart.* Still, he eagerly awaited the opportunity to glimpse the "butt" Ned had just summoned to the office. If it matched the voice, she'd have a sweet rear end—mechanically speaking, of course.

"I'm really sorry about this, Mr. Manning." The shop owner lowered himself back into the creaking chair.

Several minutes ticked by before footsteps announced Harley's arrival. She entered the room, wiping her fingers on a rag, then glanced at Jake, giving him a tentative smile.

Emerald eyes, the most vibrant green he could ever remember seeing, twinkled at him. "How's the car sound?"

Jake surveyed her. A baseball cap proclaiming Ned's Garage covered her head, but several long wisps of wheat-colored hair escaped, trailing down across her cheek. A small streak of grease on her makeup-free face added to a waifish appearance. The gray-and-black coveralls sagged over most of her frame, but fit snugly across the chest.

Ned said, "This is not about the car, Harley. This is about theft."

Harley Emerson looked from the sky-blue eyes of the Mustang's owner to her boss. A tight fear twisted her stomach when Ned levered himself up from his chair to swagger to the front of the desk.

"I warned you when I hired you, one wrong move and you were out of this shop. Now return Mr. Manning's money and his phone and get your sorry butt outta here."

As the blood drained from her head, Harley had to support herself against the doorway. "What are you talking about?"

"I'm talking about theft, you no-good ex-con, something you know all about."

Harley swung her gaze back to the blue-eyed man. He studied her intently. "I didn't take anything from your car! I swear it."

"You're the only one around this shop with a record. Now, I mean it. You return this man's property and get the hell out. You're fired!"

The whispers and cold hands of her past were clutching her life once again. Despair welled up inside Harley. She'd pay for the court's mistake repeatedly, it seemed. The people who said she'd never amount to anything would be correct. "Whatever happened to innocent until proven guilty?" Yeah, right. Who was *she* kidding? Innocent didn't mean squat. The sensation of being railroaded was a familiar one.

"You've been tried and convicted." Ned jabbed a fat, sausage-shaped finger in her direction. "Them's my coveralls and I want 'em."

"*Those* are," she corrected him, tugging at the zipper. She peeled the coveralls off her body, balancing on one foot to draw the leg over her work boot, then repeating the awkward process.

The car-owner's stare burned her skin as his eyes raked over her body. A tingling sensation followed the path they blazed and a rush of sexual energy charged the foul air of Ned's office.

What the hell was wrong with her? Accused of theft, fired from the job she so desperately needed, and she stood here, melting beneath the gaze of a complete stranger? Okay, so he had the best-looking chassis she'd laid eyes on in quite some time, what with his broad shoulders and narrow waist—but really!

She needed to get out more. Or have her head examined. Besides, the khaki dress slacks, blue-checked, button-down shirt and tie indicated he was way out of her league. A man like that would only want one thing from her.

Harley tossed the coveralls in a heap at Ned's feet. "There. I suppose you'll want your hat, too?" She whipped off the cap and flung it onto the pile of clothing. Her hair, pulled back in a ponytail, spilled down onto her neck from its previous position on top of her head.

The car-owner cleared his throat. "Look, I realize I'm the victim here, but do you have any proof that she's the one who stole my things?"

Harley shot him a grateful glance.

"She's got a record, mister. I told her when I hired her, the first time anything went missing or the cops came sniffing around, she was out. Now, something's gone missing, so she's out. I got a reputation to protect."

"Reputation? Ned, your reputation isn't worth a rat's ass without me. See the 'Vette?" Harley pointed toward the garage. "That's here because of me, because of *my* reputation, not yours. All the other classics in here recently? Because of me."

If only her entire reputation was as good as her work reputation, she'd be in great shape. Well, almost. Being a mechanic wasn't exactly a socially acceptable position for a woman. Someday she'd be able to hold her head up; someday she'd prove herself to all the people who said Harley Emerson would never make it.

"So you say. Good mechanics are easy to find. I'll replace you by Thursday."

"Not at the pathetic rate you pay me!"

The Mustang's owner took a step toward the desk. "Look, you two, I really don't want to get involved in your squabble. Ned, let's take care of my bill. I'll deduct the cash and the value of the cell phone from the total amount, and we'll be square." He retrieved a pen from his pocket and scribbled quick calculations on his invoice.

Harley stared at him. When he lifted his head and their eyes met, for a moment she thought she saw compassion. But seconds later, his expression hardened. She dropped her gaze to the pile of clothing at Ned's feet. "Ned, please, I didn't do it. Don't fire me. I need this job. I've got bills to pay."

"That's right, babe. You need *me*. I don't need *you*. I gave you a chance and you spit in my face."

"You owe me for yesterday and today." Harley raised her chin defiantly and commanded her quivering insides to settle down.

Ned bent over the desk and rummaged in a drawer, then handed her a pile of wrinkled bills. "That should cover it. I don't ever want to see you around here again."

Harley inspected the money, then crammed it into the pocket of her denim shorts. How often had she been sent packing from one place or another? Too many to count.

She stretched out her hand to place her palm on Manning's forearm. Soft, dark hair grew there, and her fingertips skimmed over it.

He paused in the act of writing out a check to glance at her.

"I'm sorry about your things. I didn't take them." She lowered her head and turned on her heel.

Her slumped shoulders and downcast eyes as she slunk from the office triggered a surge of guilt in Jake. He moved to the doorway to watch her slowly cross the bay. She stopped to kick the pile of sawdust, raising a cloud in the shop. He chuckled. There was spirit buried beneath the defeat.

A female mechanic who had a real way with classic cars. Fascinating. And she was a looker, too. Her cut-off shorts clung to a well-curved rear and exposed legs that went on forever until they met the work boots. He felt a rush of physical attraction.

He wasn't looking for a woman—not for that, anyway. But she was now out of a job because of him. And he believed her claims of innocence, based on the way she'd met his eyes when she'd apologized.

As she gathered up a few tools from a workbench, Jake turned back into the office. He tossed the check onto the desk. ''I won't be recommending your shop.''

He hustled from the garage in time to see her get into a slightly battered silver Toyota pickup truck with a black cap on the back. He slid behind the Mustang's wheel, intent on learning more about this interesting woman.

THE SCENT OF FRESH COOKIES wafted from the bakery aisle, and Harley's mouth watered. Tempting, but not on the list right now. She fingered the crumpled bills in the pocket of her shorts and scanned the price stickers on the shelf. She grabbed a large plastic jar of store-brand peanut butter.

''You little bastard!''

The harsh words were followed by the sound of a stinging slap. Harley flinched. The jar slipped from her hand, clattering to the tile floor.

She whirled in the direction of the jellies—and saw a little boy in a private-school uniform dodge another blow from an angry hand.

Her feet automatically propelled her toward the ugly scene.

"Maaa!" the child wailed. "Don't. I'm sorry!"

"I said not to open those cookies! Don't you ever listen to me?"

Harley planted herself next to the cart and waited.

The woman, clad in tennis whites and expensive sneakers, snatched the package of cookies from the child and hurled them into the cart. She did a double take, then frowned at Harley. "What are you staring at?"

"Not much."

The woman raised carefully plucked eyebrows. "Are you judging me?" She gazed down at Harley's feet, then slowly upward. "*You* presume to judge *me?*"

"Appearances can be deceiving." Harley shoved her hands into her pockets.

"Of course they can. And underneath that appearance, you're actually a Harvard graduate with a degree in child psychology." The woman grabbed the little boy by the arm. "Let's go. And next time, you listen to me or you'll really be sorry when we get home."

As the pair turned the aisle corner, the boy looked back over his shoulder at Harley, a tear dripping down his cheek. Her chest tightened, empathy for the child mingling with remembered pain of her own.

Who was she to think she could interfere? Besides, getting involved with a case like that was a risk; the child could be removed from his home. And she knew from firsthand experience that the state's idea of a better situation wasn't always so.

Foster homes could be hell.

Maybe she'd saved the kid from one more slap. That was something, wasn't it?

Harley sighed and turned, heading back down the aisle to retrieve her peanut butter from the floor. Twenty-seven years old, and she couldn't even help a child. She still struggled to help herself.

Sometimes she wondered if the words *not good enough* were stamped on her forehead.

Why did people have children they didn't want? Kids deserved loving homes, where they were cherished and cared for properly.

For sure, she wouldn't be having a kid of her own. The world was too cruel. Besides, she'd never be able to provide the ideal home she'd created in her childish dreams.

SEVERAL DAYS LATER, Jake sat in his home office, which he used a lot less now that his architectural firm could afford a downtown office. Cradling the phone between his shoulder and ear, he reached for a sheet of paper and a pencil, then laid the paper on his stepfather's old drafting table and copied the information spewing from the receiver. "Slow down, Dusty. E-m-e-r-s-o-n? Okay, what else did you find out?"

"Positive criminal record. Busted four years ago."

"Let me guess, grand theft auto?"

"No, but close. Garage that employed her at the time was running a chop-shop. She got caught in the sweep. Insisted she had no idea what was going on after hours."

"What do you think?"

"Jake, they all claim they're innocent."

Maybe she is. "What happened then?"

"First offense. Sentenced to probation and community service. The judge told her to straighten out her act. Told her if she came before his court again, she'd do time."

Jake used the sharpened pencil to scratch behind his ear. "And since then?"

"Not so much as a parking ticket."

That said more to him than the fact that she had a record in the first place. "Hmm...okay. Phone number?"

"No phone. Address is in one of the seamier sections of town."

Jake jotted down the rest of the stuff his brother read off to him, then dropped the pencil into an old coffee mug on the desk.

"Jake?"

"Hmm? I'm just thinking."

"Uh-oh, I recognize that tone. Don't you dare."

Toenails clicked along the wooden floor beside his desk, and Jake suddenly found himself with a lapful of dog. "Benji, get down." He fumbled with the telephone while gently returning the animal to the floor. "Not when I'm at the desk. You know the rules."

The wiry-haired mongrel cocked his head, offering a quizzical look made all the more intriguing because he had only one ear. Jake snapped his fingers and pointed at the floor. Benji sneezed, turned in a circle, then settled down by Jake's feet.

"Sorry, Dusty, you were saying?"

"You don't need any more strays in your life. Two dogs and assorted cats are more than enough. Stay away from this woman, Jake."

"Only one cat now. Mel inherited the other two. And you watch it or I'll come over tomorrow, take you out back and whup you. I'm the one who's supposed to be giving you advice, not the other way around."

"Just practicing. I'll be a daddy soon, remember?"

How could he forget? "I remember." He anticipated the arrival of Dusty and Kate's baby almost as much as they did. But their baby wouldn't fill the emptiness in *his* life, *his* home.

For a moment, he listened to the silence, emphasized by the ticking of the mantel clock.

He glanced up to the picture of Austin and him that hung over his desk on the wood-paneled den wall. It'd been taken by Mel at the Erie Zoo. The little boy stood on a tall flower planter, one arm looped around Jake's neck, a mint-chocolate-chip ice cream cone clutched in the other hand.

Jake sighed. "Thanks for the help, Dust. You take

care of Kate and my nephew-to-be, and I'll talk to you tomorrow.''

"Jake?''

"Yes?''

"Nothin'.''

Jake smiled slightly at what had begun as a bedtime ritual when seven-year-old Dusty had become too cool to confess love to his big brother anymore. "Back at you.''

"One more thing.'' Dusty cleared his throat. "I hope I'm as good at raising my son as you were at raising me.''

The phone disconnected—his little brother wasn't any good at what he called "sappy stuff,'' and that was as close to sappy as he'd ever gotten. But Jake couldn't think of a nicer thank-you. He hung up the receiver, still staring at Austin's photo on the wall.

A surrogate mother. That had been his lawyer's latest advice. He looked over at the stack of papers on his desk. He'd downloaded a bunch of articles from the Internet. There was one question they didn't answer, though. How the hell was he supposed to find and choose a woman to carry a baby for him? A woman who could give up her child? Generally those were the kind of women he avoided. Women like his own mother, who'd walked out on them when Jake was twelve. Dusty had only been two, Mel six.

The paper with the notes on Harley Emerson fluttered to the floor, and he bent to retrieve it. Now, there was another problem. Guilt over Harley's lost job still plagued him. But maybe this problem was more easily solved than the question of a surrogate. In fact, maybe there was one solution to both....

Nah. He shook his head. He shouldn't be thinking this way, not for a second. His surrogate should be a woman he wouldn't be tempted to care about—to fall for. He'd simply find out whether or not she had a new job. If she said yes, he could put aside his guilt. If she said no...

CHAPTER TWO

HARLEY NEEDED AN ANSWER but doubted the universe was in the mood to supply her with one. Now that she was without a job, her practically nonexistent savings wouldn't last long. Every extra cent she'd earned over the last seven years had gone to college tuition and books, the expenses of her climb to a better life. The budget would have to be trimmed again. Not that there was much left to trim.

Exhaling loudly, she slapped the checkbook shut and tossed it on top of the pile of bills.

Some days it wasn't worth getting out of bed, and this was one of them. She'd tried two other garages today, but no one needed—or wanted—a mechanic with a record. To make things worse, Ned had put the word out that he'd fired her for theft from a customer's car. Even with her skills, no one wanted her.

Unless she was willing to work in a chop-shop. Then she'd find another job easily. But she'd been innocent the first time, and she wasn't knowingly going to put her neck on the line. The slammer wasn't a place she wanted to visit ever again.

So much for next semester's tuition. That was out of the question.

She reached up to grab her ponytail, freeing her hair from the tight rubber band. The long strands cascaded down around her shoulders and she ran both hands through it. The slight pain as it returned to its natural state only heightened her sense of misery.

Harley pushed the stool back from the scarred wooden counter that separated her kitchen from the living area. One of the legs caught in a crack along the faded linoleum, nearly tipping her off. "Good, fall and break something. Add more bills to the pile. Great." She crossed the room.

The rust-and-rose-colored cushions of the battered old couch echoed her weary sigh as she collapsed onto them. White cotton curtains stirred with the breeze, while outside the window magenta streaks heralded another spectacular Erie sunset. Maybe she'd haul herself down to the Peninsula to watch. She propped herself up on her elbow to evaluate the timing, then slumped back down, deciding she couldn't make it before the sun actually set.

Closing her eyes, Harley summoned the image of the Mustang's handsome owner, an image she'd toyed with ever since their disastrous meeting. While he'd been partly responsible for her firing, she wasn't mad at him. No, she was angry with Ned and whoever had lifted Manning's cash and phone.

Manning. A perfect name for someone who was one hundred percent certifiably all man. In her mind, Harley took a step closer to him. His dark walnut hair brushed the collar of his shirt and his summer-sky eyes sparked with the knowledge of the chemistry between them. His scent, a spicy cologne, conveyed strength, as did the muscles of his exposed biceps. The loose-fitting shirt piqued her curiosity about the secrets it hid. Did he have a chest as muscular as those biceps suggested? Exactly what kind of horsepower did the man have under his hood?

Even more than the physical tug between them, the flash of compassion she'd seen flash in his eyes intrigued her. In her experience, compassion was hard to come by in this harsh world.

The sharp odor of marijuana wafted into the room, drifting along the breeze. The downstairs neighbors were starting their weekend early. Soon they'd be buzzed. She climbed off the couch to slam the window shut with a bang. The thin glass rattled.

Denied the movement of the breeze, the tiny, second-story apartment suddenly seemed even smaller. A hardcover copy of the latest Janet Evanovich mystery lay on Harley's coffee table—made from an old wire spool with a tablecloth thrown over it. *The library. That's where I'll go.* She could return the novel and check out the on-line classifieds. She scooped up the book, then grabbed her small canvas purse. Loud rap music from the house two doors down vied with the Spanish dance music from across the street as she stepped onto her porch. Harley tested the lock, then whirled to begin a careful descent of the uneven steps.

Halfway down, a blur of green polo shirt hurtled in the opposite direction. She skidded to a halt and grabbed for the banister to avoid crashing into someone. Rough wood scraped her palm; her hip banged against the railing. A splintering crack sounded, and the banister gave way. Harley found herself teetering on the edge of the stairs, arms flailing wildly.

A hand closed around her wrist and yanked her back to safety. Jake Manning's blue eyes, wide with concern, stared down at her. "Are you okay?"

What's it to you? sprang to mind first, but she bit back the retort and nodded. She peered over the edge of the steps. The shattered railing lay on the dirt and gravel below. The library book had bounced off the garbage cans beneath the stairs and landed on the narrow, newly greened strip that passed for a lawn. "Good. The lid was on."

"The lid?"

She'd forgotten all about him—odd, since the man still had hold of her wrist. She tugged it free. "On the garbage. I don't want the book to get ruined." One more thing she would've had to pay for. As it was, she knew that the landlord—who was really just one rung above a slumlord—was going to expect her to cover the damage to the railing. She sighed.

"But you're okay, right?"

Her hand stung, and Harley winced. She sank to the stairs, careful to stay on the inside, then examined her palm closely. "No, dammit, I got a splinter."

Jake sat on the step below her. "Let me see. I've taken the advanced course in splinter removal." He laid her hand gently across his own. His were warm, soft, well-manicured. Permanent stains marred her nails, and calluses announced that she made her living with her hands—and he didn't. She wanted to yank hers away and cram them into the pockets of her jeans.

"What are you doing here, anyway?" She chewed her lower lip as he probed the sliver of wood.

"Checking on you. I guess it's a good thing I was here."

"If you hadn't been, this wouldn't have happened, thank you very much. Ouch."

"Sorry. That's in there pretty good. We're going to need tweezers to get it out. Why don't we go into your apartment?"

"Yeah, right. I often invite strange men who've stalked me into my apartment. What, do I look stupid?"

The blue eyes widened and they appeared slightly…hurt? She'd hurt his feelings?

"No, you don't look stupid. Not at all."

Harley turned around and stretched to retrieve her purse from one of the upper steps. She pulled out her Swiss Army knife and opened the tweezers feature. Using the tip, she poked at the splinter held captive underneath her skin. "So, why did you need to check on me?"

Jake studied her as she struggled to remove the piece of wood. Her long hair shimmered, hanging loose around her face. This close he could smell her soft floral scent. "Just wanted to make sure you'd found another job. I feel pretty bad about what happened the other day."

"Unfortunately, no, not yet. Damnation." The tweezer point slipped across her palm.

He silently echoed her curse. She was supposed to say she'd found a new job so he could go on his merry way and sleep at night. So he could forget any dangerous and inappropriate ideas about Harley Emerson and babies... A glance around her neighborhood—shabby houses with peeling paint, empty beer bottles in the yard across the street, rusted-out cars that made her Toyota look new—only strengthened his impression that she needed a job, and badly. Where was her family and why did they let her live in such a place? He'd designed sturdier and nicer-looking doghouses, and would've had a fit if he'd found his sister living in an area like this.

"I can't get it out," Harley muttered.

"Let me have a try." He held out his hand, and she hesitantly passed him the red knife. He grinned at her. "Guess you do trust me a little, huh?"

"Very little." A slight smile lessened the sting of her words. God, she had beautiful eyes.

Which he wasn't supposed to be looking at. No, since his wife had solidified his Revolving Door theory of women by leaving him behind while she went off to pursue her rising career as a news anchor, he'd sworn off the "fair" sex. Fair. Ha. That was a joke. What was fair about a woman abandoning her family?

As his gaze slid lower, he realized he wasn't supposed to be staring at Harley's chest, either, but the form-fitting pink T-shirt that clearly defined her breasts didn't help in that department. Jake bent over her palm, blocking out all distracting views, then worked the splinter free. "There." He folded up the knife and returned it to her, then rose, wiping his hands on his pants. "I, uh, should probably be going." He pulled his wallet from his pocket and offered her his business card. "Listen, if you need anything, give me a call, okay? Or stop by my office. I'm on the corner of State and Twelfth."

She accepted the card with a wary expression. "Why?"

"Why what?"

"Why would I call you if I needed something?"

"Because I lost your job for you. You were telling the truth about not taking my stuff, weren't you?"

She nodded.

"I believe you. You have any ideas who might've taken it? Maybe we can go to Ned and get your job back."

"Yeah, right. I'm sure he'd be very happy to rehire me when I tell him I think his daughter snatched your stuff."

"Oh, crap. Really? His daughter?" Jake groaned. "Was she the kid in the front office? You know, she acted kind of weird when I went in."

"Yeah, that was Summer. And I'm betting it was her." Harley tucked the knife and his card into her purse, then got to her feet. "So, forget Ned wanting to hear that."

The stairs wobbled as Jake escorted her to the bottom. Definitely not structurally sound. Her landlord needed a kick in the butt, making tenants put up with that. Once Harley had retrieved the library book, they walked toward her truck.

"So, you'll call me?" he asked as she climbed into the pickup.

"Thanks for the concern. But I'm used to taking care of myself. Been doing it for years."

After she drove away, he glanced around her neighborhood again. She might've been taking care of herself, but she sure as hell wasn't doing a particularly good job. He slid behind the wheel of the Mustang. A pile of papers on the passenger's seat made him groan. More stuff on surrogacy, information he'd gotten from his lawyer.

He needed to find a woman he could count on to spin through the revolving door of his life, enter, give him a child, and then leave again.

He needed someone who'd do things according to *his* plan.

FINDING ANOTHER JOB—any job—was turning out to be a lot harder than she'd expected. With so many of Erie's plants closing, everybody and his aunt was out looking for work. And given a choice between Harley with her criminal record and somebody's aunt—well, the old biddies seemed to be winning out.

Harley parallel-parked the truck a half block from her apartment. New blades of grass poked through the cracks in the sidewalk's uneven surfaces. She recognized the white Mustang right away. That meant Manning was here again, for the third time in a week. His second visit had been a brief pass-through, catching her on the way to fill out an application. She wasn't sure if she should be flattered, annoyed or worried. Men like Jake Manning didn't usually take an interest in a woman like her—a mechanic from the wrong side of town—unless they wanted something. Usually sex. On the other hand, he could be a stalker. Of the two, she'd rather deal with the first.

Elbows propped on his khaki-clad knees, chin in his palm, he was sitting on the third step and— She did a double take. She could smell fresh sawdust. Small piles of wood shavings littered the ground and a black metal railing gleamed in the sunshine. Jake grinned at her. "It's about time you came home. The crew left almost an hour ago."

She gestured toward the new construction. "What's this?"

"Sturdy steps that won't collapse on you, and a splinter-free railing. Seemed like the least I could do." He patted the wood by his side. "Pretreated lumber. Won't rot out in the Erie weather."

"I—I can't pay you for this." She'd been wondering how she was going to pay the slumlord, who'd been furious when he'd found out about the railing. Now it looked as though the debt had been transferred to Jake. And Harley always paid her debts.

"I don't expect you to. Consider it a gift."

The corners of her mouth twitched upward and she shook her head. "That's a new one. Most guys go for flowers or candy. No one's ever built me stairs before."

"What can I say? I'm unique."

"Definitely." And good-looking, too. Today's indigo-blue polo shirt clung to his shoulders and torso, answering all her questions about the horse-power the man packed. The sun sparked hidden high-lights in his dark hair. "But are you a stalker?"

He laughed. "No. Jeez, you're suspicious. Hasn't anyone ever just done something nice for you?"

"No. Not without expecting something in return." Okay, so that wasn't exactly true. Charlie had become her friend and helped her out more times than she could count, and he'd never expected anything in re-turn, just that she make her life better and achieve the goals she set for herself. Damn, she missed that old man. She needed to hit a pay phone later and give him a call.

"How goes the job search?"

"Lousy. Stop asking. Even the grocery stores don't want me."

He launched himself off the steps in a hurry. "Okay, then would you mind taking a look at my Mustang? I'll pay you."

"I just fixed it a week ago. What could possibly be wrong with it already?" She frowned up at him as his shadow blocked the sunlight from her face.

"I dunno. You're the mechanic. It's making a funny noise." Jake peered down at her. He hoped she'd agree. He could slip her some money, his guilt would be assuaged and he could concentrate on more pressing matters. Like his surrogate search. Because until he got this intriguing woman taken care of, she'd no doubt continue to invade his thoughts at the oddest times, like when he was sitting at a traffic light or getting ready to fall asleep.

"And just where do you expect me to look at your car? The cops aren't real crazy about people working on cars in the streets."

"Damn, I hadn't thought about that." He snapped his fingers. "You can use my garage."

Doubt filled her eyes, and one brow rose toward her hairline. "I thought we covered the fact that I'm not stupid? I don't go to strange men's houses, either."

"Would you feel more comfortable if I arranged a chaperon for us? A woman? We could use my brother's garage. His wife's home during the afternoon, and I'm sure she'd be happy to hang around."

Her cheeks flushed. "I'm sorry. You've gone out of your way to be nice to me. Heck, you built me stairs." She took a deep breath. "You let me know where and when, and I'll meet you at your brother's house and check out your car."

"Good. Next Wednesday." That was one thing settled.

"DON'T GET UPSET." Jake made a calming motion with his hand.

"I'm not taking your money, dammit! There is nothing wrong with this car." Harley slammed the Mustang's hood, and the sound echoed through the small detached garage. "I didn't think there could be. I did my job right the first time."

"I didn't think you hadn't. I'm telling you, it's been making this funny noise. They never do it when you want them to."

She collected her socket wrench and wire gauge from the weather-beaten table against the wall. Cobwebs hung from the dirty window, dancing on the breeze. "Guess your brother doesn't spend much time in here, does he?"

"No, he doesn't," answered a female voice from the doorway. "Dusty isn't much into tools or garage stuff. He likes model trains, though. You should see the setup he has in the basement."

Harley turned to look at the very pregnant woman Jake had introduced as his sister-in-law. Kathy? No, Kate. "They do like their toys, don't they?"

"Yes. Hey, I've made some iced tea. Since it's so nice out, I figured we could sit on the back porch."

Harley wiped her hands with a rag, then laid it on top of her toolbox, along with the gauge and wrench. "Thanks, but I should get going."

The woman looked disappointed. "Please? It's not often I have company these days. I've got some brownies to go with it."

"Your special brownies, Katie? With the chocolate chips in them?" Jake asked. When she said yes, he grinned at Harley. "Don't pass those up. Come on, sit a minute. It's not like there's someplace you have to be just now, is there?"

Brownies. Harley's mouth watered at the thought. Goodies had been scarce in the pantry since she'd lost her job. "Not really. I guess I could stay for a few minutes." She held out her hands. "Where can I wash up?"

Waddling awkwardly, Kate showed her through the

little screened porch and into the sunny kitchen. Harley appraised the yellow-and-white gingham curtains and lemon walls as she washed. "Nice." Slightly blinding, but nice. It would sure wake you up in the morning.

Kate smiled. "It's small, but it's ours. Well, ours and the bank's. We got a good deal through the state because Dusty's a policeman."

"Your husband's a cop?" Cops weren't high on her list of favorite people. The night of her arrest had been the most humiliating and degrading thing she'd ever experienced, and that was saying a lot. The police had scoffed at her protests of innocence. Harley replaced the cotton towel on the oven door, then followed Kate back out onto the porch. Jake was sprawled in one of the webbed chairs, a glass of iced tea in one hand, brownie in the other.

"Yes. He loves being on the force." Condensation dripped off the pitcher as Kate poured tea into the waiting glasses. She passed one to Harley, then slowly lowered herself into a chair. "Sit down. Help yourself to a brownie."

"Thanks." The rich chocolate helped relieve some of the apprehension she felt about having tea and treats on some cop's porch. What would Kate's husband—Jake's brother—think if he knew his wife was serving goodies to a convicted criminal? Well, they certainly couldn't talk about that. No point in upsetting such a hospitable, not to mention extremely pregnant, woman. "When's your baby due?"

Kate caressed the mound of her stomach. "One

week from yesterday. Not soon enough, if you want to know the truth.''

Jake placed his empty glass on the table and slid his chair closer to Kate's. ''How are your feet doing?''

''Oh, they're fine. Not too swollen today.''

''Let me see.'' He patted his legs. ''Put them up here.''

Kate slipped off her sandals and lifted her feet to his lap. When Jake started rubbing them, she closed her eyes, dropped her head back and sighed deeply. ''Oh, that's great, Jake. I'll give you a million bucks as long as you don't stop.''

The man replaced a stranger's broken steps, worried about that same stranger's job and rubbed his pregnant sister-in-law's feet. Damn. He really was a nice guy. She didn't belong here. Harley rose. ''I'm gonna run. Thanks for the tea and brownie. It was delicious.'' The screen door squeaked as she shoved it open and headed for the garage.

She was kneeling next to her toolbox, setting her tools in their proper drawers when she felt his presence behind her.

''I really wish you'd let me pay you for checking out my car.''

She shook her head. ''If I'd done something, that would be fine. But I didn't.''

He leaned closer, looking over her shoulder at the tool box. ''Who's that?'' He pointed to the picture taped to the inside lid.

Harley slammed it shut. "Just me and my dad." The latches rasped as she closed them.

"Is he a mechanic, too?"

Her fingers traced the dents in the red metal top. The toolbox was a replica of her father's. How she wished she still had his actual set. But all she had left was the one photograph. "Yeah. He was. Taught me a lot." Her biceps flexed as she lifted the heavy box and turned to face Jake.

"Was?"

She narrowed her eyes and scowled at him. He was treading on highly personal ground.

"Okay. Hey, can I ask you a question? It might sound strange, but you seem like you were close to your dad, following in the family business and all...."

"What?" She shifted the box, using both hands to hold it now.

"Do you think a man can raise a child by himself and do a good job of it?"

Harley's throat tightened. She swallowed hard and did her best to remain nonchalant. "Yeah," she finally said. "Yeah, I think he can." She headed down the cracked driveway toward the street. "My father did."

Jake hurried after her, trying not to be distracted by the sway of her hips in the tight jeans. "Why don't you let me carry that for you?" He reached for the toolbox.

"No, thanks. I can manage." At the curb, she set her burden down and unlocked the cap of the truck.

After lowering the tailgate, she hefted the box into the truck with a grunt, then shoved it farther inside.

"What about you, Harley? You ever want to have children?" He slammed the tailgate shut, trapping her between the truck and his arm.

"Yeah, right. Look at me. I've got enough trouble taking care of myself right now. No, I don't think I'll ever have children. I'm not exactly prime mother material."

Maybe not, but despite his earlier concerns, he was definitely getting the impression that she'd make prime surrogate material. She didn't want kids of her own, she thought a man could raise a child by himself.... Maybe they could help each other out. "How would you like to go to dinner with me on Friday night? Someplace casual. I'd like to get to know you a little better."

"IS YOUR FOOD OKAY?"

She glanced from the table to his face. "What?"

His eyes sparkled at her and he broke into a broad grin. He set his hamburger back on the plate. "Your food. You've hardly touched it."

Heat flared in her cheeks. "It's fine. I was just thinking, that's all."

"About me, I hope."

Oh, yeah, she'd been thinking about him, all right. Thinking about what the hell a nice, successful guy like him was doing with a woman like her. Wondering if maybe, just maybe—her past hard-learned lessons to the contrary—he actually liked her. Was it possible that her luck with men had changed the day she'd gotten fired? Perhaps. But a wise woman didn't confess something like that, not at this stage.

"This is an interesting restaurant." She picked up a hot wing from the green plastic basket and took a tentative bite. Delicious. Just enough zing without scalding heat. She looked around, feigning more interest in the decor than in the man across the table from her.

Sports cars and motorcycles decorated the place. A blue 'Vette hung on the wall above them, while nearby a black '57 T-bird convertible rested on a lift over other diners' heads. NASCAR paraphernalia dotted the far wall, including the hood from one of Jeff Gordon's rides.

"I thought a girl named Harley who worked on cars would like it," Jake murmured. "Don't tell me you've never been here before."

"I don't go out much." She licked the sauce from her fingers.

As Jake watched her clean her fingers, a tight sensation clutched his stomach, then spread south as his body announced its appreciation of this beautiful woman. Damn, she made the idea of procreation incredibly appealing. *Down, boy. That's not how this is going to be, so get it right out of your head. If you're lucky, she'll be the mother of your child. Not your lover.*

The twinkle in her eyes made him wonder if she was tormenting him on purpose. Two could play that game. He grabbed her wrist. "Let me take care of that."

Her eyes grew wide as he raised her hand toward his own mouth—then abruptly placed it on the table, reached for a packaged wipe, ripped it open and carefully cleaned her fingers with the moist towel.

The action achieved his desired effect of distancing them, and she chuckled while snatching back her hand.

She scrubbed at her fingers with a paper napkin. "Thanks a lot. Now my wings are going to taste like soap."

"You're welcome. Couldn't have those talented fingers all messy." He picked up a French fry. "Tell me more about yourself."

"There's not much to tell."

"You could tell me about your name. Surely there's a story behind that."

"I could. There is." Her gaze dipped from his face back to the table again.

"But you don't want to tell me. Okay, I can live with that. But I think it suits you."

She peered up at him without lifting her head. "You do?"

"Yes. It's racy, it's provocative, and men do tend to refer to their motorcycles as 'she,' so it's definitely feminine."

Freshly cleaned fingers shredded the end of a napkin. "It wasn't supposed to be."

"Well, it is." The name was obviously a sore spot, and he wanted to make inroads with her, get some answers before he broached his plan. "Any luck with the job search the last few days?"

The paper-ripping increased and she raised her head to glare at him. "No." The volume of her voice rose a notch. "And I want you to stop asking."

"I'm really sorry, Harley."

She dropped the shreds to the white Formica surface of the table, folded her arms across her chest and waited.

"I didn't think Ned would fire anyone over twenty-five bucks and a cell phone."

"It's okay. It's a normal reaction. You were looking for justice."

"It's not justice when he fires an innocent person."

"Innocence has nothing to do with it." She inhaled deeply, then slowly exhaled, sagging against the booth, hands falling into her lap. "Justice is handed down, Jake. Think about it. There's a reason they use that term. It's handed down from those on high to the lower echelons."

"Ned doesn't qualify as those on high, and I rather doubt he'd even know what the word *echelon* means. So don't lump yourself in with him. Certainly don't lower yourself beneath him."

She snorted. "Beneath him…that looks like the only way I'm going to find another job."

Apprehension grabbed at him. "What?"

"Nothing. It's just that some garage owners I've seen in the past few days had rather indecent proposals for me."

A combination of emotions stirred within him: anxiety that she'd consider his proposal indecent, too, and anger that anyone had the nerve to proposition her. "That's not right. You're a fine mechanic. My car's never sounded better."

"Guess that weird noise has stopped, huh?"

"Uh, yeah." He smiled sheepishly. Okay, so he'd lied about the noise. He'd been trying to help. "But I mean it. You're terrific at what you do."

"Thanks." She fell silent as the waitress returned to their table with fresh drinks. When the woman left, she spoke again. "But nobody wants a worker with a record."

"So it was true." Jake reached for his beer, surprised as hell she'd confessed, but determined not to show it. How considerate of her to open one of the topics he really wanted to discuss.

"Yeah. In a way." Her gaze dropped back down to the table, and she removed another napkin from the tidy stack as her next victim. Elbows propped on the edge of the table, she repeated the process of reducing the paper to long strips.

"Why'd you do it?"

"I didn't do it."

"My brother says everybody claims innocence."

She snapped her head up and glared at him. "I *am* innocent. I had no idea they were running a chop-shop after hours. I didn't spend my nights in the garage."

"But you got convicted, anyway?"

"Yeah, well, the cops raided the joint and found me cleaning carburetors from chopped cars. Nobody wanted to hear that I didn't know where they'd come from, that I was only doing what my boss told me to. And the jerk of a public defender I was assigned couldn't defend his way out of a war against toy soldiers.''

''Where was your family? Why didn't they help you get a decent lawyer?''

''You ask a lot of questions for an architect. You sound more like a shrink or a reporter.'' She tossed the final napkin shred onto the pile. ''What kinds of things do you design, anyway? Let me guess, you've designed most of the lovely new strip malls around here.''

Jake hesitated over her abrupt shift in topic, but decided that letting her take the lead would help her feel more comfortable. And he certainly wanted her feeling comfortable when he popped The Question. About surrogacy. Not ''the question.'' One wife in his lifetime had turned out to be more than enough. His face warmed. ''Definitely not. I designed the new business park out on the east side, and the Spandler hotel down on the bayfront.''

''Okay, I'm duly impressed.''

The conversation drifted along in a casual manner after that, touching on the subjects of Erie's growth, the overabundance of new drugstores, and eventually a subject that made her eyes lose that wary edge—classic cars.

When they'd completed their meals, Jake brought up the other topic he wanted to cover. Satisfied that her criminal record was a fluke, no fault of her own, he crossed his fingers beneath the table and launched into the unknown.

"What's your dream, Harley?"

"Dream? What do you mean?"

"I mean, what does a beautiful, talented woman like you want out of life?" He leaned forward so he could hear her answer clearly over the clatter of dishes and the murmur of other diners.

"That's easy. I want to finish my college degree before they have to put me in a nursing home and then get a job in business."

He tilted his head and studied her carefully. "I can't really picture you in a suit at a board table."

"That's exactly the point. I'm tired of being Harley the mechanic. Nobody takes me seriously."

"The people whose cars you fix do. You did a great job with my Mustang."

A slight tinge of pink graced her cheeks. "Thanks. But society doesn't exactly look up to mechanics, especially female ones."

"So, what's stopping you?"

"There's this little thing called money. The college is pretty picky about paid tuition." A strand of her hair, loose from her ponytail and hanging down near her face, shifted as she blew out a breath. "Not to mention the other bills I have to pay."

"What about student loans? And if things are really bad, you could probably get welfare."

Talk about killing looks. The one she gave him in response to that comment could have taken out all the people in the immediate vicinity.

"I don't do government programs," she said. "I've had enough experience with them to know I'd rather starve, thanks."

"Sorry. I didn't mean to offend you. What if I told you I could help make your dream come true?"

She gave a short laugh. "I'd say this is going to be interesting." She crossed her arms. "I'm listening."

Her guarded expression warned him to tread cautiously. "Harley, more than anything in this world, I want a child."

"Why? Look around. Why would you want to bring a child into this hellhole we call a world? And what does that have to do with me?"

"There's a space in my life only a child can fill. I no longer have a wife, nor do I want to get married again. I need a surrogate, and I think you'd make a perfect one. You're beautiful, intelligent—"

"An ex-con, and this is the most unbelievable come-on I've ever heard in my life!"

The noise in their immediate area dropped and heads turned in their direction.

"It's no come-on." He stared pointedly at a gray-haired woman one table over until she returned her attention to her meal. "And if you're truly innocent, then you're not an ex-con in my book."

The shocked expression on her face vanished quickly, replaced by a glint of steel. She leaned across the table until her breath warmed his face as she spoke softly. "If you wanted me in your bed, you were on the right track before you took this sudden detour.''

An image flashed by of her in his bed, silky hair fanned across his pillow as she writhed beneath him, and he found himself struggling to erase it. ''No, no, that's not what I'm proposing.'' But hot damn, the image provoked and delighted him. ''I'm talking about artificial insemination.''

She sat back, staring at him. ''You're a sick man. That's the coldest thing I've ever heard in my life, and I've heard a lot. I'm not a prostitute, and I'm not a baby factory.''

Jake grabbed her by the wrist. ''Harley, think about it. I'll pay all the medical expenses, your full tuition, your books, even your living expenses. You could get that degree you want so much.''

''Let go.'' She tugged on her arm, but he held her firmly. ''I'm flattered, I think, that you've decided I'd make the perfect mother for your baby. But I'm not interested. There are enough children in this world. Find one whose parents don't want her and take her in.''

''Tried that. It didn't pan out. Now I want a biological child, a child I have legal rights to.''

''At least you get points for honesty. No seducing with pretty words, no declarations of love or empty promises. No, at least you've got honesty going for you.'' She yanked her wrist from his grasp and slid from the booth. ''Kids are a commitment, not a…a whim. They deserve a good home. Best of luck in your quest.''

"Spend some more time with me! Let me prove to you that I can provide a good home for a child," he called after her. "I'm reliable and responsible—"

Harley shoved past a group of people waiting in the lobby, stormed out the front door and onto the sidewalk before she remembered he'd driven. She whirled on the green-and-white racecar that sat on the sidewalk and kicked the rear tire. "Dammit."

How dare he?

A surrogate!

For once she'd thought someone like him, someone with a little class, could actually be interested in her. She should've known better. He was no different than any other man—out to get what he could from her. Although what he wanted differed from what most of them were trying to get.

A noisy cluster of patrons spilled out of the glass doors, and Harley turned to check for Jake. Fortunately, he wasn't among the crowd.

"Harley!" a deep voice boomed. A large, bald man dressed in denim and leather broke from the group and headed in her direction. "How's it hanging?"

Thank goodness, a familiar face. "Hey, Cutter. You know, I could use a ride." Just thinking about the prospect of walking all the way down Peach Street into the city made her feet ache.

"For my favorite mechanic, I think I can swing that. Come on." The big man ambled off the sidewalk and across the parking lot.

Harley scrambled to keep up, but as Cutter headed for the bike parking area, she halted in her tracks.

"Where's your Camaro? It can't be in the garage, I just repaired it."

"On a warm, clear night like tonight? Don't be crazy. I rode the bike."

She should've stayed in bed. Under the covers. Maybe tomorrow she'd do exactly that. Harley waved her hand at Cutter. "Forget I asked. I'll just walk." She changed direction, making for the road.

A booming belly laugh made her turn around. "Don't tell me a girl named Harley doesn't ride?"

"Not if she can help it," she muttered.

Cutter leaned over the back of his bike, then straightened, holding a helmet aloft. "Come on, I've got an extra brain bucket and everything."

If she didn't accept his offer, she ran the risk of another encounter with Mr. Have-My-Test-Tube-Baby. Not to mention she'd have to walk. "All right." She warily approached the bike.

Helmet secure, she mounted behind him. The motor rumbled to life, and Cutter revved it. She shouted her address into his ear. He nodded.

She flung her arms around his waist and held on for dear life. She knew altogether too well what could happen on a bike. And that a helmet didn't guarantee protection of a fragile human brain.

She'd become a ward of the state at the age of ten, along with her father, after he'd had an accident on his motorcycle one afternoon while she was at school. With no other family to make the decision, the doctors and the court had pulled the plug on her dad, and sent her to the first in a long line of foster homes.

She bit her bottom lip, hard, to stop the trembling.

As they breezed by the restaurant entrance, Jake appeared in the doorway. Harley turned her head away from him even as she unwillingly considered what his proposal could mean to her. She had no job and a pile of bills to pay. If he paid her living expenses and her tuition, plus books and everything else, she could go to school full-time and finish her degree by next spring. The new Harley Emerson could emerge and take her place in society.

But…a baby?

The thought tightened her chest, making it difficult to breathe. She buried her face in Cutter's back and tried to block out the memories of her life after losing her dad. They brought nothing but pain.

Instead, she began to imagine everything an artificial insemination entailed. Doctors and needles. Tests. Cold, sterile laboratories. A shudder made its way down her spine. Ick. Worse, she could imagine the taunting a child conceived like that might endure. Bad enough to be labeled a bastard, but a bastard test-tube baby? Poor kid.

Maybe her parents hadn't been married, and maybe her mother had walked out on her, but at least Harley knew she'd been conceived in passion, in a warm bed. She'd be a surrogate when hell froze over.

CHAPTER THREE

THE CONSTANT DRIP, DRIP, drip of rainwater leaking through the cap into the truck bed pushed Harley closer to the brink of breaking. *The devil must have his skates on, because hell's damn near frozen over.*

Unable to pay the rent, she'd been forced to give up her tiny efficiency. Though not a home in the true sense of the word, it sure beat living in the back of her pickup.

Harley huddled in the corner, as far away from the leak as possible. Her sleeping bag did little to cushion the hard metal beneath her. Damp, tired and hungry, she replayed Jake Manning's words in her mind.

Three weeks ago, the man had seemed totally insane to propose she have a baby for him; now she found herself contemplating his offer.

She picked up the manila envelope he'd sent her just days after their encounter at the restaurant and spilled the contents across her lap, lifting the various pieces one at a time toward the window to make use of the faint afternoon light that filtered through the rain. The first photograph showed Jake and two identical little blond girls—his nieces—on the train at the Erie Zoo. Other snapshots with explanations carefully penned on the backs revealed a younger version of the man. There was one with his sister, all gussied up and ready for the prom, and another with his brother, both of them holding fishing poles.

A photo of his house, where he'd lived since the age of eight, a copy of his market portfolio and a "daddy résumé" listing his qualifications rounded out his efforts to prove he'd make a good father. A résumé, for Pete's sake.

The man's organization made her head hurt.

The course catalog from the local university she attended on a part-time basis completed the package. Harley flipped it open to the business administration classes, where yellow highlighter indicated some of the ones she still needed to complete her degree. The fact that he'd gotten all this information about her college career was disconcerting, but it certainly proved how serious he was about the two of them fulfilling each other's dreams.

She leaned over and flipped open her toolbox, propping the lid against the side of the truck. She stared at the picture of her father. The handsome dashing young man straddled a motorcycle, and the little girl she'd once been—about a million years ago—stood next to him. Harley reached out to touch her father's face. "Dad," she whispered. "What am I supposed to do?"

Would it somehow balance out the cosmos if she played a part in giving one child a wonderful home? The kind she'd had before her father was killed?

"You and that damn bike, Dad. How different my life might've been, if not for that damn bike."

Never big on words, her father wasn't talking now. She needed a friendly ear.

Harley closed the toolbox, shoving it and her duffel bag out of the way, then crawled toward the end of the truck. She swung herself down over the tailgate, slammed it and the cap window shut, then bolted around the vehicle. The wind and rain churned the lake's surface, much like her indecision and confusion had her in turmoil.

Behind the wheel, Harley started the truck, giving it a few seconds to warm up. The rumble of the engine soothed and comforted her.

The drive off the Peninsula passed quickly. She swung into the parking lot of Tasty Taco. Inching the pickup alongside the payphone, she eased the stick shift into neutral. She shut off the engine and fumbled for her wallet. Several cards tumbled out as she unfolded it.

Jake Manning's lay on top of the pile.

Running a finger over the raised blue letters, Harley sighed, then slipped it into the breast pocket of her short-sleeved denim shirt. "I'll get to you later."

She sifted through the rest until she found the one she needed. Stuffing the others back in her wallet, she held up the card with the scribbled number on the back. The window groaned as she cranked it open. Phone receiver cradled against her shoulder, Harley punched the required numbers, then waited for the operator to answer.

"Collect from Harley."

"One moment, please." At least it was a real person, not a computer.

"Harley Emerson, you're late checking in." The gravelly voice washed over her like the final rays of sunset; the familiar phrase brought a half smile to her lips.

"I didn't think I had to check in with you every week anymore, Charlie."

"Don't get fresh with me, girl. I missed hearing from you last week, that's all."

Harley partially rolled up the window to keep the drizzle from coming in. "Well, I hate to run up your phone bill. How's Florida?"

"Hot as hell and stickier than a honey bun."

She laughed. "You're the one who wanted to trade in beautiful Erie summers for that, remember?"

"No, I'm the one who wanted to trade in Erie winters, remember? If you don't now, you will when the snow flies. Just keep in mind when you're freezin' this winter, kid, there's a room here for you if you want it."

Tempting. Right now the room was very tempting. But she didn't want him taking on more of her problems. God knows the man had solved his share of them in the past. "Charlie, you know I can't afford to relocate and transfer schools. I'd lose too many credits."

"How are things going?"

"Fine." Crossed fingers accompanied the white lie.

"What classes you taking this fall?" Charlie coughed, then cleared his throat.

She listened carefully to his breathing. Repeated bouts of bronchitis last winter had finally prompted him to retire and make the move to a warmer climate. Harley suspected they'd both shed private tears over his departure. "You sick, Charlie? That didn't sound too good."

"I'm still adjusting to the air down here. Don't change the subject—it doesn't work with me and you know it."

No, it didn't. He'd been able to get around her circular conversations from day one. "I'm not sure what I need for next semester yet, Charlie. But don't worry. I'm gonna make you proud of me, you old goat."

The gruff voice softened. "I already am proud of you, kid. How many times do I have to tell you—it's not a piece of paper that's important, it's who you are and how you act. Get it through that damn thick skull."

Harley's nose tingled, and a mist that had nothing to do with the rain interfered with her view of the parking lot. "I didn't call for a lecture. I just called to touch base." *And to hear your voice, old man.*

Charlie cleared his throat again. "How's life at the shop?"

"I've got things under control." Another lie, but it couldn't be helped. No matter what he said, he sounded sick, and if that was the case, he sure didn't need more of *her* problems. As much as she really didn't want to be part of Jake's plan, she hoped he hadn't found someone else. "Listen, Charlie, it's raining, and I'm getting wet. I gotta go. I'll talk to you soon."

"You do that, kid, and don't worry about the phone bill. I'll hear from you next week."

"Sure thing. Bye." She gingerly replaced the receiver. "I *will* make you proud, Charlie."

Not normally given to self-pity, Harley couldn't help noting what a sad reflection it was on her life that everything she owned lay in the back of her pickup and the only real friend she had in the world was her former parole officer.

She'd been terrified of him the day they'd met. He'd been chewing some guy out for violating conditions of his parole, and Harley had watched as two cops came in to drag the moron back to jail. On the spot, she'd vowed never, ever to mess up on her parole. It had taken her almost two months to learn that Charlie was more bark than bite, at least with her. For some reason, one she'd never been quite able to figure out, he'd believed in her innocence and taken her under his wing. He'd helped her find jobs when she needed one, scholarship money when tuition was hard to scrape up, and he listened when she needed to talk.

Her father was a fleeting memory, but Charlie filled some of the empty space he'd left behind.

THE RETURN ADDRESS ON the envelope matched the neat white house, and she recognized it from the picture he'd sent. Green shutters and trim accented the windows and doors. Yellow flowers grew in a circle around a black lamppost near the sidewalk, and the shrubs along the edge of the property were perfectly shaped. A red Jeep was parked on the side of the garage; a basketball hoop hung over the double garage door.

All it needed was a white picket fence.

And obviously, as far as the owner was concerned, a child to play in the backyard.

On the outside at least, it was the kind of home she'd longed for herself as a child.

Now she needed to discover the truth of what lay inside.

Harley stared at the house for several minutes, debating her next move. Talking to him didn't mean she'd actually agree to his plan. Charlie, bless his crotchety self, was still an ace in the hole for her, but one she'd play only with no other option.

She'd never wanted to bring a child into the world, knowing firsthand what a cold and treacherous place it could be—and fearing she'd be a mother like her own.

Still, in this case, that could actually work in her favor. After all, that was what this man wanted. He wanted her to give birth, hand the baby over to him and go about her life as if the child had never existed. If family history played its part, she could do that.

Couldn't she?

She'd checked out the implications. Pennsylvania had nothing on the books regarding surrogacy, so she wouldn't be breaking any laws. That was important.

She shivered at the memory of Judge Ephraim's pronouncement and his finger wagging in her direction. Nope, a courtroom was a place to be avoided at all costs. So was a jail cell.

The opportunity to grab for her dreams, to finally bring them to reality, lay before her in the cute white house. She would finally be able to hold up her head in the face of all those who had looked at her with disapproval, and proclaimed that the only thing Harley Emerson would ever make was license plates.

"Success is the best revenge," she muttered, toying with the bottom button on her shirt. "I'll show them if it's the last thing I do."

But the price of her success was a baby. She didn't know what kind of father Jake Manning would make, despite all his pictures and his daddy résumé. No way she'd even consider doing this for a man who wouldn't care for the child properly. And what if something happened to him? Who would care for his child then?

A lot of questions needed answers before she could agree to this...this *plan* of his. And she had some conditions of her own.

The button came loose in her hand, and she glanced down to see she'd twisted the tail of the shirt into a tight coil. At the same moment, her stomach growled.

"Oh, you shut up. It's not like you haven't been hungry before. You've been spoiled lately." Harley yanked the keys from the ignition, then dropped them and the button into her pocket. Straightening her posture, she glanced out at the house again.

This Millcreek neighborhood, unlike some, didn't consist of identical, cookie-cutter houses. Several bikes lay in the driveway across the street, left out in the rain by kids who obviously had other things on their minds.

It was a far cry from the area she'd recently vacated, where an unattended bike was an open invitation for theft. This suburb looked like an ideal spot to raise a family—if you were interested in that kind of thing.

Harley had a sudden vision of the handsome architect standing on the front porch, a beautiful child in his arms, a warm smile on his face—a smile directed at her as he welcomed her home.

Home. There'd been no real home for Harley since she'd lost her dad.

What are you doing, stupid? she chastised herself. *He's out of your league, remember? You're not good enough for him. He's interested in you for one reason and one reason only—and that's your ability to give him what he wants. A baby. Get real! There are no white knights, no nice guys, only pretty words and empty promises.*

Her stomach rumbled again, reminding her exactly what reality meant. It meant being cold and hungry and lonely. It meant being a nothing.

It meant getting her damn butt out of the truck, crossing the tidy lawn to the house, and seeing what she could do about making her own dreams come true.

JAKE GRINNED DOWN AT the baby in his arms. Matthew Jacob Manning, his new nephew, named after Dusty's father—and Jake. "He's a cute kid, Dust."

His brother beamed at him from the love seat on the far side of the room. "You think he looks like me?"

"Nope, he's all Kate. That's what I said. A cute kid." At Jake's side, Kate chuckled.

"Guess he told you, brother," Melanie said, laughing and giving Dusty a pat on the arm. Dusty mock-scowled at the room in general as the rest of the family—Melanie's husband, Peter, and their twin daughters—joined in the laughter. The little girls had no clue what the fuss was all about, but if everyone else was laughing, they'd add their shrieks of joy, too.

The dogs jumped to their feet, barking and staring up at the picture window that looked out onto the screened front porch. Jake followed their lead, glancing at the window, discovering a pair of emerald-green eyes, wide with fright, staring back at him.

He handed the baby to Kate. "Here, take him. I'll be right back."

Dusty was already opening the front door. The dogs bounded past him, onto the porch.

A scream of unholy terror sliced through the air, followed by the sound of the screen door banging shut.

Jake slid into his loafers in the foyer. "I'll handle this, Dusty," he said, rushing after his ill-behaved pets. The second slam of the screen door informed him that Pepper and Benji were now on the loose in the neighborhood and hot in pursuit of the woman for whom he'd spent the past week searching.

The drizzling rain turned the front lawn into a series of squishy patches, some muddier than others. The dogs danced around a still form on the grass. Jake pulled up short, muttering curses under his breath.

"Pepper, Benji, sit. Back off, you guys."

He grabbed the Labrador by the collar and hauled him away from Harley, who lay in the grass curled into a ball with her hands over her face. "Harley, it's okay. They won't hurt you."

He crouched and ran his palms over her back, surprised at the way she was trembling.

Her hands muffled her response. "Hell, yes they will. That big dog wants to eat me and the little one is hoping for leftovers."

Jake bit down on his tongue to stifle his laughter. The last thing he wanted to do at the moment was alienate her. "Get up. I'll protect you from them." He straightened.

She lowered her hands cautiously, then peeked around him. When Pepper woofed an enthusiastic greeting for this newfound playmate, she jumped to her feet and threw herself into Jake's arms. "Don't let it bite me."

"They don't bite." Mud ran down her face, and water dripped off the tip of her nose. She smelled of the outdoors, a wild, uninhibited aroma of rain mingled with woodsmoke. He wrapped one arm around her waist, and with the other, brushed a strand of hair off her cheek, tucking it behind her ear. Even in such a sorry state, she was beautiful.

The dogs cavorted around them. Harley muffled a shriek and pressed her body so tightly against his, a sheet of graph paper couldn't have come between them. Jake lost himself in the heavenly sensation.

"Everything okay out there, Jake?"

He turned his head to see Dusty on the porch steps, umbrella held over his head, ready to dash out to his big brother's rescue. His sister was also watching the scene from her vantage point behind Dusty. "Fine. Open the garage door, will you?"

"No problem." Dusty disappeared into the house.

Jake waved a hand at Melanie, shooing her back inside, as well. "All right, Harley, let me introduce you to the dogs." He reluctantly released her from the embrace. "Sit, boys."

She turned to face the dogs, but hovered close to him.

"The black dog is Pepper, and the little one is Benji."

"Great, wonderful, pleasure to meet you," she muttered. When Benji lifted a paw, she backed into Jake's chest. "What happened to his ear? Did the big dog eat that, too?"

"No. Benji lost a fight with a coyote before he came to live with me. Look, he wants to shake your hand."

"Too bad. That big one's too close."

The automatic garage door rumbled to life, and the

dogs took off like a shot in that direction. Harley exhaled loudly and sagged against him.

"Come on, let's go inside." He wrapped an arm around her shoulder and nudged her toward the back of the house.

"Do we have to go this way? Can't we go in the front door?"

"No, we're wet and muddy, so we're going through the back." Jake's loafers squished a soggy rhythm as they slogged up the driveway.

He guided her past the Mustang. The dogs waited at the bottom of the steps that led to the kitchen door. Just as Jake and Harley reached the car, Pepper leapt to his feet and shook himself, spraying water in every direction.

Harley ran the back of her hand over her face and glared at the dog. "Look what you did to his car!"

From the doorway, Dusty said dryly, "I can see your priorities are in order."

Melanie peered over Dusty's shoulder.

Jake looked pointedly at his siblings. "Don't you have something to see to in the living room? Like kids?"

"Uh, yeah."

They hurried into the house.

Jake turned his attention to the dogs. "Since you were both so eager to get out, you can just *stay* out until you dry off."

The wooden steps creaked beneath his tread. He pulled open the screen door, pausing to press the button for the overhead door. Glancing over his shoulder, he saw that Harley remained off to the side, as far away from the dogs as she could possibly get in the enclosed space. "Aren't you coming?"

She gestured at her clothes, then looked back up at him. "I thought maybe I had to stay out here until I dried off, too."

"Not this time."

JAKE HAD CHANGED INTO dry clothes, and his sister, brother-in-law and the twins were already gone when his brother dropped the duffel bag onto the gray-slated entryway floor. "Here." He frowned over Jake's shoulder. "Your new stray's clothes. How long you keepin' this one?"

Jake arched an eyebrow at Dusty. "How do you know she's a stray and that I plan on keeping her at all?"

Dusty ticked off the reasons on his fingers. "One, you've driven me nuts trying to find her for a week. I'm guessing the reason you haven't is that she's been living in the back of her truck." He raised another finger. "Two, I see the way you look at her, and can't say I blame you. She's easy on the eyes. Three, you're just a bighearted softie."

"Am not."

"Are too," Dusty insisted.

"If Kate kicks you out, I'm not taking *you* back in, so you'd better get her and that new baby home. Don't keep her waiting out in the car."

Dusty poked Jake in the chest with his index finger. "Watch your back, your wallet and your car. Not to mention your heart. I don't want to see you go through another mess.''

"You don't have to worry about me, little brother. I learn from my mistakes. Now, get going.''

"Listen, you've been moping around since you lost Austin and that birth mother changed her mind. You're vulnerable right now, whether you know it or not, and—''

"Goodbye, Dusty. Give Kate a kiss for me.'' He shoved his brother out the door and slammed it, bending over to pick up the maroon duffel bag.

Moping? He wasn't moping. Real men didn't mope.

He was planning. Big difference.

Was Harley really living out of her truck? If so, it was his fault. He'd been the one to get her fired. How the hell could he make that up to her?

Deep in thought, he made his way to the bathroom and knocked on the door. "Harley?''

The hiss of running water conjured up images of her, erotic, exciting images. The realization that she stood naked in his shower, with his bar of soap gliding across her wet skin, caused an instinctive, hormonal reaction. He rested his forehead against the door. Dusty had been right: she was damn easy on the eyes.

Lifting his head and raising his fist again, he rapped harder. "Harley?'' The water ceased abruptly. "I've got your stuff.''

The shower curtain rings clinked against the rod, and he closed his eyes, fully able to envision the scene inside as she climbed from the tub. A moment later the bathroom door opened a crack and steam rushed into the hall.

"Thanks. And I appreciate the shower." Her hand snaked around the door.

The scent of her freshly washed skin rose to tantalize him. Damn, that soap never smelled as good on him. "No problem." He placed the handles in her palm, then curled her fingers around them. "Here you go. I'll be in the kitchen when you're through."

"Okay, I'll be right out."

"Take your time."

He wandered into the kitchen and occupied himself with the task of cleaning up from his family's dinner gathering, a celebration of his nephew's birth. Kate had been eager to get out of the house, but Dusty refused to take her and little Matthew anywhere public yet. The new daddy was too afraid the baby might catch something from strangers.

Not that Jake blamed him. He understood the fear of bad things happening to those you loved. He rinsed off some silverware and loaded it into the dishwasher. Dusty would lighten up as soon as he realized that babies were a lot hardier than people thought. Why, Jake's main concern when Dusty was small had been to keep him from eating dirt. The big brother chuckled at the memory.

"You know what they say about people who laugh to themselves, right?"

Her voice sent a shiver of delight down his spine.

The woman really should've been a radio deejay, with a sultry voice like that. "No, what?"

"They're not firing on all cylinders." She leaned against the door frame and toweled off her hair.

Oh, boy. She wore that clinging pink T-shirt again, the one that accentuated the curves of her breasts. Jake let his gaze slide lower, taking in the form-fitting black jeans that hugged her hips. She was temptation personified, every man's fantasy. And she was standing barefoot in the entrance to his kitchen. He still couldn't quite believe his good fortune. He'd assumed he'd never see her again when his latest envelope was returned to him, stamped Undeliverable.

Her stomach rumbled, and her cheeks flushed as she lowered her hand to cover her midsection. "Sorry."

Jake smiled at her. Definitely a stray. They usually came to him hungry. "Can I get you something to eat?"

"Um, sure. That'd be great."

"Turkey sandwich? Tuna? Peanut butter and jelly?"

She shrugged. "Whatever. I like PB&J."

"Okay, peanut butter and jelly it is, then." He pulled the fixings from the cabinets and thumped them down on the counter. "So, Harley, what brings you here?"

"Actually, I…well, I…"

"Yes?"

"I wanted to talk to you about your proposition."

His heart rate increased. The knife in his hand

trembled slightly as he spread grape jelly across the whole wheat bread. "Oh?"

"Yes. I've studied your daddy résumé, and I've been thinking about it."

"And?" He slapped one slice of bread over the other. Placing the sandwich on a paper plate, he turned to her.

"Well, I really need to know you a lot better to begin with. Résumés have been known to be padded." She twisted the end of the towel in her hands. "And I've got two conditions that are absolutely non-negotiable."

Jake swallowed hard and crossed the kitchen. "Okay, come and sit at the table and tell me what they are."

She followed him to the dining room, sinking into the chair he pulled out for her. Once he was seated, she nudged the sandwich, breaking off small pieces of the crust.

"Well?" he prompted.

"First, you marry me for the duration. You can divorce me later. I'll sign whatever prenuptial agreement you want, but I will not bring an illegitimate child into the world."

A little flash of pain flickered in her eyes; the set of her mouth indicated something more than she was saying.

"I'll consider it. The second term?"

"No artificial insemination. We make this baby the old-fashioned way."

He was grateful she'd waited until he was sitting down.

CHAPTER FOUR

JUDGING BY HIS WIDE EYES and slack jaw, he hadn't expected that. Harley's fingers flicked the edge of the paper plate as she worked on devouring the sandwich.

"No," he finally said.

Trying not to choke, she washed a chunk of bread down with the orange juice he'd provided. "No? No what? No marriage? No standard conception? No baby?"

Now what?

"Are you living in the back of your pickup?"

"What does that have to do with anything?"

"Everything." He eyed her plate and the remaining crust. "Are you finished?"

She nodded.

His pushed his chair backward. "Come with me." He leaned over and grabbed her duffel bag from the floor, then rose with a fluid grace.

Harley shoved away from the table. "What are you doing with my stuff?" She scurried after him as he vanished down the hallway, past the bathroom and around the corner.

He flung open a door and strolled into the room.

She hesitated.

The far wall boasted an oak dresser with a long mirror. On either side, floral curtains flanked the windows; the last vestiges of twilight floated in. About two feet from the opposite wall stood a twin bed with a bookcase headboard; it was covered with a bedspread that matched the curtains. A border in the same pink-and-lilac floral pattern edged the room at ceiling height.

Harley's heart tried to crawl into her throat. At eight, she'd begged her father to paint her room this exact shade of purple. After two weeks of her pleading, he'd finally caved in, and they'd spent an entire Sunday—the only day the garage was closed—painting the room together. But this…this was even prettier.

Jake dropped her bag on the foot of the bed, then leaned against the dresser. "This was my sister's room. You can stay here until we find you another job and another place to live."

"We?" She raised her eyebrows.

"Yes, we. I'm not about to take advantage of your situation."

"I thought you wanted a baby?"

His face softened and a wistful light appeared in his eyes. "I do. Listen to how quiet it is here, Harley. My home needs the sound of a child's laugher to bring it to life again."

He pushed off from the dresser. "This isn't something we have to discuss tonight. I know some people around town. Tomorrow I'll make a few phone calls and see what I can do about helping you find a new job. Until then—'' he gestured toward the bed ''—make yourself at home.''

"At home," she murmured with a small sigh.

He paused in the doorway beside her, so close the warmth from his body made her cheeks flush. The lingering scent of his spicy cologne hung in the air between them. How was it that he made her feel like a teenager in the throes of adolescent hormone-rush? His gaze settled on her mouth, and for a moment she feared he was going to kiss her—and at the same time she feared he wouldn't....

Kissing was not something she was supposed to be thinking about when it came to Jake Manning. Making a baby, yes; kissing, no. Kissing implied a relationship. They were just going to have sex. Eventually. Maybe. Her flush deepened.

"Good night, Harley. I'll keep the dogs in my room, so you don't have to worry about them bothering you."

The dogs. How could she have forgotten? *Easy. Out of sight, out of mind.* "Your dogs don't have rabies, do they?"

His rich laughter flowed over her, then suddenly stopped. "You're not joking, are you?"

Her hand covered her stomach. "No."

"What happened to you?"

She couldn't resist the genuine concern in his eyes. "I was attacked by a dog when I was little. They never found it, so I had to have rabies shots."

"Ouch. From what I hear, that's pretty painful."

"It was." Besides pain, the strongest memory of

the experience was her father's callused hands, smelling of soap and lingering grease as he comforted her.

"I'm sorry. But honestly, my dogs won't hurt you. And neither will I." He brushed the back of his fingers across her cheek.

Startled by the unexpected contact, she flinched. *That's what they all say,* she reminded herself. *Pretty words and empty promises. Why did you tell him all that?*

He shoved his hand into his pocket. "Like I said, make yourself at home."

He slipped away and headed down the hallway, back toward the dining room.

Harley closed the bedroom door and turned the old-fashioned lock.

She surveyed the room again. Hands down, it qualified as the most beautiful room in which she'd ever stayed. But make herself at home? She didn't have a clue what that meant. Should she do the dishes and sweep the floor? Chores had been a requirement in most of her foster homes.

A cold sweat broke across the back of her neck. The price for this lodging was going to be steep—although he hadn't pressed the baby issue, nor had he mentioned her "demands."

She decided to ignore her worries about the price. *For tonight, I'm going to sleep in a nice, comfortable place. Tomorrow is soon enough to worry about tomorrow.*

She stripped down to her T-shirt and panties, shoved the bed against the wall, then climbed in.

THE SOUNDS OF WILD LAUGHTER drifted through the open window and prodded Jake upward toward consciousness. He lifted his head and opened one eye to peer at the numbers on the clock. "Damn!" He bolted upright.

Summer vacation had begun, and the sound of screaming kids playing outside should've been his first clue that he'd overslept. Overslept! He never overslept. Of course, he didn't usually toss and turn three-quarters of the night, either.

We make this baby the old-fashioned way.

Her words rattled around in his brain, as they had all night long.

What the hell had he gotten himself into?

Throwing back the sheet, he slid from the bed. The dogs scrambled to their feet. "I suppose you guys want to go out?" he asked as he padded to his dresser. They whined in response. He pulled on a pair of navy cotton shorts and walked quickly toward the door.

After they'd taken care of business, he shut them back in his room and headed for the shower. No running or workout at the gym this morning.

The bathroom door snapped open as he reached it, and a towel-clad Harley exited. She stopped short before they collided. The curves of her breasts peeked seductively over the towel. His thin cotton shorts did little to conceal his sudden arousal; he hoped she wouldn't notice. He cleared his throat. "Good morning."

"Morning."

Roses. He leaned closer and inhaled deeply. "You smell good. What is that?"

"My shampoo. I hope you don't mind that I took another shower."

Jake lifted his gaze from the towel to really look at her. Her eyes were wide and filled with...concern? Fear?

"You're welcome to use the shower whenever you want."

"I thought you'd already left. I won't use any more water."

"Water's cheap. I told you to make yourself at home."

She clutched the towel with one hand. "Whatever that means," she muttered.

"What?"

"Nothing. I'll get dressed and get out of here."

"Where will you go? I told you, the room's yours until we find you someplace else to go and a job to support you."

"And then what?"

"Then we talk about my baby again." His gaze swept over her. "And about your terms."

He stifled a groan as uncertainty clouded her eyes. He couldn't allow himself to feel for this woman. This was a business arrangement, no matter how they decided to play it out. "I'm behind schedule. I have to hit the shower now."

She hesitated, then nodded and turned toward Melanie's room. He did his best to ignore the sway of her hips and the long, lean legs that taunted him until she disappeared behind the bedroom door.

He bolted into the bathroom and twisted the cold water tap wide open. Maybe that would clear his head. Maybe that would subdue his hormones. But he doubted it.

BEGGARS CAN'T BE CHOOSERS. Harley knew it, had embraced it as her part of her life's credo, but she hated it. Hated it with a passion. At least there was some challenge to being a mechanic, and damn it, she was good at what she did.

But this?

She plopped down on an overturned plastic bucket and braced the course catalog on her knees. Both overhead doors to the narrow garage that housed the Quik E. Lube stood open, and a sticky breeze flowed through, circulating the smell of oil.

Officially she was an "oil change technician." Unofficially, she was a grease grunt making even less money than Ned's lousy pay.

The one advantage was that the owner trusted her enough to leave her alone in the place. The fact that he knew Jake probably helped.

Harley ran a finger over the list of courses she still needed for her degree: business policy, several more business electives, another literature class—thirty more credits in all. The breeze rustled the pages.

The purr of a finely tuned engine grabbed her attention as a car pulled into the garage. "Oh, yeah!" She dropped the course catalog beside the upturned bucket and stood. "You've got to be kidding me," she said to the convertible's driver. "A Mercedes SL500, and you bring it to Quick E. Lube for work?"

The blond man in a dark suit that screamed money slipped off a pair of dark sunglasses and flashed a perfect set of teeth. "Not the most impressive job of salesmanship I've ever heard."

Harley ran an appreciative eye over the silver car. "Sorry, just telling the truth. This car starts at eighty-thousand—"

"Eighty-three."

"Whatever. If you can afford this, you can afford to take it to the dealer for service. I don't think I even have the parts in stock." She crossed behind the car and headed to the work counter and the computer.

"I don't have time to wait around for dealerships. Time is money and I don't waste either." The man stepped out of the convertible and strutted around to the passenger side, leaning against the door and folding his arms over his chest. "Check quickly."

Harley felt the weight of his stare as he slowly looked her over. She focused on the computer screen as she typed in the model number. "Nope, sorry. Don't have the filter."

"Well, now, that is a loss for me. I would've liked to see you bent over my engine."

Harley's face heated. *I'll bet.* "Not today."

He straightened away from the car and sauntered around the short counter separating them. "A shame indeed. You know, it's not easy to find a gorgeous woman who appreciates a fine car. I've had bimbos who like the way it looks, but never one who knew the model and price tag just by sight.''

Her mouth went dry as he advanced on her. She backed against the wall. ''No customers behind the counter.'' Eyes locked on his, and not liking the predatory stare she found there, she cast blindly across the counter with her left hand.

''I'd like to be more than a customer, baby. I appreciate fine cars, fine wine and fine women.'' He lowered his gaze to her chest. ''And you are one of the finest women I've seen in a long time. I can take you places you've never been before. I came for a lube job—'' he ran his tongue over his lips ''—and I'd really like to get one. What do you say?''

She found what she was searching for and tightened her grip. ''I say, unless you'd like a wrench upside that thick skull of yours, you'd better get back in your car and get the hell out of here.'' She held the wrench out in front of her.

Pretty Boy stopped in his tracks. ''You wouldn't.''

''Care to bet those capped teeth on it?''

He slowly—scornfully—looked her up and down again. ''Come to think of it, you're not worth the effort. And these teeth probably cost more than you make in a year.'' He smoothed his suit jacket. ''No, now that I take a good look, I don't think a woman with grease under her stubby fingernails is something I need. Not even for a quick lube job.'' He cast her a final, disparaging glance as he opened the car door. ''And I certainly wouldn't have wanted anything more than that from you.''

The engine roared and his tires squealed as he tore out of the garage.

The wrench trembled in her hand, and she placed it back on the counter. On slightly unsteady legs, she crossed the garage and retrieved the course catalog. "Success is the best revenge," she muttered. She would be more than this. Harley Emerson would be somebody worthy of people's respect. And right now it looked like there was only one way to make that dream come true.

DELIGHTED GIGGLES GREETED Harley as she trudged into Jake's house, and she remembered his early-morning comment about babysitting his sister's twins, Grace and Hope, for the evening. She'd met them briefly the day she'd arrived.

This would be the perfect time to check out the truth of his daddy résumé. Would the reality match the hype? After the run-in with Pretty Boy this afternoon, she hoped he'd be able to give a child the happy home she'd always envisioned. The fact that he hadn't pressured her into the surrogacy had already scored him points.

So had the job he'd helped her get, and the fact that he'd invited her to stay until she could accumulate enough money to rent a new apartment. Which would take a few more weeks. Part of her already regretted the day she'd have enough to leave.

The dogs raced to the foyer, skidding to a stop when she pointed a finger in their direction. "No! Sit! Stay!" She unlaced her work boots with a wary eye on them. Tails wagging, they disregarded her commands and ran back the other way.

Harley rounded the corner to find Jake on his hands and knees, a pair of blond "cowgirls" dressed in sleeveless white shirts and tiny jeans riding on his back. The "horse" bucked gently, carrying the toddlers around the living room.

"Now, there's a sight," Harley announced.

Jake started and the little girls shrieked with delight, apparently thinking it was part of the act. "Okay, girls, off you get. The horse needs a rest."

"No," said one twin.

"No," repeated the second.

"Yes. I'll give you another ride later." Jake slid the children off, then rose to his feet, brushing dog hair from his knees. "How was your day?"

Harley clutched the course catalog to her chest. Jake's face was flushed with exertion and excitement, emphasizing his high cheekbones. His normally fastidious clothes were rumpled from his romp with the children, and she decided he'd never looked more appealing.

"Harley?"

"Oh, my day was fine." If you didn't count being bored to death, accosted by a rich jackass or afflicted with PMS. She waved the book at him. "Let me go put this away."

His nieces had wandered off to the sofa, where they were turning a big canvas bag upside down and shaking out the contents. Diapers, powder and other items she couldn't identify tumbled to the floor.

"Girls!" Jake dashed toward them.

Harley chuckled and turned on her heel, walking down the hallway to her room. She eased open the door, then shut it behind her before either of the two dogs or the cat could scoot in. She'd learned quickly that the only way to avoid an animal on her bed was to keep the door closed at all times.

She dropped the course catalog on the dresser and threw herself down on the twin bed. She loved this pretty purple room.

One week in the place had given her a new appreciation for the word *home*. For this home in particular and for the man who owned it.

"Harley? Did you eat?" Jake called. "We're having pizza if you want some."

Harley pushed herself upright and clambered off the bed. "Sounds good to me."

The twins sat on booster seats attached to the dining-room chairs with straps. As Harley walked in, Jake deftly fastened a bib around one of the girl's necks. He tossed another bib at Harley. "Here, you put on Hope's while I get the pizza."

"Peeza!" Grace shrieked as Harley snatched the bib from the air.

She approached the tiny child with trepidation, turning the bib in various directions. Okay, she was mechanically inclined; she could figure this out. The snaps didn't look that difficult.

Closing them around the neck of a wriggling child, on the other hand, was something else entirely. "Hold still a second, Hope."

Each time she brought the pieces together, the child moved. Fearing she'd choke the little girl, Harley flung the bib on the table in disgust. She glanced at the frilly white blouse and envisioned pizza sauce all over it. "I've got a better idea." She grabbed the bottom of the shirt, tugging it up over the little blond head. It came off easily, and Harley nodded in satisfaction. "There."

She sank into a chair at the end of the table, a twin on either side.

"Peeza!" Grace shrieked again as she pounded her palms on the tabletop. "Me want peeza!"

"Me too, peeza," Hope echoed, mimicking her sister's motions.

"It's coming, squirts, be patient!" Jake emerged from the kitchen, holding two paper plates. He set one in front of each child, cleared his throat when he saw Hope, then raised his eyebrows at Harley.

"What?"

"I asked you to put her bib on, not strip her half-naked."

"Relax. Skin cleans up easy, a lot easier than that white shirt would. You were going to give them a bath tonight, anyway, right?"

Jake nodded.

"There you go. So, you give her a bath, the pizza sauce comes off, and you don't even have a bib to wash."

Jake offered her a half smile. "I have to admit there's a certain logic in that statement."

"Thanks…I think."

By the time supper was over, he definitely conceded the logic of her approach. The twins not only had pizza sauce covering their bibs, or in Hope's case, her chest, but they had it smeared all over their faces, and plastered in their hair. For some reason, feeding them had never been such a messy chore. Of course, Harley's laughter every time they made a mess had encouraged the slovenly eating, but he hadn't had the heart to chastise any of them for it. Harley's laughter delighted him no end.

"I'm going to get their baths ready. You entertain the troops while I'm gone, and whatever you do, don't let them down from those chairs until I call for them."

"I think I can handle it." Harley pulled a bite-size piece of pizza from Grace's hair, then flicked it onto the paper plate. Grace giggled and grabbed it, hurling it to the floor, where Benji immediately raced in to snatch it.

"Don't feed the dogs pizza," Jake admonished.

"Don't tell me, tell your niece. I wouldn't feed the dogs anything. They'd probably take my fingers with it."

Hope, always one step behind her sister, threw a square of pizza at Pepper. "Dog!"

Harley laughed.

"Stop encouraging them, Harley."

She covered her mouth, stifling a chuckle. "Sorry." When her hand came down, her face was a mask of seriousness. "Ladies, this behavior is totally unacceptable and must cease. No more pizza-throwing.''

''That's better.'' He turned and strode down the hallway, gathering towels from the linen closet as he passed. He tried to ignore the implications of the giggles he heard behind him.

Soon he had the tub filled and all the supplies lined up. ''Harley! I'm ready. Bring in the dastardly duo.''

He debated going to help her. Sometimes getting them both to move in the same direction could be a real challenge.

''Yay!'' screamed Grace as she charged into the bathroom, Hope hot on her heels. ''Bath!'' Grace held her arms over her head, and Jake peeled her shirt off.

Hope plopped onto the floor and yanked off her pink socks. ''Me too, bath.''

Jake glanced up at Harley, who leaned against the doorjamb. ''Okay, how'd you get them both in here so fast?''

She smiled. ''That's our little secret, right, girls?''

Blond heads bobbed agreement.

''I've been overrun by women.'' Jake growled at the twins, inciting shrieks of delight. ''All right, if you're so good at hustling them in here, maybe you should give them their bath.''

The color drained from her face. ''No, I think I'll clean up the dining room and kitchen instead. You deal with the bath.'' She turned quickly and vanished.

Jake finished undressing the twins and then lifted them into the tub, his thoughts miles away.

Harley obviously had little experience with children, but what she lacked in actual knowledge she made up for with pluck and improvisation. He still knew almost nothing about her family life, and suspected a few more skeletons might fall out of her closet if he rattled it hard enough, but he knew enough to admire her. She was intelligent, spunky and resourceful. She'd make an excellent surrogate.

Images of making that baby occupied his mind far more than he cared to admit. But he felt a sliver of fear, too. What if she turned out to be different from most of the women he'd known? What if she had a hard time spinning through the revolving door and out of his baby's life?

He needed to consult his lawyer again and make sure his biological rights, in addition to the agreement he'd already had drawn up, would be enough to assure him custody if Harley changed her mind about giving up the child.

When would she feel convinced of his fitness as a parent? When could he be sure she was no longer a woman desperate enough to agree to anything? The job was a good first step.

However, keeping her in his house while she carried his baby wasn't a bad idea. He'd be able to monitor things much better that way, bond with the baby before it was even born.

A splash of soapy water hit his face, and Jake blinked, then rubbed his eyes. "Keep the water in the tub, you two. Let's wash your hair and get out of here."

Ten minutes later, he pulled two clean, fresh-smelling toddlers from the tub, then let the water drain. While he wrapped Hope in a towel and began to dry her, Grace seized the opportunity to run naked from the bathroom. "Hey!"

He dried Hope quickly, then wrapped the towel around her and picked her up. Before he could leave the bathroom, Harley appeared in the doorway, Grace held firmly around the middle and tucked under her arm like a football. Grace giggled and kicked her feet wildly.

"I caught this dripping-wet streaker jumping on the sofa. What do you want me do with her?"

Jake grinned. "Dry her off and follow me." He tossed a fluffy yellow towel at her and carried Hope to the living room.

He spread out another towel on the floor and laid the toddler down on it, reaching for the diaper bag. Harley sat on the couch, Grace held captive between her legs while she dried the squirming child. Jake felt her eyes on his every move as he diapered and dressed Hope.

"You're pretty good at that."

"I've had plenty of practice."

"Oh?" She ran the terry cloth over Grace's hair.

"I took care of Mel and Dusty a lot when they were little." Jake scooped Hope off the floor and set her on her feet. "There you go, squirt." He glanced at Harley. "Your turn."

"Oh, no, I'll leave it in your capable hands." She passed Grace to him.

Jake placed the second twin on the towel. "You haven't been around kids much, have you?"

"No."

"No brothers or sisters?"

"No." Her face was taking on that wary expression again.

"Where'd you grow up?" Jake fastened the diaper tabs around Grace's middle.

"Here and there."

He raised his head to meet her gaze and locked eyes with her, refusing to let her off the hook this time. He knew from the day at Dusty and Kate's that she'd lost her father at some point, but surely there were other relatives? "Where's your family now?"

"I—I don't have any."

"None?"

She shook her head. "None to speak of. My—my mother might be out there somewhere, but I don't know where."

He grunted. "I know that feeling."

"You do?" Her eyes widened.

"Yup." Jake guided Grace's foot into the bottom of her lightweight summer pajamas. "My mother took off when Dusty was two. Decided she'd had enough of motherhood. Left the three of us to 'find herself' with a new boyfriend. How old were you when yours took off?"

"Not even one."

So, her own mother had gone through the revolving door. That explained why she believed a man could raise a child by himself. "What about your dad?"

"Killed in a motorcycle accident when I was ten."
She stared at the floor.

Jake lowered Grace to her feet and she ran off to
play with her sister and a pile of blocks. He leaned
back on his heels. "What happened to you then?"

She lifted her chin and looked deep into his eyes.
Unspoken pain sparked briefly in hers, then a shim-
mer of determination replaced it. "Jake, let me ask
you this. If something happens to you, will your sister
and brother take care of your baby? Like it was their
own?"

Your baby. That was an excellent choice of words
in his opinion. "Of course they would."

"Good." She rose from the sofa. "Now, I have to
go and finish cleaning the dining room. There are tiny
red handprints on the woodwork." She glanced at
him over her shoulder. "But once you get those two
settled for the night, we need to talk."

CHAPTER FIVE

"ALL RIGHT, THE TWINS are on the sofa watching a video. They'll probably be asleep in five minutes. Let's talk." Jake took the sponge from Harley's hand as she wiped the last of the pizza sauce off the wood paneling in the dining area.

Her stomach gave a little flip at the thought of what she was about to do. She cleared her throat and stood up. "Can we do this in your office? After all, it's— it's business."

An eager light flashed in his eyes. "Business, huh? All right, go on in. I'll be there as soon as I get rid of this sponge."

She entertained herself by checking out all the stuff hanging on the walls in his office. Her fingertips brushed reverently over the frame of his Bachelor of Architecture degree. A master's certificate hung next to it. This, *this* was why Jake Manning had the chance to hold a respected place in society. *Yeah, this and the fact that he doesn't have a criminal conviction.* The conviction she couldn't do anything about, but getting a piece of paper like this was something she could—would—do.

Blueprints of houses also dotted the wall, along

with an impressive poster-size photo of the new hotel down on the Bayfront. But it was the picture of Jake beside a little boy with a precariously held ice cream cone that captured her attention. She lifted it from the wall to examine it carefully. Man and boy shared silly grins with whoever stood behind the camera. Why hadn't he included this photo in his daddy résumé package? "Who's this?" she asked as Jake came up behind her.

He sighed. "That's Austin. I tried to adopt him about a year ago."

"What happened?"

"Social worker decided he'd be better off in a two-parent home."

Harley looked over at him. Longing flickered in his eyes, but then he shrugged. "Nothing I could do about it."

"Social workers." She wrinkled her nose. "Get a good one, and you're lucky. Get the average over-worked, underpaid, frantic one, and…" And you ended up shuffled from place to place, and in some homes that shouldn't have been allowed to take in a vicious dog, let alone a child.

While good people and good kids were separated.

She handed Jake the photo, then touched his fore-arm. The same tingling sensation she'd felt when she'd touched him in Ned's garage surged up her fin-gers. "I'm really sorry. I'm sure Austin was, too."

The picture rocked briefly as he hung it back on the wall. He straightened it, then turned and waved at the chair in front of his desk. "Have a seat." He settled on the stool by the slanted table.

Harley perched on the edge of the chair. "After seeing you with your nieces tonight, I know you were telling the truth. You'll make a great father."

Jake slowly released his breath. "Good." He didn't dare say more.

"You know what my terms are. Have you thought about them?"

Thought about them? He'd dreamed about them, awakening with a hard-on that wouldn't quit. "Yes, yes, I have."

"Okay, so then you realize that marrying me is a good idea for your baby? So he or she is legitimate?"

Good idea? No. But one he was willing to concede. After all, it was a marriage on paper only. Besides, marrying her also meant his insurance would cover the pregnancy and delivery. "That's fine. As is your other, um, condition."

She jumped from the chair to pace the room. "Okay. So how do we do this?"

"My lawyer is completing the paperwork. First, I want you to have a medical exam. We can get the name of Mel's OB/GYN, unless you have someone else you prefer."

Her face lost some of its color and she stopped in the middle of the room. "OB/GYN?" She tossed her head in apparent indifference. "No, Mel's doctor is fine. Whatever." She started walking again.

"I think I'd like you to keep staying here. That

way, I have a chance to be close to the baby and bond with him before birth."

"What?" Her head bobbed a crazy pattern, not quite a nod. "You want me to *stay?* Here? Uh, okay. I'd like that." She halted in front of his diplomas, stealing a quick glance at them. "And I get to go to school full-time, right? You'll pay for as many credits as I can handle?"

"Well, I don't want you overdoing it. Too much stress isn't good for an expectant..." *Mother* wasn't really the word he wanted to use, since she wasn't going to really be a mother. "Woman," he finished.

"I'll keep working at the Quick E. Lube part-time, too."

"I don't think so." Jake came out of his chair. "I don't think a garage is the right environment for an expectant woman, either."

Her eyes revealed disappointment. "But I need the money. I have other bills to pay, insurance on my truck, stuff like that."

"I'll take care of anything you need."

She shook her head. "I don't want a handout, just the tuition."

"Look, Harley, I'm not going to argue with you. Whatever needs you have will be my responsibility. For the duration of our agreement, your problems are my problems."

This time skepticism filled her eyes.

"I'm serious."

One of the twins screeched from the living room. "Uh-oh. I'd better go check on that. We'll get things rolling, okay?'' Jake reached out and touched her arm as he passed. ''Thank you, Harley.'' It didn't seem like enough, but how did you thank a woman for agreeing to have your baby?

Jake hustled toward the living room as another screech pierced the air.

ABOUT A WEEK LATER, as Jake sat in his downtown office, tires squealed on the pavement outside. He whirled in his chair, peering out the window just in time to see a car on State Street narrowly miss getting rear-ended by another. His corner second-floor office allowed a view of both State and Twelfth, and accidents were just one of the many distractions.

''Jake, you still there?''

He grabbed the receiver, deactivating the speakerphone. ''Yeah, I'm here.''

''Sorry to put you on hold for so long.''

''As long as you stopped the clock while you did it. I'm not paying for you to talk to somebody else.''

His lawyer laughed. ''No, I'm not charging you for hold time. Now, I've gotten your prenuptial drawn up. All you need to do is drop by the office with your intended and sign it. You're absolutely sure this is the way you want to go, not with a surrogate contract?''

''The mother-to-be won't have it any other way.''

''There are other surrogates out there.''

''I want this one.'' Man, did he want this one. The house suddenly seemed too small, and no matter which way he turned, she was there. He occasionally found strands of her hair in the bathroom, and her toothbrush lying next to his on the counter presented a picture of domestic tranquility he found hard to ignore. He raced home from the office in the evenings and was disappointed if she wasn't there.

Watch your heart, watch your heart, watch your heart. Dusty's words echoed in his mind. He had to admit his little brother had a point. When Stacy had gotten the offer to be a news anchor in a bigger market, she'd decided that being married to him didn't mesh with her new opportunity; he hadn't known such pain could exist. He'd believed she was content—content with her life as it was. Finding her stuff gone had been quite a shock. So had realizing he hadn't been as much in love with her as he'd thought. The new catch-phrase for it was a "starter marriage." Which actually applied now that he was facing matrimony for a second time.

"Jake? Have I lost you?"

"Huh? Oh, yeah. How soon can we drop by? I want to get this done." It had already been almost a week since they'd agreed to go through with the plan.

"Come anytime, Jake. Tomorrow would be fine."

"Okay, thanks." He replaced the receiver and turned back to his computer, where the contemporary house he was designing for some very wealthy clients awaited his finishing touches. He keyed in some changes.

Mrs. Witherby had specifically requested—no, demanded—a cupola. Jake grimaced. It threw off all the lines. He'd repeatedly pointed it out to both Witherbys, but they'd been adamant. Well, they were the clients, and the clients were always right, even when they were ridiculously wrong. The fees he charged them would pay for Harley's fall semester tuition. So, he wouldn't include this house in his folio. There were plenty of other buildings he was proud of— buildings he could use to attract future clients.

A tapping on his office door diverted him from the design. "Come in."

Harley waltzed in, stunning in a pale yellow T-shirt dress. It clung to her curves and set off her emerald eyes. She dropped into one of the chairs alongside his desk and crossed her legs, dangling a sandal off her toes. It was a far cry from her normal work boots, jeans and T-shirts. He'd never seen her look more feminine.

"I hope you're happy," she said.

"Happy?"

She shuddered. "I just came from my appointment with the OB/GYN."

He glanced at the clock on the wall. "Oh, right. I'd forgotten about that."

"Too bad I didn't forget." She scowled at him.

"And?"

"And I'm perfectly healthy, and the doctor sees no reason we shouldn't be able to conceive a child. He did remind me that it could take six months to a year, and that given your age, if we don't conceive within a year, we should take 'appropriate action.' His words."

Jake leaned back in his chair. "Six months to a year just to conceive?" That was far too long. He'd already realized that the longer he stayed in contact with her, the more danger he could be in. The very last thing he wanted was to fall in love with her. Damn it, why did she have to be so *likable?* "It didn't take Dusty and Kate that long, or Mel, either, for that matter."

"And they're all younger than we are."

"I'm thirty-five, for crying out loud! You're twenty-seven. Since when is that ancient?"

"Look, don't shoot me, I'm just the messenger. And hey, it wasn't you on that damn table today, so give me a break." She shuddered again. "I hate doctors."

"I guess you'll have to get used to them. We can swing by my lawyer's office and take care of the pre-nuptial, and we'll get this show on the road."

"Careful, you'll make me think you're either eager to get rid of me or eager to get me into your bed."

The way her voice dropped on the word *bed* sent a jolt of desire coursing through him, one that made him grit his teeth. It'd been a long time since he'd taken a woman to his bed. Two years, two months and seventeen days, to be exact. But who was counting?

He turned his chair back to face his computer, saved the final changes to the Witherbys' house, then started burning a backup CD. "Tell you what, since you had such a terrible day, why don't I make it up to you by taking you out for dinner? Seems the least I can do."

"Sounds good to me. How about the Peninsula for the sunset afterward?"

He looked at her sharply. "I thought that was your favorite quiet time? You told me you liked to spend it alone."

"That's true. But I wondered if you'd like to take a break from analyzing things to just enjoy something for a change."

"I suppose I could give it a try." Jake took the backup disk from the computer and slipped it into a plastic case. Crossing the room, he placed it in the drawer of a metal filing cabinet. "Okay, let's go."

THE WIND STIRRED HER HAIR, fanning it into her face. Harley tucked the strands behind her ear, wishing she'd put it in a ponytail before coming down to the beach.

Gulls whirled overhead, their piercing cries carried away by the breeze off Lake Erie. The clouds began their nightly show of colors, the reds and golds appearing first. Harley slid her bare feet deeper into the sand and closed her eyes. Peace, an elusive thing in her muddled life, embraced her like a long-lost friend. The trees rustled behind her, soothing, calming.

Jake exhaled loudly and stirred restlessly beside her.

She opened her eyes and turned to look at him. Still wearing his powder-blue, button-down shirt, black circle-and-star tie, gray dress slacks and black split-toe oxfords, he looked as out of place on the beach as she would at a gala ball in her mechanic's coveralls.

She shook her head and moved to the edge of the blanket at his feet. "You're not getting into the spirit of the exercise, Jake. You really need to loosen up." She tugged on the laces of his shoes, untying both at once.

"What are you doing?"

"I'm loosening you up. Close your eyes and listen to the birds, the water, the wind." She peeled off his socks, then rolled the bottoms of his pant legs up three turns. Pushing aside the blanket, she pressed his feet down. "Feel the sand."

She crawled back up to his side. Her hands shook as she reached for his tie. Did she dare? *Just do it.* After all, the man intended to make a baby with her. Removing his tie was a little thing in comparison. She worked her fingers into the knot and pulled.

His eyes flew open and he caught her hand. "What are you doing now?"

She swallowed hard at the dusky look he gave her, then ran her tongue over her lips. "Still loosening you up?"

"Actually, I think you're tightening something," he murmured, caressing the back of her hand.

The contact sent a flash of pure fire up her arm and down into her stomach. She pulled harder on the tie, got it free and dropped it to the blanket. The buttons at the top of his shirt challenged her quivering fingers, but she finally managed to open them. His caress traveled farther up her arm, distracting her from the task. "There," she whispered. "That's better, isn't it?"

He shifted closer to her. "Yes. Much." He grasped her gently by the forearms and drew her to a seated position. "That's even better."

Harley could see the setting sun reflected in his eyes. She could see other things, too: a tenderness, an echo of the compassion she'd seen when Ned fired her...and desire.

She trembled, unsure of herself. What was this knot in her stomach, this tightness in her chest? It was more than a physical response; that much she knew. But surely it wasn't...love? Was this what it felt like? Had she really begun to fall for him?

What kind of idiot falls for a man who only wants a surrogate? A woman to give birth to his child? All right, so he was tender, and compassionate, and he'd believed in her innocence at the garage. Still, he'd already made plans to remove her from his life.

Harley sighed. Goodbyes she knew how to handle. Perhaps she should just enjoy this while it lasted. A small piece of heaven was better than some people ever got, and definitely more than she'd ever had before.

She closed her eyes again and leaned in toward him.

Jake recognized her intention immediately, and despite a stab of apprehension, followed suit, closing his eyes and easing forward to meet her.

First contact was soft, hesitant.

The warmth of her lips drew him deeper, and he

wrapped his arms around her and pulled her against him. The pounding of his pulse in his ears overwhelmed the cry of the gulls, the sounds of the water. Her tongue danced along the edge of his lips, and he opened his mouth to let her in.

Passion, more powerful, more heated, than he'd ever experienced, grabbed him and dragged him under, a strong current he should have struggled against, but didn't. He'd willingly drown in her arms.

Her hands slid around the back of his neck and she ran her fingers through his hair, pressing him deeper, urging him onward. The kiss took on a life of its own and the world around them came to a sudden halt.

After what seemed an eternity, she pushed her palms against his chest. They both gasped for air, eyes now open and gazes locked. The desire in hers rattled him, though he was sure his own must hold the same smoldering fire.

"Holy…" she breathed.

"Smokes," he finished for her. "I think we might want to move that wedding day up."

CHAPTER SIX

HARLEY'S WEDDING DAY ranked right up there as another one of those should've-stayed-in-bed days. She couldn't escape the courthouse fast enough. She scrambled out the heavy glass doors and onto the sidewalk.

The hot end-of-July sun reflected off the windows across the street, making her squint. Midday traffic crawled, someone's brakes screeched, and she winced at the rotor damage the fool was probably causing; the sounds of people laughing and talking surrounded her. She couldn't breathe.

Her husband finally caught up to her. "I'm sorry, Harley."

"It doesn't matter."

"It matters to me. I just had no idea."

She flipped open her purse and pulled out a pair of sunglasses, shoving them onto her face before she turned to him. "It's done. That's all that matters."

"The judge I wanted was on vacation, and if I'd known Judge Ephraim had been the one to sentence you, I would've made sure—"

"I said it's okay. Let's just forget it." Easier said than done. Her stomach tightened as she recalled the sneer on the judge's face. He hadn't forgotten her any more than she'd forgotten him, and he'd made it his business to ensure that her groom knew all about her criminal record before he read the vows. Thank God she'd talked Jake out of asking his family to attend the ceremony. As it was, the two secretaries they'd snagged to act as witnesses had goggled at her when the judge launched into his lecture about her past. Why did it seem that no matter what she did to start a new life, the old one popped up to haunt her?

Jake groaned and Harley looked up at him, then followed the direction of his eyes. A uniformed cop strode in their direction. Jake slipped an arm around her waist and pulled her close. "Smile. Our secret wedding is about to be a secret no longer. I thought we'd have more time before I had to explain this hasty marriage."

"Jake, Harley." Dusty gave Harley a quick once-over. "What are you doing at the courthouse?" He arched an eyebrow at her.

"It so happens, little brother, that congratulations are in order. Harley and I just got married."

"You *what?*"

"You heard me." Jake squeezed her tighter, as if he knew her fear of his brother, the cop. Every time Dusty looked at her, she couldn't shake the feeling that all he saw was her record.

"No, I don't think I heard you. At least not correctly." Dusty raised his arm and peered at his wristwatch. "I have to run, I'm testifying. But I'll be by later so we can talk about this."

Jake took a step toward him. "There's nothing to talk about, and I'll be rather busy this evening, so don't bother, *little* brother." The emphasis on *little* rang loud and clear.

Dusty shot her a glare that would have withered a lesser person, but Harley had become immune to those kinds of looks. She smiled politely at him, hoping it would irritate him more than anything she could do or say. Dusty whirled on his polished black heel, then stalked to the courthouse door.

"Sorry. He's a little possessive and overprotective of me. He'll get over it." Jake took her elbow and guided her down the sidewalk in the direction of his Mustang.

"I hope so, for your sake. Maybe you should just tell him the truth."

Jake halted mid-step. "No. You were right. I hadn't thought about the implications of an arrangement like this for the baby. I don't want Dusty or Mel looking at my child like he's somehow different from their own. A child of divorce or adoption is completely understandable in this day and age, but a baby by arrangement is still a little suspect. The truth is between you, me and my lawyer, and I want it to stay that way."

"Whatever works for you." They resumed their trek toward the car. "Are you going back to work?"

He paused in the act of inserting the key into the lock. "It's my wedding day. I'm taking the afternoon off."

"Oh." Damn it, he had no right to be so handsome,

and he had no right to tap into her fantasies without permission. She'd hoped for a reasonable facsimile of a wedding, and so far it had been a day from hell. But his sparkling eyes held promise, maybe her wedding night wouldn't be quite the disaster her day had been.

HE'D BEEN A FOOL TO SUGGEST the fancy restaurant for a late lunch. Harley had looked the part of an elegant lady in her simple short white dress, the dress he'd insisted she buy. She'd carefully watched his every move regarding silverware, and she'd eaten everything placed in front of her. Which turned out to be the biggest mistake of all.

Jake pulled the Mustang into the garage and glanced over at his wife. *Wife.* Damn, that word took some getting used to again. The ashen pallor of her normally pink complexion concerned him. "Here we are, Harley. Home at last."

"Thank goodness." She climbed out of the car. "I'm going to lie down."

The dogs barked from inside the kitchen and she hesitated on the top step, waiting for him. "You go first."

"How do you get in the house when I'm not here?"

"I yell at them. A lot. And I'm not up to that." She raised her hand to massage her temple.

Jake opened the door and shoved Pepper aside. "Come on, who wants a cookie?" Like the Pied Piper, he marched across the kitchen with the dogs trailing behind, tongues lolling, tails wagging a mile a minute.

Harley kicked off her sandals and trudged from the kitchen without another word.

Jake changed out of his dress clothes into a pair of jeans and a polo shirt, then busied his hands with minor tasks. He fed the dogs, mopped the kitchen floor, straightened magazines. Anything to keep his mind off the track it continually wandered—Harley Emerson, a gorgeous, tempting woman soon to carry his child.

She'd looked beautiful today, at least until her face had blanched the same color as her dress. Between the shock of seeing that judge and the rich food he'd foolishly forced on her, it was no wonder she didn't feel well.

Jake's left hand curled into a fist, and he scrubbed the bathroom counter harder. The judge had raked over Harley's scrumptious body with his beady weasel eyes and Jake had clenched his teeth to avoid any trouble. Who the hell did the man think he was, looking down his pointy nose at her? Jake suddenly understood the comment she'd made about justice being handed down.

The puzzle pieces of her life were beginning to fit together to make a very sorry picture, despite the gaping holes still left in the center of the image. What other pieces were left for him to discover? He still didn't know what had happened to her after her father's death, although he had a pretty good idea. Especially given her comments about social workers, and the way she'd looked at Austin's picture.

The doorbell chimed. Jake tossed the sponge under the vanity, rinsed his hands, then grabbed a towel from the bar near the tub. In the foyer, he peered through the window alongside the door as he dried his hands.

Melanie stood on the screened porch, balancing a large white box while the twins clung to either leg. Peter waved at him from behind Mel, then shrugged his shoulders, a universally male sign that he had no more of a clue about what was going on than Jake did.

Jake draped the towel over his shoulder, opened the door and the crew rambled into the house. "Hi, Mel, Peter." He leaned over. "Hi, squirts. Do you have a hug for your uncle Jake?"

Grace lifted her arms, and he scooped her up.

"Me too!"

"Yeah, you too, Hope." He wrapped his other arm around the second toddler and hoisted them both to his chest. Their sweet baby-shampoo scent filled him with longing. Being an uncle was great, but it wasn't the same as being a daddy. If things went according to plan, he'd soon know the difference.

Mel bussed him on the cheek and breezed by him, carrying her white box to the dining room.

"To what do I owe this unexpected pleasure?" he asked, following her.

"Cake!" Hope sang.

"Big cake," Grace added. "No happy birfday cake."

Peter brushed past him, setting the twins' diaper bag on one of the chairs. "No, it's not a birthday cake."

Jake looked to his brother-in-law for assistance, but Peter just grinned at him and spread his hands, clearly indicating that Jake was on his own. Mel carefully untied the red string around the box and peeled away the cardboard to reveal exactly what his nieces had proclaimed—a big, white, one-layer wedding cake with *Jake and Harley* intertwined in flowing green script across the top.

"I see Dusty didn't wait long to call you," he murmured, setting the twins down on the floor. "Go play with your blocks. Now, Melanie, before you start in on me—"

"Start in on you? Why would I do that?" His sister enfolded him in a hug, then slapped him on the shoulder. "You mean, besides the fact that you didn't invite me to your wedding?"

"Now, Mel, this snuck up on us. It was kinda impulsive, you know? Besides, after my last wedding and its results, I didn't want any fuss. And look, here you are, fussing." He smiled to mask the pain of lying to her. "I already know how Dusty would've reacted...."

"Yes, I know what Dusty would've done." She shook her head. "He's not happy about this. I, on the other hand, am very glad for you. You deserve some happiness. I saw this coming. I mean, when I looked out that day and saw her in your arms, I just knew. Harley seems like a really nice woman, and I—where *is* your new bride?'' Mel backed away from him and swiveled her head, checking the kitchen.

''She's lying down.''

Mel covered her mouth with her hand, her eyes widening. ''Oops. We didn't interrupt anything, did we?'' She sent him a piercing look, and he nearly squirmed beneath her frank scrutiny. ''I mean, with the twins, we can't get anything cooking until after they've gone to sleep, so I didn't think—''

''Thanks, Mel, that was more than I really wanted to know.''

Both she and Peter laughed. ''What?'' Mel said. ''My big brother, the one who taught me all I needed to know about fending off a guy, is squeamish about his sex life?''

''No, I'm squeamish about *your* sex life.'' Jake struggled with the urge to wipe the knowing smirk from Peter's face. ''I think I'll go get Harley. I'm sure she wouldn't want to miss the party.'' His sister's chuckles rang in his ears as he hurried down the hallway to Harley's room.

He rapped lightly on the door, then swung it open. ''Harley?''

Her first night in his house, she'd moved the twin bed to the far side of the room. Now he saw why. She slept with her back pressed firmly against the lavender wall, a pillow clutched in her arms, guarded securely both front and back. His heart went out to her, wondering again what had happened in her life to make even her sleep so insecure.

He lowered himself to the edge of the bed. "Harley?"

Her arms tightened on the pillow and she shrank farther against the wall. Jake felt certain she'd have melted into it if possible. Her eyes flew open.

"It's just me."

Her features softened. "Jake."

He loved hearing his name in that sexy, husky voice. His libido kicked into overdrive and he fought the impulse to gather her into his arms and make his sister's fears of interrupting something a reality. "I'm sorry to wake you, but my sister and Peter are here with the kids and they brought us a wedding cake."

"They did?" She tossed the pillow aside and stretched, then sat up on the bed and smoothed her hair.

He reached out to brush the long, silky strands off her cheek, tucking them behind her ear. "Have I told you how much I love your hair?"

She blushed, and the roses in her cheeks set off her creamy skin. He skimmed his fingertips over the flushed patches. Not even his newborn nephew had softer skin. "Are you ready to act the part of a newlywed?" he murmured.

"Ready, willing and able," she whispered.

He didn't think he'd have much of a problem with it himself.

JAKE CLOSED THE FRONT DOOR behind his sister and heaved a long, exaggerated sigh. "I thought they'd never leave.'' He grinned at Harley. ''Now, her re-action was a damn sight more pleasant than Dusty's.''

Harley shifted on the beige-and-brown sofa, tuck-ing her long legs underneath her. ''They both love you, Jake. You're lucky to have them.''

He sank into the cushions at the opposite end of the couch. ''Yes, I am. But they don't really need me anymore. Dusty's been married for more than two years, and he's got a son. Mel and Peter have the twins.''

''And now you want someone to need you again.''

''Does that sound foolish?''

''No. You're really good with children. You—you should have one of your own.'' She rose up on her knees and moved closer.

The aroma of the pink soap she'd left in his shower drifted through the air around him, a clean, feminine scent that made everything else recede.

The analytical part of his mind tapped him franti-cally on the shoulder, reminding him that he had no idea where she was in her cycle, or what their current odds of conception were.

Everything male in him rejected that observation.

He reached for Harley, pulling her into his arms. The delightful softness of her curves against him warmed his blood, made his senses sing. ''I want something from you, Harley.'' He brushed the back of his fingers over her lips. ''Do you know what it is?''

The vivid green of her eyes darkened as she shook her head.

"I want to make love to you. Tonight it's just you and me, with no thought about tomorrow or the future or anything else." He dipped his head and skimmed her mouth with his, a light, teasing kiss. "Can we do that?"

She nodded this time, and the desire in her eyes pushed his pulse rate to a higher level.

"I want to do this right for you. Wait here one second." He eased her off his lap, strode to the bedroom, then returned with the pink box he'd stashed under his bed several days earlier.

"Take this. And give me ten minutes." He set the gift on the couch next to her and knelt on the floor. He kissed her again, more urgently, reveling in the way her breathing hitched as he pulled away. "One more thing, sweetheart." He ran his fingers through the silky strands of her hair. "Put this back up for me."

"You like it better up?"

"No. I just like the idea of taking it down." He framed her face with his hands and brushed his lips over hers one more time. "Trust me."

He rose to his feet. "Ten minutes. My room."

Harley picked up the box and clutched it to her chest, contemplating his physique as he walked across the living room in the direction of the hall. His broad shoulders and narrow waist were perfectly formed. The hour he spent in the gym every morning clearly paid off.

She carried his gift to her room, closing the door gently behind her. A shiver of delight and anticipation ran through her as she thought about what would happen ten minutes from now....

Her insides melted to the consistency of warm motor oil.

She lifted the top of the box to expose a delicate glass bottle lying on tissue paper. Perfume. She hoped that wasn't his way of saying she smelled bad. She drew the stopper from the bottle and sniffed. Exotic flowers, with an oriental flavor. The label read Endless Possibilities. Once upon a time, long ago, she'd believed in endless possibilities. She dabbed the end of the stopper on her wrists and behind both ears.

Setting the bottle on her dresser, she returned her attention to the box, moving aside the layers of tissue paper. She caressed the smooth fabric—white satin—she found there. Unfolding the garment, she held it in front of her. A long, flowing nightgown with thin spaghetti straps.

A rueful smile tugged at her lips. He'd given her a virginal nightgown, when the truth was she'd lost that at a too-early age. To the son of a new set of foster parents. A boy she'd believed when he'd spoken words of love.

Harley shut her eyes for a few seconds. No point in dwelling on the past—but those lessons were something she needed to keep in mind. Jake and his nice-guy compassion had a way of getting deep into her head—and her heart. This was going to be about sex, about making a baby in a warm bed as opposed to a cold doctor's office. That she could handle. She'd had a few lovers after the boy who'd taken her virginity, but she'd never again confused sex with making love.

She quickly peeled off her clothes, then slipped the gown over her head, pausing to study her reflection. He'd judged the size perfectly. A long slit raced up the length of her right thigh, and the V neck took a daring plunge. She retrieved the perfume to apply one more dab just between her breasts.

She'd never felt sexier in her life.

She worked bobby pins into her hair, pinning it up. If that was how he wanted it, that was what he'd get.

She felt a touch of apprehension as she glided down the hallway toward his room, her bare feet padding softly on the polished wooden floor. Would she meet his expectations? She tapped on his door.

''Come in.''

Hand trembling, she turned the knob—and entered a true fantasy. Candles lit the room, casting flickering shadows across the king-size bed he'd already turned down. A pair of long-stemmed glasses and a bottle of champagne waited on the night table near the door. Soft instrumental music drifted from the stereo on his dresser.

Jake had her seduction planned to a ''t.''

And she was flattered beyond belief.

The tightness in her chest had nothing to do with the physical event about to take place and everything to do with the man himself. No one had ever been as thoughtful, as considerate.... The virginal nightgown was appropriate, after all, because she knew that for the first time in her life a man would truly make love to her.

And that scared the hell out of her. All the cynical lessons she'd learned in the past were forgotten. Foolish, crazy, stupid beyond belief—all those words applied to a woman who fell in love with a man who'd already set a term limit on their relationship, but Harley didn't care. Closing her eyes, she begged the fates for one tiny favor…and hoped that for once in her life, they'd listen. *Please, please, let it take me months to get pregnant.* The longer she postponed that, the longer she postponed the inevitable—leaving this home, and this man.

"You look beautiful."

She opened her eyes to discover he held a half-filled glass in her direction. "Thank you."

The tenor sax on the CD wove a sultry spell in the background as they sipped the champagne. Anxiety prickled along the nape of her neck. As if he knew how she felt, Jake took her glass and placed it back on the night table, along with his own. "May I have this dance?"

With a smile, she nodded. He pulled her tight against him, wrapping his arms around her waist.

She clasped her hands behind his neck and swayed with him to the seductive rhythm. Nuzzling his throat, she inhaled his spicy aftershave. Smooth skin greeted her questing lips as they strayed across his jawline.

Jake and Harley lost themselves in the music, allowing their hands and mouths to explore each other with tantalizing slowness. Harley slipped her fingers inside his black silk robe, caressing the soft hair on his chest. His low hum of approval encouraged her, and she slid her hand lower. "Why, Jake. You've got nothing on underneath this robe."

He clamped his teeth gently on her earlobe when she brushed his arousal. "Do you have a problem with that?"

"Not at all."

He stroked her breast through the flimsy material of the gown. Harley gasped and arched her back, pressing forward.

Exquisite. The woman was absolutely exquisite, and he'd never get enough of her. Her breast filled his hand perfectly. With the other hand, Jake reached around behind her and plucked a pin from her hair. "Look at me, Harley."

Like sparkling jewels in the candlelight, her eyes met his. As he removed the rest of the pins, her hair cascaded over her bare shoulders. "You are the most beautiful woman I've ever seen."

She dropped her gaze.

"You are." He planned to spend the hours until dawn convincing her. Shoving the thin strap of the gown aside, he planted smoldering kisses along the slope of her shoulder. She shuddered in response. He moved the other strap, and the gown slipped from her body to pool around her ankles. Jake let his own robe fall to the floor.

For a moment, everything stopped as he admired her naked form in the candlelight.

A heartbeat later, he scooped her into his arms and

placed her in the middle of the bed, following her down.

She grabbed for the sheets.

"No." He stilled her hands. "I want to see you."

He set off in slow exploration of her body, touching every inch of her and reveling in the experience. The jasmine perfume he'd chosen suited her perfectly and drove him wild. He wanted her so badly he ached with his restraint, but he was determined that this night would wipe clear any memories she had of other lovers. He might not be her first, but by damned, he'd be the one she remembered for the rest of her life. After all, his ego—his proficiency in the bedroom— was on the line. And that was the only reason he'd gone to such trouble in creating the perfect seduction.

Jake ignored the tiny voice in the back of his head calling him a liar, and instead began to lavish the attention of his hands and mouth on her sumptuous breasts, kissing, caressing, sucking. Her moans and tiny whimpers of response pleased him. Her hands skimmed his shoulders as he kissed a path down her flat, smooth stomach.

She twitched beneath him and gasped, then went deadly still. He smiled in anticipation. Lowering his head, he flicked out his tongue and caressed her in the most intimate way, slowly. Maddeningly.

She bucked, clutching the sheets and gasping his name in that sultry voice he loved. It sounded even sexier when she couldn't catch her breath.

He continued his loving torment until her entire

body tensed in climax, then she collapsed, panting for air. "That...that was..." she said weakly.

"Fabulous?" he offered, grinning up at her.

A satisfied smile lit her face. "Definitely fabulous."

She grabbed his head in her hands. "Please, come up here. I need you inside me."

"Soon." He teased her first, gliding his erection across her slickness—but not entering—waiting until she trembled with need and he could no longer resist the urge to plunge inside her. "Ask me again, sweetheart."

"Jake, please! Now!"

"Since you ask so nicely." He slipped inside her warmth, burying himself completely. An intense rush of pleasure stormed him, and he couldn't breathe. She cradled him perfectly, as if she'd been custom-designed just for him.

"Jake." Her eyes shimmered with desire, her honey-wheat hair fanned out across the pillow—his pillow—the reality of it ten times better than the fantasy had been.

He crushed her mouth with his own, claiming her lips as he claimed her body in the most powerful fashion.

They moved together. Their pace began with a leisurely tempo that quickly dissolved into a frantic, heated frenzy. Her whimpers threatened to spin him over the edge.

"Harley, open your eyes."

Her eyelids fluttered, then opened. Pupils wide, she locked her gaze with his. "Yes! Oh, yes!"

He watched her fall, eyes closing, head thrown back, throaty moan rumbling her satisfaction.

"Yes, baby!" A few more deep strokes triggered his own orgasm.

After regaining his breath, he tucked her under his arm and snuggled her close. When her smooth, even breathing indicated she'd fallen asleep, he crept from the warm sheets to douse the candles.

Jake slid back into the bed and gathered her once more into his arms. He drifted off to sleep, to dream of a baby—*his* baby. Someone to share his life, his home.

But in his dreams, the baby's eyes weren't blue like his. They were emerald green.

Like Harley's.

CHAPTER SEVEN

"HARLEY."

Jake's warm breath stirred the hair next to her ear, and Harley struggled upward from the best night's sleep she'd known in ages. She began to stretch.

"No, don't move. Just lie still and open your mouth."

Open her mouth?

His fingertips brushed across her cheeks. "Come on, open up."

Still groggy, she obeyed. He slipped something cold and narrow under her tongue. She brought her lips together at his urging. "There, now, don't move. Just lie there until it beeps."

She opened her eyes to glare at him, hoping to communicate her question and her unhappiness with this rude awakening.

"No, close your eyes and relax, Harley. We want a perfect reading."

Perfect reading? He'd stuck a thermometer in her mouth! What in the world was the man up to now?

The bed shifted as he rose from her side. "I'll be back in a minute."

The fragrant aroma of freshly brewed coffee drifted

into the room, and she hoped he'd gone to bring her a cup. If so, maybe she wouldn't kill him for waking her like this.

Time crawled with agonizing slowness before the thermometer beeped, coinciding with Jake's soft footsteps crossing the bedroom floor. She opened her eyes as he sat beside her and withdrew the thermometer.

"What the heck is that all about?" Harley clutched the sheets to her body as she sat up.

Jake reached for a clipboard on the night table. "Basal body temperature. Now, when did you start your last period?"

"What?" Harley didn't much care for the shrieking quality in her voice. She took a deep breath.

He stared at her, pencil poised over the sheet of graph paper on the board.

"You're serious, aren't you?"

"Absolutely. I need to maximize our chances for conception, and that means knowing exactly where you are in your cycle. So—" he tapped the paper with the pencil "—when was your last period?"

"Wait and I'll check my day planner," she drawled, rolling her eyes.

He scowled at her.

"All right, let me think. I was definitely PMSing the day that jerk wanted a lube job."

"What?" Jake looked slightly flustered.

"Nothing. The day you baby-sat the twins and we decided to go ahead with this. So I probably got my period the next day."

"All right. That was July 18, which makes this

approximately day twelve of your cycle." A smug smile spread across his face as he scribbled on the chart. "Not bad. That means you should ovulate in about two days. Provided your cycles are twenty-eight days. Are they?"

Harley slumped back into the feather pillows and yanked the covers over her head. "This is far more than I told the gynecologist, Jake." Obviously the man's romantic soul had faded with the dawn. No more Mr. Nice Guy. No more Mr. Seduction. Now she was back to being a baby factory.

Jake pulled the sheets and comforter away from her face. "How many days, Harley?"

"Twenty-seven, twenty-eight, twenty-nine?" She gave him a shove. "Take your chart and go, so I can get dressed. I've got an appointment with my student adviser this morning."

"All right. Look, I'm going to put this thermometer on the night table next to your bed. You have to take your temperature every morning, just like I did today."

Ah. So he no longer wanted her sleeping in his bed. She was being returned to the guest room. She closed her eyes to hide the hurt, the regret. By damn, she wasn't going to let him see it.

"Yeah. Right."

Jake's footsteps retreated from the room, and Harley rolled over onto her side to burrow deeper into the bed. The scent of his aftershave lingered on his pillow.

She'd been returned before, found wanting in some

way. It wasn't like that was anything new. Time to rebuild the walls. She wouldn't allow Jake Manning to break her heart, she'd allow no one to do that, ever again. And Jake's generally caring and compassionate attitude would make it even worse. He was too easy to love.

Whatever last night had been, it was obviously over.

She jumped from the bed, grabbing the nightgown that now lay neatly draped across the end. Satin caressed her flesh, sliding over her shoulders with a faint whisper. Inhaling deeply, Harley lifted her head. Today she was starting a brand-new life, and her adviser would help her plan it.

JAKE LEANED AGAINST the kitchen counter, clipboard in one hand, oversize mug of steaming coffee in the other. From all the research he'd done, he knew basal body temperature was a fairly reliable tool for aiding conception. It didn't work as well in preventing conception, but it could help them get pregnant faster.

And after last night, after the way she'd rocked his world and blown his mind, he wanted her pregnant as quickly as possible. With as few trips to her bed as possible. It would be far too easy to get used to having her around, to having her warm, tender body cradled against his through the night. No, he wasn't going to let it happen. He'd been there, done that, paid the price.

Still, the warmth he'd experienced last night had been wonderful.

A plump black-and-white cat stalked across the countertop, rubbing his arm.

"Irving, get off the counter." Jake shooed him with the clipboard. Nose in the air, the cat jumped to the floor, arched his back and skulked from the room.

A stray. Like some strays he took in, Harley was a temporary boarder. Best for all concerned if she got pregnant right away, then he could keep his distance from her, or as much distance as the small house would allow.

But the vision of her face as she'd cried out his name in passion would be hard to forget.

Watch your heart. He didn't intend to get burned again.

"Still playing with your chart, I see." He breathed in the scent of jasmine mingled with freshly scrubbed skin as Harley moved past him, heading for the automatic coffee machine.

"Yeah, we architects love anything we can draw lines on."

"Ah, yes. You architects are planners, while we mechanics, we're doers. Hands-on approach, you know?"

The image of her hands-on approach last night seared his brain.

Opening the white cupboard next to the sink, she removed a mug and poured herself some coffee.

Jake set his on the counter, along with the clipboard, and walked to her side. He plucked the mug from her hands, then dumped the contents down the drain.

"Hey! What are you doing?" She clenched her fists and propped them against her hips.

"No coffee. Caffeine's bad for you, and it's especially bad for a developing baby. Kick the habit now."

The way she glared at him, if looks could kill, the new Mrs. Manning would be a widow. "No caffeine?"

"No."

"Fine." She stalked across the kitchen, retrieving the blue mug he'd left on the countertop. "What's good for the egg is good for the sperm." With a quick twist, she inverted the cup over the sink, splashing black droplets all along the nearby countertop, even getting some on the window that overlooked the backyard.

She smiled at him, setting the now-empty mug in the sink. "Have a nice day. I'll see you later." Her work boots squeaked on the yellow-and-green linoleum as she whirled and left the kitchen.

Jake grabbed the sponge to wipe down the countertop. "That went well," he muttered.

HARLEY SURVEYED THE scattered piles on the dining-room table—the fall semester's course schedule, the catalog and a list of classes she needed to finally obtain her business degree. She rested her chin on her palm and sighed. She needed thirty more credits to graduate in the spring. But she was having problems juggling the timetable. The business policy class she had to have conflicted with the American literature class she needed to fulfill the English requirement, which meant she was probably going to end up taking poetry. She groaned. Poetry was definitely not her style.

The adviser had been very little help, except to obtain permission allowing her late registration for a full-time fall semester.

Jake probably wouldn't have any trouble with this. He'd turn the whole mess into a coherent and workable schedule with one flick of his wrist.

The black-and-white cat rubbed against her ankles. Harley reached down and scooped him onto her lap. Contented purrs rumbled in his throat as she scratched behind his ears. "What do you think, Irving? Should I ask Mr. Planner to use his clipboard to help me?"

The cat stretched on her lap, then shook and Harley laughed. "No, you're right, I can manage this by myself."

Irving rubbed his head against her chin.

The front door of the house rattled open, and Harley glanced at her watch. It was far too early in the afternoon for Jake to be coming home. She dropped the cat gently to the floor and pushed her chair back, looking through the living room toward the foyer.

Dusty stood there. He was in uniform, lines impeccably pressed, face contorted in a scowl. Wordlessly he strode across the living room toward her.

A sense of panic descended on Harley. "What? Is something wrong? Did something happen to Jake?"

"Yeah, something's wrong. My brother married

you.'' The young cop halted a few feet from her and folded his arms across his chest, staring down at her.

''Don't do that to me. You scared me into thinking he'd been hurt.'' She tilted her head back to meet his eyes.

''Like you'd really care?''

''Of course I would. What kind of question is that?'' A question she should've expected, and probably would've asked, too, if she were in his shoes.

''An honest one. After his first wife ran off, my brother vowed he'd never marry again. And yet, a little more than two years later, we have you, the second Mrs. Jake Manning. What kind of scam are you trying to pull here?''

Harley twisted the plain gold band around the ring finger of her left hand. ''No scam, Dusty.''

''So you love my brother?'' He leaned forward, icy-blue eyes piercing.

''Your brother is the kindest, most compassionate man I've ever met.'' Harley swallowed the lump in her throat. Truer words had never been uttered, even if he *had* stolen her coffee.

''My brother's a bighearted softie who takes in strays, but he usually limits himself to cats and dogs. What possessed him to take you in?''

Harley decided to toss the big issue right onto the table. ''My stellar past?''

Surprise flickered across Dusty's face, then a slow feral smile curved his lips. ''Doubt it.''

''According to the courts, Officer, I've paid my debt to society.''

"You may have paid that one, but if you're up to something here, I can promise you won't like the next payment plan. Probation and community service are a cakewalk compared to doing hard time."

Sweat broke out on her forehead. If he discovered the marriage wasn't on the up-and-up, could he arrest her? Was it fraud? She needed to stay strong. "Is that a threat, Officer?"

"No, a promise. My brother's had enough heartache. He doesn't need any more."

"Yeah, right, I'm sure your lives were just so awful." Harley waved a hand around the room. "I know for a fact that Jake's lived in this house since he was eight years old. That's not exactly an unstable life."

Dusty grunted. "And he watched two women who supposedly loved him walk out that door. Are you going to be the third?"

Yes, actually that was the plan. But she couldn't let him know it. She groped for a way to gain control of the conversation. "I really don't think your brother would be happy to know you're here interrogating me."

"One more question. Are you pregnant?"

Harley straightened and arched an eyebrow at him. "Well, after the wedding celebration your brother and I had last night, I very well could be."

Dusty's cheeks flushed ever so slightly.

Score one for me.

He regained his composure. "If you're gonna leave, you do it now. My brother wants a child in the worst way. If you get pregnant and then take his baby, Jake'll shatter. And I don't want that to happen.''

She had to admire his protectiveness. She knew if she'd had someone like Jake to take care of her after losing both parents, she'd feel the same way.

She and Dusty had a lot more in common than the young cop would ever want to admit.

The heels of his polished black shoes beat a retreat across the wooden floor. He paused in the foyer for a moment to look back at her. ''And *you* don't want it to happen, either.'' The door slammed behind him, his implied threat hanging in the air.

Would Jake feel even a tinge of regret the day she walked out? Or would he cling to his child and merrily wave her out of his life?

Who would pick up the pieces if *her* heart shattered? Or was there really enough of her mother in her to prevent that from happening?

Shoving aside all negative thoughts about the future, Harley picked up the course schedule from the table and flipped the page.

CHAPTER EIGHT

SHE WAS LATE.

Jake stole a glance at the clock mounted on the wall over his computer, just on the outside chance the computer clock was wrong.

It wasn't. She was late.

The fall semester was already several weeks under way, but the idea of her on campus at night, alone, made him anxious. Which made no sense at all, given that up to this point, all her course work had been done during night classes. *She's a big girl. She can take care of herself.*

Pepper and Benji sprawled on the floor near the office fireplace. Off in the distance, he heard the front door open. The dogs jumped up and raced out of the room, tails wagging.

He sighed in relief.

"No. Sit, and I mean it!" Harley's voice carried to the back of the house. "If you want a cookie, you'd better sit."

Jake chuckled. She'd finally learned that edible rewards ensured doggie obedience. He heard her walk into the kitchen and the squeak of a cabinet door.

"There. Now, get lost." A trace of warmth rang in

her voice; Pepper and Benji had finally pushed their way past her fear.

She appeared in the open archway to his office, a backpack slung over one shoulder. Her black jeans—his favorite pair—defined her shapely curves. Jake imagined she easily gave the younger co-eds a run for their money when it came to beauty.

Tonight, however, she looked tired. Her eyes held no sparkle and weary lines marked her face. "Are you okay?"

She dropped the book bag, then crossed his office, sinking down into the leather recliner. "I'm wiped. I had no idea going to school full-time could be so tiring. Maybe I'm too old for this."

"Yes, you look positively decrepit."

"Well, I feel decrepit." Irving circled her ankles and she leaned forward to pet him. "I've got something else to tell you." She looked up, then quickly refocused on the cat.

"Oh?" He pushed his chair from his desk. "What?"

"I—I think I'm getting my period again." Her cheeks flushed pink and she stroked the cat more intently.

Damn. He turned back to his desk and opened the bottom drawer, pulling out her charts. "Harley, are you sure?"

"I'm spotting, and that's usually the start. Why?"

He ran his finger along the line of the graph. "Something's absolutely not right here. Your temperature has been almost exactly the same since we started charting two months ago. It should be lower in the first part of your cycle, and then go up for the second part. That hasn't happened.''

Harley vacated the recliner to peer over his shoulder. ''So?''

''So, that's not right.''

She wrapped her hands around his shoulders and began to knead them.

Jake stifled a groan.

''Maybe we just need to relax, Jake. You've turned this into a science experiment.''

''No, there's a problem with the ovulation predictor kit, too. Didn't you notice that the color has stayed the same each day we did it this month?''

''No, I haven't. I leave all that junk to you.'' She lowered her hands from his shoulders.

He grabbed her fingertips. ''Don't stop. It feels really good.'' It did. Her touch, even on his shoulders, caused warmth to radiate down and lodge in his groin. The woman affected him like no other ever had. Being in her bed during the fertile part of her cycle and then trying to keep his hands off her the rest of the month made him crazy.

She resumed rubbing.

''I think we need to make another appointment with Dr. Hansen,'' he said. Her thumbs dug into a tender spot in his muscles. ''Ow! Hey, take it easy.''

''Sorry.'' This time, she lowered her hands and they didn't come back. ''Why do I need to see Dr. Hansen again?''

''I just want to touch base with him.'' He held up

the charts. ''Something's off here and I want to figure it out now.'' He spun the chair in her direction.

The remaining bit of color faded from her face, and Jake slipped to the edge of his chair, ready to catch her, afraid she was about to keel over on him. Then she lifted her chin, avoiding direct eye contact. ''Fine, make the appointment. Just be sure you keep my schedule in mind. I can't afford to miss even one class.''

She offered him a dismissive smile, then turned and strode to the arch, where she leaned over to retrieve her backpack. ''I've got some reading to do and after that I'm going to bed. 'Night.''

'''Night.'' He watched her go, puzzling over the expression in her eyes when he'd first turned around.

JAKE SLOUCHED AGAINST the wall of the tiny exam room at Dr. Hansen's office. Harley, clad in a hospital gown with a sheet over her lap, sat on the end of the table on the opposite side. Her feet tapped an erratic beat against the step stool.

If he didn't know her any better, he'd have said she looked ready to cry. But that couldn't be the case. In the time he'd known her, he'd never seen her come close to shedding a tear.

Was she worried they'd find something wrong with her? Jake tensed at the thought. What if she *was* ill? What if she had some serious condition that threatened her health? Surely she didn't think he'd turn her out into the cold?

A quick rap on the door announced Dr. Hansen's

arrival. The door swung open and the OB/GYN rushed into the room. "Sorry to keep you waiting. Back so soon, Harley? That didn't take very long, did it?" The gray-haired man scanned the file in his hand.

When she didn't answer, Jake did. "Actually, Doc, we're here because something seems...not right."

The physician set the chart on the counter and turned to Jake, hand extended. "Mr. Emerson, it's a pleasure to meet you. It's always nice to see a husband here to support his wife."

"Um, that's Mr. Manning." Jake shook the doctor's hand.

"Oh, sorry." Dr. Hansen nodded over at Harley, who twisted her wedding band around her finger. "I can't get used to this newfangled idea of wives keeping their own name. I apologize."

"No problem." Jake shifted his feet. "We've been charting Harley's basal body temperature, and it's been almost the same since we started more than two months ago. She's had periods, but even the ovulation predictor kits don't seem to be working right." He handed the doctor his charts.

"Well organized, aren't you, son?" The older man chuckled. "I can see you two are very serious about getting pregnant."

After scanning the notes with some head-nodding and chin-stroking, Dr. Hansen sat down on the stool by the exam table and tapped Harley on her sheet-covered knee. "Don't you have anything to say?"

"Not really."

"How have you been feeling?"

"Fine."

"Really?" He peered intently at Harley. "You look kind of tired."

"Yeah, I am. Full-time college has turned out to be a little more than I expected." Harley picked at the paper covering underneath her thigh.

The doctor patted her knee once again, then folded his hands in his lap. "There's something you're not saying, Harley. Do you want your husband to leave the room?"

She shook her head.

Jake's pulse rate increased. What the hell was going on?

"Can you think of a reason your hormones might be out of whack, Harley? You're not taking any kind of medication, are you?"

She shook her head again, eyes cast down. "There's one thing I didn't tell you the last time I was here."

Jake and the doctor waited expectantly.

"I—I had an ovarian cyst."

"When was this?"

"I was sixteen."

"What symptoms did you have? Mid-cycle spotting? Sharp pains in your side?"

"No."

"Well, how did your doctor discover it?"

She murmured something under her breath, fingers picking faster at the paper table-covering.

Jake leaned forward to hear better.

"What was that?" Dr. Hansen asked. "Did you say you were in the hospital?"

She nodded.

"Why were you in the hospital?"

If she lowered her head any farther, Jake thought, it was going to fall off her neck. She muttered another reply.

"What was that, Harley?"

Finally she lifted her head. "I said, I'd been beaten."

Jake leaned back against the wall and closed his eyes. Beaten. That explained a lot of things, like the moved bed, and her distrust when they'd first met.

"What did the doctors say?" Dr. Hansen asked.

Jake's eyes shot open to watch her response.

"They said it shouldn't affect my future fertility."

Dr. Hansen gave her leg another reassuring pat. "And I'll bet they were right. But I'd like to run a few tests and examine you again, and we'll see if we can't solve the mystery, okay? And even if you have another cyst, that doesn't mean you can't have a baby, so just relax for now."

Harley nodded her head and followed the physician's instructions to scoot down on the table. Mind whirling at the implications of her revelation, Jake studied the floor at his feet while the doctor examined her.

"Mmm-hmm. Okay, Harley, you can sit back up. You brought in a urine sample?"

She nodded.

"I'll be back in a few minutes. Don't go anywhere.'' The doctor peeled off his latex gloves, tossed them in the trash, then proceeded to the sink and washed his hands. He gave Jake a light slap on the shoulder as he passed him on his way out the door.

Harley couldn't bear to look at Jake. Head down, she continued to pick at the edge of the paper table-covering. What was he thinking? Did he hate her for keeping this secret?

''Why didn't you tell me?''

''It doesn't matter.''

''It matters to me.''

''I was afraid you wouldn't let me try to have your baby if the doctor's report wasn't perfect.''

''Who beat you, Harley?''

She glanced over at him. His eyes were full of that tender compassion. How could she *not* tell him when he did his Mr. Nice Guy thing? ''A foster father.''

Jake cursed under his breath. ''What happened?''

''He found out my older foster brother—his son— had seduced me. Of course, it wasn't his kid's fault, it was all mine. I was a no-good tramp who came from trash and wasn't worthy of…of sleeping with his son.'' The paper in her hand gave way with a loud tear, and she twisted it around her fingers. ''I thought Jimmy loved me. But he just stood there while his father beat me.'' And that had been when she'd lost faith in the idea of love, and white knights who rescued damsels in distress. When she'd been forced to realize she wasn't good enough for certain types of other people. People like Jake.

''Who helped you?''

"Who else? Me. I got hold of a phone later that night and called 911. The first-aid squad and cops showed up and took me to the hospital. At least the Kesslers weren't allowed any more foster kids after that. But the charges against Steven Kessler were dropped on some technicality, some screw-up with his arrest."

He cursed more loudly and colorfully this time. He took a step in her direction.

"No." She held up a hand to stop him. Dammit, she didn't want to see pity in his eyes. But it was there. "Don't look at me like that!"

"Like what?"

"I don't want your pity. I don't need it. I got enough of that in the hospital afterward. Poor little orphan girl, knocked around by her foster father. Well, I learned one lesson quickly, Jake. Acting tough made one hell of a great cover for being scared."

No wonder she didn't like doctors. How long had she been in the hospital?

The foster care system had let her down, big time. Thank God Austin was out of the system, even if it wasn't the way Jake had intended.

He finished closing the distance between himself and Harley and gathered her into his arms. She was stiff and unyielding at first, so he stroked her hair and murmured soothing nonsense into her ear. "You don't have to act tough with me, Harley." He of all people should have recognized the signs of a battered stray. After a short while, she relaxed, allowing him to cuddle her. She'd turned to him in passion before, but never for comfort. She probably hadn't had anyone to comfort her since she'd adopted the whole tough-independent-woman persona.

Anger flared as he considered everything she'd been through. "That boy—Jimmy—took advantage of you."

"I let it happen. By then I was so starved for love in any form, I believed his pretty words and empty promises when he said he loved me. I was stupid."

"You were young and trusting." If Jake could get his hands on either guy, he'd show him a thing or two about how to treat women.

"I'll leave tomorrow," she mumbled into his chest.

"And go where? Don't be ridiculous."

"But if I can't give you a baby—"

"Shh. I'm not going to throw you out of the house. Hey, Benji's only got one ear, and I let him hang around."

"You didn't have a deal with Benji to provide you with puppies and find out he couldn't."

Jake chortled. "You're right. But let's not rush things, okay? It's going to work out."

The polite knock sounded at the door again, and Dr. Hansen returned. "All right, I need to run one more test to give you a diagnosis. Harley, pull the strings of that gown a little tighter, and Jake, you might want to walk behind your wife. We need to take a little stroll down the hallway. I want to do an ultrasound."

The doctor handed Harley a liter of water. "First, bottoms up. You need to drink all of this."

Harley accepted the bottle from him. "*All* of it?"
"All of it."

Harley unscrewed the cap and saluted them both with the bottle. "Bottoms up." She gulped down some of the cool liquid.

ANY MINUTE NOW, she'd certainly explode. "Have my eyes turned yellow yet?" Harley asked Jake.

He peered at her closely. "Nope, not yet. They're still that beautiful green."

"Where the heck is he? If he doesn't get in here soon, I'm leaving and going to the bathroom."

"I heard that." Dr. Hansen entered the ultrasound room, and Jake stepped out of the way. "Remember that when you call me with an urgent question you're sure won't wait."

Harley fidgeted on the exam table. "No question could possibly be as urgent as the fact that I really have to—"

The doctor's sharp laugh cut her off. "That's good news. It means your bladder's full enough for me to do the exam now."

"Then let's do it and get it over with, before I embarrass myself on your table." Harley lay back, and Dr. Hansen tugged the gown up over her stomach. A sheet covered her lower body, but self-consciousness engulfed her with Jake standing there. Strange. It wasn't like the man hadn't seen all of her, but something about this particular situation made her edgy. She wished the doctor would hurry up and explain what was going on.

"This might be a little cold," Dr. Hansen warned.

Harley gasped as he applied a thick gel to her stomach. "Uh, yeah, you could say that."

The doctor smiled. "Now, let's take a peek inside." He rotated a round object across her lower abdomen, studying the small monitor before him.

Jake moved to stand behind Dr. Hansen's shoulder.

"Mmm-hmm. Yes, that's what I thought."

"What is it? Do I have another cyst?" Harley couldn't stand the waiting any longer. If the doctor didn't talk soon, she'd have to throttle him.

Dr. Hansen pointed to the static-filled black-and-white monitor and glanced over his shoulder at Jake. "Do you see this fluttering, son?"

Fluttering? Inside her? Cysts didn't flutter, did they?

Jake leaned closer to the screen, then reached out to place a finger near it. "Here?"

"Yes, right there. Know what that is?"

Jake shook his head.

"Hey, I can't see," Harley complained. "What's going on?"

"That, son, is your baby's heart, beating strong and perfect. Congratulations, you're pregnant."

Harley struggled to sit up. "Pregnant?" she squeaked. "But…but that's not possible. I had my period."

Dr. Hansen pushed her gently back onto the table. "And what were these periods like? Lighter than usual?"

"Yeah, I guess they were. The last one was just

spotting.'' The reality of the situation hit her like a NASCAR crashing into the wall. Her body cradled a baby—the baby of the most wonderful man she'd ever met, a man she knew without a doubt would make a fantastic father. But she wouldn't be around to watch him be that father.

The truth of the situation made her nauseous—she'd sold her baby and her soul for a college degree. And it looked like her heart, not her body, would take a beating this time.

Harley watched Jake's face. His gaze was fixed on the monitor, eyes wide with wonder as he stared at the screen. The corners of his mouth turned up and he shook his head slightly. ''A baby. We did it. We made a baby.''

Dr. Hansen removed the device from her stomach, then picked up her file, tracing his fingers along Jake's temperature graph. He began to chuckle. ''I'd say you made a baby very quickly. Judging from your chart and notes, I'd say you made this baby on the very first try.''

Jake puffed out his chest with exaggerated pride. ''No six months to a year for us.''

''I'd say not. So, that makes your baby due in April. April 25. But remember, that's an estimated due date.''

Harley pulled the gown back over her abdomen. ''I don't feel pregnant. I haven't been sick or anything.'' *At least, not until I just realized what I've done.*

''But your tiredness may have less to do with college, and more to do with this baby,'' the doctor replied.

Harley caressed the surface of her stomach. Two months pregnant. The clock already ticked downward on her time with Jake. Obviously the fates hadn't listened to her on that magical night. But then, when had they ever?

She carried his child within her, and in seven months, she'd deliver the baby and be expected to leave them both.

Harley swiped the small tear from the corner of her eye before anyone could see and lifted her chin. Defiant bravado in place, she muttered, ''April 25. Our timing stinks. That ought to put me right around spring semester finals.''

Jake frowned at her. ''Harley! We're having a baby. Is school all you can think about?''

No, but she wasn't going to let him know that.

CHAPTER NINE

A CLOUD FORMED AS JAKE'S breath condensed in the cool October air. He rested on his rake for a moment, surveying the front yard of Melanie and Peter's old farmhouse. Scattered heaps of red-gold-and-brown leaves dotted the lawn. Most of his family was busy creating the piles. Kate sat on the weathered front steps with baby Matthew in her arms, swaddled in a blanket.

On the far side of the yard, beneath a tall thin poplar, Harley struggled to maintain the order of her pile. The twins helped her. Or so they thought, anyway. He couldn't resist a smile as the little girls used their small purple rakes to create havoc in the leaf mountain Harley had just finished.

His amusement fled quickly when she mopped her brow, then pressed her hand against her stomach. After propping his rake against the trunk of a white oak, he strode across the yard. "You're overdoing it," he murmured into her ear, gently disengaging the tool from her grip. "Are you all right?"

She nodded and glanced around at the others before answering him. "Just a little queasy. I think I'm hungry—again." Her eyes narrowed and she pursed her lips ruefully. "Nobody bothered to inform me that I'd be starving all the time."

Jake chuckled. "Nobody informed you because you didn't ask." He lowered his voice. "I think it's time we told them."

Her gaze darted across the yard again, lingering on his brother.

He placed his hand on her arm. "Harley, don't worry about him. The family's going to be thrilled, you'll see."

"Sure, just like Dusty was thrilled about the marriage."

Her vulnerability never failed to get to him. Jake wrapped his arm around her shoulder and dropped a casual kiss on her forehead. At least, he hoped it seemed casual.

The scent of jasmine and roses mixed with the crisp, earthy smell of the fall air, and he struggled against the impulse to sweep her into his arms and kiss her properly. That part of their relationship was over. Or so he kept telling himself. Trouble was, he had a hard time believing it. He still wanted her, wanted her with an ache that had become a near-permanent condition. And most disconcerting was that the ache didn't always have the good sense to stay below his belt. On occasion, it was distinctly higher. Like mid-chest.

His family believed his marriage was the real thing, and a few kisses would reinforce the illusion. But she didn't look well. Now was not the time.

He cleared his throat and shouted across the yard.

"Hey, Mel, how about a break? I think we could all use some hot chocolate."

"Yay! Hot chocowet!" Grace threw down her rake and raced as fast as her pudgy legs could carry her toward the front porch.

Hope took a different approach than her sister had. The younger twin gently lay down the plastic tool, then ran and threw her arms around Jake's legs. "Up, Unka Jake," she demanded.

Jake freed Harley, bending over to scoop up his niece. "As you wish, pretty lady."

"Me too, hot chocowet?" She patted his cheeks with her tiny palms.

"Yes, you too, Hope."

Harley tugged on his sweatshirt sleeve. "Me too, hot chocolate?"

Jake drew his eyebrows together and pretended to consider it. "Well, you really shouldn't.... What do you think, Hope? Can Harley have some hot chocolate, too?"

"Yes, her can!"

"Oh, you women always stick together, don't you?" Jake tickled the little girl and she dissolved into a squirming, giggling mass in his arms. "All right, Harley can have some, too."

"Yes!" Harley offered him a triumphant smile and pushed past him toward the front porch. "Last one in has to rake with the twins later." She launched into a trot.

"No fair!" he called after her. "I'm unduly burdened." At that moment Hope planted a sloppy, wet kiss on his cheek. He grinned. How anyone could ever see a child as a burden was beyond his understanding.

Dusty took his son from Kate's arms and helped her up. She smiled at him, an expression so full of love, Jake felt a moment's twinge of regret. A baby, a daddy and a mommy, a trio of people who created a family. Maybe he was wrong in wanting a child of his own with no mother in the picture. Then again, it was easier on the child if the mother left early. He recalled Dusty's tear-stained little face when, night after night, the toddler had called for his mommy. Only mommy wasn't there. No, his plan was the best thing for his child—and himself.

The screen door slammed shut and Harley wandered down the hallway toward the large kitchen in the back. Cow magnets adorned the fridge, cow pictures hung on the walls, and a knickknack shelf in the corner boasted ceramic cows of all sizes. Melanie removed a cow-shaped teapot from the stove and held it under the sink.

"So, Mel, I guess you like cows, huh?"

Jake's sister laughed. "Actually, this all started out as a joke between Peter and me. You can see the joke's taken on a life of its own and gotten a little out of control."

Harley arched an eyebrow. "A little?"

"Okay, a lot."

A gray cat rubbed across Harley's ankles.

"That's Smoky," Mel said. "He's one of the cats

I inherited from Jake. Patches is probably hiding somewhere.''

Smoky shot out of the room as the rest of the family clattered into the kitchen, filling it with amiable chitchat and laughter. Oak chairs scraped against the linoleum as everyone gathered around the large table. Jake unzipped Hope's jacket and tossed it onto a bench near the back door, then lifted the child up and deftly fastened her into a wooden high chair. Harley marveled at his skill with the little ones. She'd never have that kind of easy ability with a child.

It doesn't matter, because you won't be getting the chance. The thought gnawed at her, and she shoved it out of her mind. Her stomach rolled and she swallowed hard, then turned her attention back to Melanie. ''Mel, do you have any crackers or anything? I hate to admit it after that wonderful lunch, but I'm hungry again.''

Mel settled the second teapot on the stove to heat the water for their hot chocolate. ''Of course I do. They're in the bread drawer. Help yourself. In fact, pull them out and put them on the table. Get the cookies, too, while you're in there.''

Harley walked in the direction Mel was pointing. She pulled out the large, metal-lined drawer and examined the contents. A newly opened package of Oreos lay nestled beside the bread and crackers. She cast a furtive look over her shoulder to check on Jake. Ever since the confirmation of her pregnancy, he'd become the nutrition police. He took the whole thing a bit too seriously in her humble opinion, though given his personality and the fact that he'd done his best to change her diet right from the start, she hadn't been too surprised.

The Oreo cookies called to her. Biting back a grin, she reached into the bag and grabbed one, stuffing the whole thing in her mouth.

"I saw that." Jake's baritone directly at her ear made her jump.

"Saw what?" she mumbled.

"You're eating a cookie."

She swallowed, then ran her tongue over her teeth, hoping to remove any evidence. She turned around to face him. "Surely you're mistaken."

"I don't think so." He leaned closer, forcing her to take a step backward. "Don't think you can hide it from me. I have ways of finding out these things."

The edge of the counter pressed into her back. "Oh? Like what?"

A strange expression crossed his face, and he quickly glanced at his family. "Like this." He slid his arms around her and moved his body into contact with hers.

Her knees quivered. He hadn't been this close since he'd comforted her in the doctor's office, and she'd missed the warmth of his arms, his body, his kiss. She tilted her face expectantly, closing her eyes.

He lowered his head and brushed his lips across hers, nibbling at the seams, probing gently with his tongue. Her breasts tightened against his chest and a warm pool of desire flooded her body.

He deepened their kiss, and the heat intensified.

She felt like one giant hormone, and she craved him far more than chocolate cookies. No one had warned her pregnancy would make her feel so aroused, either.

"Get a room, would you?" Dusty growled at them.

Harley tore her mouth from Jake's, opening her eyes to meet his sky-blue ones. The lust-darkened irises and dilated pupils betrayed his desire. "I knew it," he whispered. "Oreo cookies."

Dusty scowled at his brother. "If you want to know what she's been eating, ask. No need to shove your tongue down her throat. Children are present."

Jake glanced around the room again. "Yes, but the only one who seems to have noticed is you."

Dusty's scowl intensified and he turned, stalking back to the table.

"He's going to have a fit," Harley murmured.

"Too bad. He'll get over it. In fact, let's just get our announcement out of the way now, shall we?"

"Now?"

"No time like the present." Jake released her from his embrace and turned around to stand next to her. He reached down and threaded his fingers through hers. "Everyone? Could we have your attention for a moment?"

The clamor in the kitchen was reduced to a dull murmur, all adult eyes focused expectantly on Jake and Harley. Her face grew warm under their frank stares.

"We have some news. The family is about to increase again. We're having a baby in the spring."

Melanie quickly left the stove to gather Harley in

a hug, gushing congratulations, then embracing Jake. Peter and Kate also made their way over to offer congratulations, and Dusty followed reluctantly. Harley could see the wheels turning in his head, and knew she'd pegged his response correctly. Jake could fool himself all he wanted. She knew the truth—his little brother was less than thrilled with their announcement.

After the fuss had died down, and they'd enjoyed their hot chocolate break, Harley excused herself, wandering down the hallway to the half bath located beneath the front stairs. When she came out, Dusty was waiting for her. Arms crossed over his chest, he leaned against the wall, storm clouds apparent in his eyes.

She nodded at him and headed back to the kitchen.

His hand darted out and he grabbed her arm. "No, you don't. I wanna talk to you."

"Fine, Dusty, let's talk." She yanked her wrist from his grasp. "What shall we talk about? The weather? Your job? How many tickets did you write this month? Bust anyone for running a chop-shop lately?"

His eyes flashed a warning. "I was thinking more about the news my brother just dropped on the family. He didn't say—when's the baby due?"

"April 25. Would you like me to help you count to nine?" Harley watched as he did the mental calculations himself.

"Damn close. Now I understand your answer when I first asked if you were pregnant. You got knocked up to trap my brother, didn't you? He took you into his house, but that wasn't enough.''

She shook her head. ''You have it all wrong.''

''Yeah, I'll bet. I'll bet my pension, too, that this baby's going to be born earlier than April 25. Exactly when did you get pregnant? Is it really my brother's baby you're carrying or somebody else's bastard, and you found Jake a convenient target for fatherhood?''

Overhearing his brother's words, Jake skidded around the corner in time to see all the color drain from Harley's face.

''Bastard?'' she whispered, hands fluttering protectively around her middle. ''This baby is no bastard.''

Jake closed his fingers around the back of Dusty's neck. ''Outside!'' he roared. ''Now.'' He half shoved, half dragged his younger brother toward the front door.

Once outside on the porch, Jake released him with a final push in the direction of the stairs. Dusty rubbed his neck, maintaining a wary eye on his brother. ''What the hell are you doing, Jake?''

''I might ask you the same thing. How dare you interrogate my wife like she's some kind of thug!'' The crisp autumn air did little to cool his anger.

Dusty moved toward the far corner of the wrap-around porch. ''Did you see her face? She's hiding something.''

''Of course she's hiding something, you idiot! Did the thought ever occur to you that she's got a sensitivity to that word because she's illegitimate herself?'' Jake's hands curled tightly into fists. ''And let me assure you, the child she carries is mine, one-hundred-percent, absolutely, positively mine.''

"Listen, Jake—"

Jake held up his hand, palm out, and shook his head. "Don't you 'Listen, Jake' me. That is a pregnant woman you were just grilling. I thought I raised you better than that! How would you have felt if I'd done the same thing to Kate while she was carrying Matthew?''

Dusty clenched his hands and his face darkened.

"Exactly. I'm about an inch away from hauling off and letting you have it. If you were anyone else, you'd already have my fist in your face.''

"It's just—"

"It's just nothing! You've had it in for her since you met her. You didn't even give her a chance. Anyone would think you'd never made a mistake in your life, the way you treat her.''

Dusty stared at the plank floor. "I don't have a record.''

"First of all, she's innocent of those charges. And second, I seem to recall a certain fourteen-year-old boy who took my Mustang out joyriding one night. What do you think would've happened if I'd called the cops?'' Jake crossed the creaking floorboards to stand directly in front of his brother. He poked him in the chest. "I didn't call the cops because I was afraid that in addition to charging you with grand theft auto, they'd take you away from me. Luckily, you dumb ass, you brought yourself and my car home in one piece.''

Dusty had the grace to look slightly abashed. "I was a juvenile, not an adult."

"Oh, so a few years makes a difference? Give her a break and trust my judgment. I'm not asking you, I'm telling you. If you ever, *ever* talk to her like that again, the whupping I gave you that night will look like a walk in the park."

The brooding eyes lightened and a slight smile twitched on Dusty's face. "You could try. I'm not fourteen anymore."

"No, you're not. You're a grown man with a son of your own. Try to act like it." Jake stepped back. "Now, get inside and apologize to Harley. And mean it." As he turned to face the house again, the curtain over the window in the living room shifted. Which member of the family had decided to watch the show?

THE JEEP JOLTED ALONG the back road, causing Harley to grit her teeth. *Next time we're taking my truck.* For a split second she wished she hadn't urged Jake to put the Mustang to bed in the garage for the season quite this early. Anything beat being jounced around in his Jeep.

"You okay?" Jake asked.

"If you don't want a wet seat, watch the bumps." She pressed her thighs together.

He chuckled. "You should've gone before we left Mel's house."

"I did, Mr. Smarty. You try bouncing down the road like this with a baby in your belly and see if it doesn't make you have to go, too."

A companionable silence enfolded them again on the ride back to Millcreek. Harley carefully considered how to bring up the subject of Dusty. Did Jake realize part of his brother's behavior came from jealousy? That Harley and now the baby were taking Dusty's place with his big brother, the man who'd raised him? Probably not. Men, even men as sympathetic as Jake, were thickheaded when it came to stuff like that. But still, the way he'd defended her to his brother made her feel...cared for? "How did you know?" she asked.

"Know what?"

"That I was a bastard."

Jake shot her a quick glance. "Ah, so it was *you* listening at the window."

She dropped her eyes to her lap and nodded.

"Well, I can't say I blame you. If I'd been you, I'd have gone to watch. I'm sorry if I disappointed you, though."

"Why would I be disappointed?"

"Because I didn't let Dusty have it."

"Yes, you did."

"Not really. And don't use the word *bastard* to describe yourself. That word means someone very undesirable. It doesn't apply to you."

"You still didn't tell me how you knew."

Jake moved his hand from the stick shift to place it on her knee. "Sweetheart, it was written all over your face. I kind of figured that was the reason you were so adamant about getting married in the first place."

"It was." She slumped in the seat and stared unseeingly out the window. "I've lived with that label all my life. I'd never want any child to hear the taunts I heard growing up. You know, even in a children's home, there's a pecking order."

She didn't say she'd landed at the bottom of the pecking order. Nor did she confide that Steven Kessler had used the word *bastard* repeatedly while he'd beaten her. She could hear his taunting as though he were in the Jeep with them. She hadn't been good enough for his son. And Jimmy had stood in the corner of her bedroom and watched while his father reinforced his words with his fists.

"The only person who ever paid any attention to me was my dad," she murmured. "And I didn't even get to share his last name. They were never married, and my mother insisted I have her name. After she took off, I think Dad figured it was all I had left of her."

Jake downshifted as they rounded a curve, but quickly returned his hand to her knee, squeezing gently in support. "Names are important. I wasn't always a Manning myself."

She looked over at him.

"Manning was my stepfather's name, Mel and Dusty's father, Bud. He was a hell of a man and the only father I ever really knew." He withdrew his hand to grip the steering wheel tightly. "When our mother left, he could've easily tossed me out, too. But he didn't. He let me stay. 'Course, I helped by taking care of Mel and Dusty. But he kept a roof over our heads. He never made me feel like I was less to him than they were. He was a hell of a man.''

Jake fell silent.

''What happened? How'd you become a Manning?''

''The day I turned eighteen, I went to court and had my name legally changed. I wanted to acknowledge him. Bud's the one who started me on the path to becoming an architect. I wanted to be like him.''

''What happened to Bud?''

''He died of a massive heart attack a few weeks after I finished my master's program.'' Jake exhaled loudly. ''There I was, twenty-two, with a fourteen-year-old sister and a twelve-year-old brother to care for, and an architecture internship to complete—which I was supposed to do with Bud.''

''That couldn't have been easy.''

''No. There were times I was ready to pull my hair out. Especially with Mel. But somehow we survived. I wasn't about to let them be taken by the state.''

Harley winced.

''Sorry. I didn't mean that the way it sounded.''

She shrugged and turned back to the view out the window. How lucky for Mel and Dusty that Jake had been there for them. Made her wish she was a Manning, too. Maybe she *should* have changed her name when they got married. Jake certainly was a better role model of caring than her mother had been.

''How did you end up in foster care, Harley?'' Jake's voice was soft.

''You know, Mel really has her hands full with

your nieces. They're hilarious. Did you see Grace stuffing those leaves into poor Hope's sweater?''

"I guess there wasn't anyone else to take care of you after your dad died, huh?''

A small ache, a reflection of the one she'd felt years ago, blossomed in her chest. Surely it was the hormones making her so sensitive these days. She'd buried her emotions under layers and layers of control, but since Jake Manning had walked into her life, that control was hard to come by. "No. There was no one else. They tried to find my mother...."

"And?''

The pain throbbed a little harder. She forced herself to answer him. "She told them she had no interest in me, that she'd washed her hands of me years earlier. She signed away her parental rights and that was that.''

"I'm sorry, Harley.''

"Hah. Don't be. Hey, you should be grateful to my mother. You know what they say, 'The apple doesn't fall far from the tree.' Basically, I'm going to do the same thing she did—abandon a child. So I guess you owe my mother for having a daughter who can follow in the family footsteps.'' Her hand slipped to her waist. His child. *His*. Not hers, not theirs.

The heartache increased.

How would she ever follow through on the agreement?

It didn't matter. She'd given her word, she'd signed a contract and she'd do what she had to do. Besides, she'd make a lousy mother, and Jake would be a wonderful father. He'd already proven himself with Dusty and Mel. He had backup support, a stable career that allowed him to set his own hours, and he could offer a secure home. She, on the other hand, could offer a child nothing.

Nothing.

Story of her life.

Jake clutched the steering wheel harder, her words ringing in his ears. "You're not abandoning the baby, Harley. You're relinquishing custody to me, the baby's father, someone who's very capable of caring for him."

"Same difference. Your mother relinquished custody of you to your stepfather. Tell me it didn't feel like abandonment."

"I can't, because it did." It hadn't been any better the second time she'd turned her back on them, either. He'd tracked her down—at Mel's request—so she could be invited to Mel and Peter's wedding. The reconciliation had fallen flat. She'd been furious with Jake for "dredging up old pain"—and because her current husband had no idea she had grown children.

"I rest my case."

"This is different, Harley."

"How so?"

Jake fumbled for words. *How indeed?* Because he wanted it to be different? Because the child would never know her—so couldn't miss her? His knuckles went white over the steering wheel. She wouldn't back out like the others had, would she? He couldn't really see her initiating a custody battle that would land them in court, not with her background. Not with the way she'd reacted to the judge the day they were married. He glanced over at her.

"Oh, Jake, chill out. I'm not about to renege on our arrangement."

She didn't sound as certain as he'd like.

Damn it to hell, she'd gotten under his skin. Well, he wasn't allowing her to inflict pain on him—or on his child. His plan would proceed as designed. It was the only viable possibility. A splinter under the skin needed to be removed as soon as possible to prevent it from causing greater damage.

The next six and a half months were going to be very difficult.

He just had to keep reminding himself that she was off limits. He should not admire her courage or tenacity, not feel sympathetic toward her, and certainly not desire her.

CHAPTER TEN

DESIRABLE. TEMPTING. SINFUL. Blissfully, utterly, completely sinful.

Eyes closed, Harley eased her lips around the fork and slipped the chocolate cake into her mouth. Rich icing clung to her teeth and the roof of her mouth. She swirled her tongue, savoring each trace before opening her eyes to target her next forkful.

Big mistake.

She snapped her eyes shut immediately, hoping the old "if I can't see you, you can't see me" trick would work.

"What are you doing?"

Nope, it didn't work. She opened her eyes again and offered Jake a tentative smile. "I thought you'd left for the gym?"

Have mercy, the man had no right to look like that in the morning. And how dared he flaunt his physique in front of a hormone-loaded, sex-starved pregnant woman? His walnut hair still tousled with sleep, wearing only a pair of rumpled gray sweatpants, he looked good enough to eat. Suddenly chocolate cake lost its appeal and *sinful* took on a whole new meaning.

"Don't try to change the subject. What are you doing?"

"Eating breakfast?"

He gestured at her plate. "You call that breakfast?"

"I'm drinking milk with it." She raised the glass, saluted him with it and gulped down a slug.

Jake continued to glare at her.

"It's got eggs in it. And wheat—"

"Spare me the Bill Cosby routine. You know very well that doesn't constitute a nutritious breakfast for a pregnant woman. You've got a baby to think about."

Baby. How she wished for once he'd think about *her.* "How do you know it's not the baby who ordered the chocolate cake for breakfast?"

Jake folded his arms and shook his head at her. "A good parent doesn't let a child make decisions like that, especially a child who's not even born yet."

"There you go. I never claimed I'd be a good parent. That's your job."

"A job I'm trying to do." Jake settled into the chair beside her at the dining room table. He reached over to hold her hand. "You've got to take your nutrition seriously. The baby is depending on you to provide what he needs."

"You need to take everything a little *less* seriously, Jake. I take my vitamins every day. I'm drinking enough milk to support my own dairy herd. I eat fruit and vegetables like never before, and I haven't had any caffeine since you dumped my coffee down the drain."

His lips twitched at the corners and his eyes twin-

kled at her before he composed his mask of seriousness once again.

"I mean it. I'm being very careful. I think some
chocolate now and then isn't irresponsible. Lighten
up. You're such a stick-in-the-mud."

"Stick-in-the-mud?" His brows drew together, and
the corners of his mouth drooped. He released her
hand. "Is that how you see me?"

"We-e-ll—" she dragged the word out "—sometimes." She gave him a once-over, letting her gaze
linger on his well-defined pecs. "Not always. For ex-
ample, your attire right now is definitely not stick-in-
the-mud."

"What's wrong with what I'm wearing?"

"Absolutely nothing. That's my point. You look
natural like that. Approachable." *Not to mention sexy,
desirable and gorgeous.*

"What else?"

Harley dipped the fork back into the cake and lifted
a piece. "Enjoy the little things, Jake. Remember the
night we watched the sunset on the beach?"

Remember? How could he forget? The kiss they'd
shared that night would be burned into his memory
to the end of time. "Yes."

"Okay, so trust me now. You eat chocolate cake
for breakfast today, and I promise not to have any
sweets for the rest of the week."

His lips twisted into a wry smile. "Harley, it's
Wednesday already."

She shrugged. "Take it or leave it."

A stick-in-the-mud, huh? All right, it wouldn't kill

him to lighten up just a little and eat the cake. Especially if it meant his baby would be getting only nutritious foods for the next four days. "Okay, deal."

He leaned forward, reaching for her plate, but she snatched it away from his questing hands. "No, I want to make sure you do this right. This is an experience, not something to be shoveled down. Now, close your eyes."

He scrutinized her warily.

"Stick-in-the-mud."

Jake closed his eyes and settled back. Her chair scraped against the wooden floor and suddenly she was sitting on his lap. "Harley—"

The tip of the fork touched his lips. "Shh. Smell the chocolate. Now, open up."

He did as she ordered, more aware of her warmth and the floral scent of her freshly washed hair than the chocolate cake. He closed his mouth and she slid the fork from between his lips.

"That's it. Slowly."

Her sexy voice vibrated in his ears, sending the familiar jolt of lust racing through him. He swallowed the sawdust cake in an effort to keep a groan from escaping his throat. The only texture and taste he wanted to experience belonged to her.

She shifted, her well-formed bottom brushing against him. His body hardened in response. "Mmm."

"See? It's good, isn't it?"

"Oh, it's more than good, Harley." It was bad. It

was wrong. It was exactly what he'd promised himself he'd never do again.

Her fingertips outlined his lips. "Want more?"

Damn straight he wanted more. He nodded.

The fingers vanished, leaving behind an emptiness at their absence. But they reappeared quickly. This time as they traced his lips, they left behind light smears of icing.

"Open up."

He opened his mouth again, expecting the fork to return, but instead, her chocolate-coated finger slipped in. Instinctively he closed his lips around it, allowing his tongue to skim the surface before he sucked gently.

She moaned, and wriggled on his lap.

He opened his own eyes to discover the emerald eyes he so admired smoldering with flickering desire. He slowly withdrew her finger from his mouth. Wrapping his left arm around her waist, he pulled her closer. "You got icing all over my mouth," he murmured.

"Yes, I did." She leaned over and rested her forehead against his. "Shall I fix that for you?"

His pulse thundered in his chest and between his thighs. "Absolutely."

Her warm breath carried the scent of chocolate and the promise of sweetness, a promise quickly fulfilled when she opened her mouth and met his lips with hers. "Harley—"

"Shh." She pressed her index finger against his lips. "Don't. Just experience."

She stood and pivoted quickly, then straddled him in the chair. He shifted his hips, pressing his erection into the V between her thighs. Sweats met denim. She threw her head back, a blatant invitation.

Her exposed neck proved too tempting. He inched forward to trail his tongue along the hollow of her throat. He felt her heart rate pick up noticeably, and a surge of masculine pride flooded him. "Harley, Harley," he groaned into the creamy skin over her collarbone. "What you do to me, woman."

The tip of her tongue traced the curve of her ear. "What? What do I do to you?"

"You make me forget myself, forget everything but how much I want you."

"That's good. Go with that impulse."

He slipped his hand under her sweater, cupping her breast in his palm. Beneath the cotton fabric of her bra, her nipple tightened in reaction to his caress.

She gasped and bucked against his hardness.

He grabbed for sanity as his erection throbbed in response. "We should stop, Harley," he whispered. "Tell me now."

"No. Don't stop." She crossed her arms to grasp the bottom of her sweater, pulling it up and over her head. Another quick motion, and her bra joined her sweater on the floor beside the chair.

The last shred of self-control he possessed vanished with the sight of her swollen breasts. The nipples, enlarged and darker in color, cried out for his attention. Using his mouth, he eagerly obliged.

Harley clutched his shoulders and ground her lower

body against his with near-frantic urgency. "I need you." She pressed closer against him. "Please, Jake, I need you." She whimpered when he thrust his hips upward to meet hers.

What normal male could resist that? Desire pounded through his veins, thundering in his head, making his entire body ache for her. He clasped his arms around her and rose from the chair, taking her with him.

Three quick strides brought him to his office. He sank to his knees on the rug before the fireplace, lowering her carefully onto her back.

He slid his fingers beneath the elastic waist of her jeans—and the reality of the situation hit him. She wore elastic-waist jeans. Her old tight jeans didn't fit anymore. She was nearly three months pregnant with his child. He pulled back. "Harley, we can't. The baby—"

"We can't hurt the baby, Jake. Please." She sat up on the rug and placed her palm against his chest. "The baby will be fine." She dipped her head and licked his nipple.

He gritted his teeth until he could speak coherently. "You're sure?"

"Absolutely."

Jake reached for her.

The phone rang.

"No! Just ignore it." Harley brought her arms around his neck and pulled him down onto the rug.

He willingly followed, cradling her neck in the crook of one elbow while his other hand explored her curves. The ringing phone faded into the background when she thrust one hand into his sweats and grasped his erection. He groaned.

The answering machine clicked on, and his own voice filled the room with the recorded message.

Beep.

"Mr. Manning, this is Theodore Spandler."

Jake lurched upright on the rug, struggling to extricate Harley's hand from his pants.

"I wanted to discuss the possibility of your designing several more hotels for us."

Jake jumped to his feet and grabbed the phone. Several pencils rolled from the desk onto the floor. "Hello?" He stabbed the button on the answering machine. "Mr. Spandler? I'm here."

Harley inhaled deeply, held her breath a moment, then exhaled. A shiver raced across her body. She continued to slow her breathing, having gone from fourth gear to Park without the benefit of downshifting. Not that she could blame him. Theodore Spandler owned the Spandler hotel chain, and if he wanted Jake to design more hotels, that was a very big deal.

Still, she couldn't resist silently cursing the man's timing.

She turned her head to watch Jake settle into his desk chair. His eyes sparkled with excitement. Had she caused it—or had Mr. Spandler? If she were a betting woman, she'd have to lay odds on Spandler, though Jake had seemed very interested in her just moments ago.

She rolled onto her side, then pushed herself to her

feet. Being half naked in his office didn't seem appropriate anymore. She headed back to the dining room to retrieve her clothes—and drown her frustrated libido in chocolate cake and milk.

HARLEY SLID THE LAST BITE of cake into her mouth as Jake dropped back into the chair at her side. His eyes no longer held the same sparkle. Did he regret their interrupted lovemaking as much as she did? *I'm not going to mention it unless he does.* "What's wrong? For an architect who just got a phone call from a major mogul, you look downright glum."

His hand curled into a loose fist and he hammered on the table. "Oh, it's a fantastic offer. It means major money, not to mention the possible doors it can open for me."

"So, what's the problem?"

"They want me in Virginia Beach at their corporate headquarters."

"So?"

"For the next few months."

"Oh." Harley licked the last remnant of chocolate from the back of her fork, then placed it on her plate.

"*Oh* is right. I can't stay away for a few months."

"Why not?"

"Why not?" He waved a hand around the room. "I've got obligations here. The dogs, my family and there's you."

Me? For a blissful moment, Harley luxuriated in the idea that Jake Manning didn't want to leave town because of her. What an incredible feeling to be included in that list, even if she did rate behind his family and the dogs. "Me?"

"Of course, you. You're pregnant with my baby. What kind of guy goes off and leaves a pregnant woman alone?"

Ah, yes, good old reality. The fact that she was the incubator for his child qualified her for the list—nothing more. "Plenty of them, if statistics are to be believed." Harley leaned back in her chair. "Listen, I'm a big girl. I've been taking care of myself for years." *Or I did, until you started doing it for me.* "I'll be fine. No need to worry about the animals, either. I'm sure I can manage them, too."

Doubt appeared in his eyes. "You're going to look after the dogs?"

"You don't think I can? Hey, I even get along with the big beast now. No problems. We'll be fine. You can't pass up this opportunity." She wouldn't let him. This was one way she could repay him for all the kindness he'd shown her—a way that didn't involve the child growing in her belly, a way that would be her personal gift to him.

"You can't clean the cat box. Maybe Melanie and Peter will keep Irving." Jake began to consider the idea. "And the business—well, the Witherbys are all taken care of, and I've only got a few other projects pending. I think I know a hungry young architect who might like a house design or two."

He turned his attention back to Harley. Determination burned bright in her eyes. If she could hold down the fort at home, it would also give him the chance to secure a reasonable financial reserve before the baby came. After the birth, he'd have a healthy cushion to rest on while he got used to being a parent.

Harley would be gone then.

That thought caused a tightening in his throat. He'd come to admire her tenacity, her spirit and her attitude about life. He loved the smell of her, loved just having her around. And her sensuous body certainly added to the attraction.

The green eyes no longer held flickering flames of desire, and for that, he felt regret. But he'd promised himself that he'd keep his hands off her once she was pregnant—and he'd been doing a damned poor job of it. The chemistry between them was simply too intense to ignore.

Maybe going away for a few months wasn't such a bad idea. He needed to develop some resistance toward this woman, needed to get himself back on an even footing. By the time he returned home, his baby inside her would be so obvious, it would diminish the physical chemistry between them, and he'd be able to keep his distance again—both physically and emotionally.

Yes, maybe this was exactly what they needed.

So, why didn't he feel better about leaving her?

"Jake?"

"Hmm? If you're sure you can manage everything, I'll give Mr. Spandler a call this afternoon and discuss terms with him."

"I'm sure."

He wished he could say the same.

"When do you think you'll be back?"

He did some quick calculations. "I'll be home for Christmas...."

CHAPTER ELEVEN

JAKE SANG ALONG WITH the carol playing on the radio, a grin pulling on the corners of his mouth. Damn straight he'd be home for Christmas, and it wasn't going to be a dream, either.

Flurries drifted from the gray Erie sky. The traffic light turned green, and the tires from the car in front of him kicked up slush. He hoped Dusty had fulfilled his promise to keep the driveway and sidewalks clear for Harley. Jake certainly didn't want her shoveling snow or, God forbid, falling on the slippery ground.

Spandler loved the hotel design, and Jake had a hefty paycheck to carry him through the baby's birth. He'd managed to limit himself to a few weekend trips home. The twins' third birthday party wasn't something he could miss, and Mel had pitched a fit when he'd tried to avoid coming home for Thanksgiving. But the plan was supposed to be to stay away from Harley, not see her every time he turned around.

Their communication during his absence had been restricted to a few phone calls and more frequent e-mails. She kept him up-to-date on the animals, the house and the baby. But he learned more about Harley when he spoke to his sister. "Harley's really slogging through all this class work," or "Harley seemed especially tired today," or "Harley tuned up my van."

He'd missed her a lot more than he'd expected. A lot more than was wise.

The Jeep rounded the corner, and his house came into view. Only a few inches of snow covered the driveway, so Dusty had lived up to his promise.

Harley's battered Toyota was nowhere to be seen. A wave of disappointment washed over him. "Damn it, get a grip. It's probably in the garage."

It wasn't.

It took him twenty minutes to unload, haul everything into the house and stow it in its proper place. The dogs made things more difficult by constantly getting underfoot, trying to show how happy they were to see him. Jake didn't even mind the puddle Benji made as additional proof.

He was rummaging through the refrigerator for something to drink when the phone rang. "Hello?"

"Is Harley there?" a gruff male voice asked.

"No, she's not. Can I take a message?"

"Who is this?"

Annoyance shot through him. "This is Jake Manning. Who is *this?*"

"Oh, you're the husband. You know, you really shouldn't leave a looker like Harley alone for so long." A chortle passed through the phone line. "You never know what could happen while you're gone."

Jake's hand tightened around the receiver. "Who did you say this was?" He peered at the caller ID.

Charles Rafferty. Jake didn't recognize the area code, so it wasn't local.

"It's Charlie. Leaving a new wife alone for two months is no way to start a marriage. You'd better be good to her or you'll answer to me."

"I don't know who the hell you think you are, but—"

"Just tell her that Charlie called to wish her a Merry Christmas a few days early. And tell her if she finds it's too cold for her there, it's plenty warm here and she's always welcome."

The caller disconnected, and Jake stared at the receiver for a moment, sorting through the emotions that gripped him. Did she have a fling while he was gone? The idea of her in another man's arms—he clenched his fist and shook his head. No, she wouldn't do something like that. Would she? He hadn't been jealous in a long time, and he didn't like the bitter taste it left in his mouth.

At least the guy wasn't local, so an affair seemed unlikely. But who the hell was he?

A door slammed outside. The dogs raced to the foyer, barking.

"All right you guys, settle down. Don't knock me over."

The husky voice created the usual reaction in his body—and a strange pull on his heart. Maybe absence really did make the heart grow fonder. Would she be as glad to see him?

"Jake? Where are you?"

He left the kitchen and wandered into the living

room as she came from the foyer. She dropped several mall shopping bags next to the couch. "You made it! I was worried about the roads. I heard there was a pretty good storm down near Pittsburgh."

She yanked on the zipper of her coat. His coat, actually—his old beige winter jacket. She looked damn cute with the sleeves trailing too far down her arms and the bottom hanging just above her knees. "Damn, this zipper is a pain in the neck."

"That's why I got a new coat. Why are you wearing my cast-offs?" He offered her a half smile. Charlie's words still rang in his ears as he crossed the living room to take the zipper tab in his fingers.

"Mine doesn't close anymore, but for a different reason."

"What?" He yanked on the zipper and it suddenly gave way. The fabric parted, revealing her rounded stomach protruding beneath a green plaid flannel shirt. "Aah, I see."

"I guess I'm a lot fatter than at Thanksgiving."

He stared at the evidence of his child, growing within her. "Not fat, Harley, pregnant." He forced himself to look up at her face. Her eyes flashed uncertainty. Studying her, he saw that her features were slightly rounder and her hair appeared a shade darker than when he'd left. He reached out to stroke it. There was still a rosy tint in her cheeks from the cold air. Just as the cliché had it, the woman positively glowed. "I must say, pregnancy does agree with you. You look more beautiful than ever."

He wanted to smack himself the moment the words

left his mouth. This trip had accomplished one task—creating a nest egg—but it obviously hadn't helped him create a buffer between himself and this woman. Damn it, how was it possible for her to grow more beautiful?

She smiled hesitantly at him. "Thanks. Most days I feel like a cow, and Mel tells me it'll only get worse." She shrugged out of the coat. "I'm going to hang this up."

"No, don't. I'll do it. You sit down, put your feet up." His hand brushed hers as he took the jacket from her, and electricity traveled up his arm. "So, you were out shopping? School's over for the semester, right?"

Harley wrinkled her nose. "Yes, thank goodness. I thought I was going to die from terminal boredom. Some of my professors could give the sleep-aid industry a run for its money. Especially the guy in my poetry class." She groaned. "And accounting. I hate the accounting classes."

Jake tossed the garment onto the coat tree in the foyer, then returned to the living room, sinking down on the sofa next to her. "Doesn't sound like it's what you thought it would be."

She shook her head. "Doesn't matter. I'm another giant step closer to that respectable career and the all-new Harley. Only fifteen more credits to go."

"But is it what you really want? I kind of like *this* Harley." His eyes fastened on her stomach again, and his fingers twitched.

Harley noticed the direction of his gaze. "Go

ahead, you can touch,'' she murmured. ''Jeez, everybody else does.''

He looked up at her, eyebrows climbing toward his dark hair. ''Everybody?''

She nodded. ''A pregnant woman's belly seems to be considered public property.''

His mouth thinned, and she could tell that idea didn't sit well with him. Taking his hand, she placed it on her abdomen. ''Now, just wait.'' She breathed slowly, moving his palm to the spot where the baby fluttered within her. ''Feel that?''

''No, I —'' His eyes widened and a slow grin curved his mouth. ''I feel it! I can feel the baby moving.'' He brought his other hand reverently to her belly, then leaned closer. ''Hello in there! This is Daddy. Everything okay in there? Accommodations okay? Food arriving on schedule? Nutritional needs being met?'' He grinned up at Harley. ''Just joking.''

''Daddy'' looked like a kid who'd awakened Christmas morning to find he'd received everything he wanted. Conflicting emotions pulled at her—pride that she'd given this wonderful man his dream, dismay that she couldn't provoke the same reaction in him, and a warm sensation that had to be love. God help her, even after a two-month separation, the man still had a hold on her heart.

Jake jumped from the sofa, pacing to the entertainment center on the far wall and back again. ''Harley, this is incredible. *My baby*. I could feel him moving around. Is he very active? What does he feel like inside you?''

"It could be a her, you know. She's fairly active, and it's progressed from feeling like butterflies to a kitten tumbling around. Mel assures me that in another month or so, it'll feel like having a soccer player inside me." *Incredible* was right. Ever since the baby had begun to move, she'd been in awe of the miracle. A child was growing inside her. Their child.

"You spent a lot of time with Mel while I was gone, didn't you?" Jake continued pacing the room.

"Yes, she's been great. I really like your sister." And she felt guilty as hell about cultivating a friendship—the first woman-to-woman friendship in her life—under false pretenses. What would Mel think of her if she knew the truth of the arrangement?

"Christmas Day is going to be fantastic—" He skidded to a halt near the front window, then slowly turned and scanned the room. "Where's the tree? Where are the decorations?"

She shrugged. "Wherever you put them last year."

He dragged his hand through his hair. "Harley! We're having Christmas dinner here in three days and there are no decorations up! Didn't Mel tell you to put the stuff out?"

"Nope. I'm not a big Christmas person, Jake. It's just another day as far as I'm concerned."

A muscle twitched along the side of his jaw and he stared at her. After a moment, he shook his finger. "You know what happened to Scrooge with that kind of attitude, right?" He hurried to the sofa, grabbed her arms and pulled her to her feet. "Come on. We've got a tree to find."

Harley groaned.

"It'll be fun, I promise." He stopped to face her, then stroked her cheek. "You're the one who told me to lighten up and enjoy the experience. Well, Harley, I'm going to make this a Christmas you'll never forget."

The bones in her body turned liquid, and she nearly melted into a puddle of slush at his feet. She'd never in her life had a real Christmas, not even with her dad. Holidays didn't mean anything around her house as a child, except that the garage was closed for a day, although sometimes they'd tinker around in there, anyway. Many times she'd watch TV, wishing for the big family gatherings shown in holiday commercials. As a foster child, she'd been to several different celebrations, but always on the outer edges. And there'd been two Christmases with Charlie. One they spent serving dinners at the City Mission, and last year they'd shared frozen dinners in front of the TV, watching a football game. Come to think of it, that was the one she'd enjoyed the most.

She was afraid to hope for the Christmas Jake had promised. "Bah, humbug," she muttered theatrically.

"You keep that up, and you'll be hearing chains rattling soon." He helped her back into his old coat while humming a Christmas carol. "Don't let me forget the mistletoe, Harley."

Mistletoe? She was all in favor of mistletoe. Maybe she'd get another kiss from him, after all.

SOMETHING HIT HIM SQUARE in the back. Jake whirled from the tree he was inspecting but saw only an innocent-looking Harley, gloved hands shoved deep into her pockets. She rocked back and forth on her feet. "What's the matter?" she called. "Does that tree have a hole in it, too?" A cloud of dragon smoke drifted from her mouth. "Jake, I'm freezing to death. Pick one and chop it down, will you?"

"Fresh air is good for you and the baby. Be patient. It has to be just the right tree." A shapely Douglas fir grew two rows over, and Jake moved in its direction.

The second snowball knocked off his wool cap. This time Harley was nowhere to be seen, although a stifled snort revealed her general location. "Harley?" He crept cautiously around the plump evergreen, snatching the blue hat from the ground on his way and returning it to his head.

Another snowball hurtled toward him. Jake deftly dodged right, and it sailed past. "Missed me." He scooped up a handful of snow, packing it lightly so it wouldn't hurt on impact. The last thing he wanted to do was hurt her. Still, he couldn't let an attack like this go unanswered.

"Jake, I found a good tree," she called from somewhere behind him.

How does she do that? He turned in the opposite direction. "Where?" The snow missile was ready for launching.

"Over here."

Following her voice, he wandered through the evergreens until he found her.

"It looks like me, short and fat. I like it. Can we go home now?" Her eyes widened as she spied the snow in his hand. "Hey, you can't throw that at me. I'm pregnant, you know."

He flashed her an evil grin. "Should've thought of that before. Prepare to be pelted." He lifted his hand, and she shrieked. Instead of throwing it, though, he rushed her, grabbing her around the middle and pulling her close. He dropped some snow down the back of her collar.

She shrieked again, wriggling and dancing in his arms. "Oh, that's cold!"

Cold? It felt plenty warm to him. The layers of clothing kept them separated, for which he was very grateful. The rule of hands—and lips—off loomed in his mind and he reluctantly released her. "People who don't like the cold shouldn't throw snowballs."

She sent him an innocent "who me?" look that dissolved into a broad grin. "You're right."

In direct opposition to his silent commands and curses, the warmth spread north to his heart.

Jake slapped his gloved hands together, then circled the tree she'd selected. "Well, it's not what I normally look for in a tree, but if it's the one you want, we'll take it." He glanced around. "Now, I just have to go back and find where I dropped the saw."

"THINK YOU'VE GOT ENOUGH lights on there?" Harley sat back on the sofa, cradling her mug of decaffeinated tea and watching as he put the finishing touches on the tree. Christmas carols swelled from the strategically placed speakers.

"You can never have too many lights."

"So, if the entire city of Erie goes black when you flip that switch, that's gonna be your defense?"

He grinned at her. "Yup."

"With that crummy defense, I hope you get a better lawyer than I did. Maybe you should just plead guilty."

"I'll keep that in mind." Jake stepped back from the tree, surveying his work. "There we go. Now—" he walked to the switches by the foyer, then turned out the room lights "—let's see how we did." Squatting down on his heels, he leaned behind the tree to plug it in.

Multicolored twinkles filled the room. Some of the lights shone steadily, while others blinked on and off. The colors were reflected in the front picture window, enhancing the effect.

Harley set her mug on the table, then clapped her hands. "Bravo! I have to admit it's beautiful."

"You can't appreciate it from over there. Come here and I'll show you how to really enjoy a Christmas tree."

"You're the expert." She pushed to her feet and crossed the living room to stand by his side. "Now what?"

"Now, we do this." He sank onto the floor and lay on his back, staring up at the decorated evergreen.

"You're nuts."

"You're a stick-in-the-mud."

Harley gasped and clutched her hand to her chest as though mortally wounded. "You dare call *me* a stick-in-the-mud?"

"Yup." A broad grin filled his face and he offered his hand to her.

Harley lowered herself slowly to the floor, sitting cross-legged beside him.

"No, you have to lie down here and look up at the lights. Come on."

She sighed and swung her legs out, then eased onto her back. He moved closer until their sides brushed. She glanced up at the tree. "I feel like a Christmas present."

Jake rolled onto his side and propped himself on an elbow. He smiled down at her. "No comment." What he really wanted to say was how he'd love to unwrap her, peeling away her clothes like so much colorful paper.

"You're not looking at the tree anymore."

"I'd rather look at you."

Her cheeks flushed pink. The lights twinkled in her eyes. Her flannel shirt, the top two buttons open, exposed the delicate lines of her neck. He reached out to caress her throat, forgetting all about the hands-off rule. "Tell me about your favorite Christmas memory."

"Like I said, Christmas doesn't really mean much to me."

"All right, then tell me the story of your name. How'd you end up being called Harley?" His fingers wandered up the curve of her neck to trace the outline of her ear.

"My dad loved bikes, especially Hogs. I told you he was a mechanic. He had his own shop." Her expression became wistful. "He taught me all the basics before he died. Anyway, he was convinced I'd be a boy. His name was David." She looked up at him expectantly.

"And?"

"Do I have to draw you a picture? Harley, David's son?"

Jake groaned. "Oh, that's bad. I take it your father had a strange sense of humor?"

A tiny smile blossomed on her lips. "You could say that. Anyway, when I turned out to be a girl, my mother thought Harley would still be a good name for me. I think she wanted to rub it in my father's face that he didn't get what he wanted." Her eyes grew somber. "Jake, you keep referring to the baby as 'he.' Will you be disappointed if it's a girl?"

He placed his right hand gently on the swell of her stomach. "Are you kidding? Sweetheart, whether it's a boy or a girl, I'm going to be ecstatic."

"What if…what if something's wrong with her?"

"What?" Fierce protectiveness rose within him and he spread his fingers wide over her belly, as if he could somehow shield their child from harm. "Did Dr. Hansen say there's something wrong?"

She shook her head. "No. Just…what if?"

Deep inside her eyes, old pain flickered with the blinking of the lights. With a flash of insight as clear as an Erie-winter sky, he understood her fear. She'd never measured up, failing first to meet her father's expectations, then being rejected twice by her mother, and finally, enduring repeated failed foster placements. And she feared a similar fate for the child in her belly.

"Oh, Harley. No matter what, I'm going to love this baby. I already do." And he loved her, too. Despite his wariness, his caution, a two-month separation—he had to face facts. He'd fallen in love with her.

He was playing with fire that would surely burn since her leaving was part of the plan. But at the moment, all he wanted to do was erase the pain in her eyes. He lifted his hand from her belly and cupped her face in his palm. His thumb caressed the silky skin over her cheekbone. "Harley. Sweet Harley."

The tenderness in his voice, in his touch, warmed her. Her name sounded wonderful on his lips—feminine and, for the first time she could remember, appropriate.

He lowered his head, and she closed her eyes. His lips brushed over hers, so gentle, so soft, she was afraid she'd imagined it. Feather-light kisses covered her cheeks, her nose, her eyelids, then his lips returned to her mouth. This time he took possession more surely, ravishing her with a kiss that sparked combustion.

He trailed his tongue down her neck. "Jake..." The man certainly knew how to get her motor running. She ran her fingers through his hair, then pulled gently, tipping his head back up. She pressed her mouth against his, this time claiming him.

"You make me crazy," he murmured against her lips. "Going away was supposed to put this fire out, Harley."

She opened her eyes and looked directly into his. The summer blue darkened; his pupils widened with desire.

"Burn, baby, burn," she whispered, running her finger over his upper lip.

He lightly nipped at her. "All I want for Christmas is you." His hand stroked her breast, and her nipple hardened, betraying her need. He fumbled with the buttons on her shirt. "And I'm not waiting until December 25 to unwrap you."

His breath heated the base of her throat, mouth ministering to her flesh. He finished the buttons, and she struggled upright, hands clutching the sides of her shirt together. "Maybe—maybe this isn't such a good idea. Maybe we should go into the bedroom." *The dark bedroom.*

Jake looked at her with an arched eyebrow. Understanding dawned in his eyes. "You're beautiful, Harley." He clasped her fingers and pulled them away from her shirt, then parted it himself. "Beautiful." He moved back. "Show me just how gorgeous you are. Unwrap the package yourself."

Heat scorched her cheeks. Surely he was joking? She wanted him, wanted to lose herself in his arms, the one place she'd ever felt secure—but here? There was too much light in the room with all those strings on the tree.

"Harley, look at me. See what you do to me." She followed his gaze to his lap, where his erection strained against the fly of his khaki pants. "You are a highly desirable woman, now and always."

"Pretty words," she whispered.

"True words. Pretty woman. Let me see you."

She got to her feet, more self-conscious than she'd ever been in her life. Her shirt hung open, exposing glimpses of her swollen belly, her dull white maternity bra. She glanced at his face. He smiled at her. Warmth and desire shone in his eyes.

With unsteady fingers, she unfastened the sides of her jeans and allowed them to slip to the floor. The tails of the shirt trailed down her thighs, providing fleeting coverage. She turned her back on him, reaching beneath the shirt to shimmy out of the cotton maternity underpants she suddenly detested. For a split second she longed to be back on their wedding night, when they'd conceived the baby nestled within her. She'd felt sexy in the white satin nightgown. Not like now. And the Christmas carols weren't exactly what she considered mood music.

But she reached around her back and unfastened the bra, then pulled her arms up inside the shirt to remove it, still within the comforting shelter of the soft flannel. She held the edges in one hand and turned back to face him. She held her other hand out to him. "I…I can't. You'll have to finish the unwrapping."

Jake took her hand and kissed the back of it, surprised to find it quivered beneath his lips. There it was again, a little indication of her hidden vulnerability that he found so endearing. He rose to his feet, then leaned over to give her a slow, smoldering kiss. Finally satisfied that her trembling had more to do with desire than anxiety or fear, he grasped the shoulders of the shirt and peeled them back, exposing her creamy skin, her breasts. "Let it go, Harley."

She straightened her elbows and the garment fell to the floor.

The soft lights from the Christmas tree flickered on her skin, her round belly and delightfully curved body taking on a magical quality. "That is truly the most amazing Christmas present I've ever seen." He gently took her chin in his palm and forced her to meet his eyes. "I told you pregnancy looked good on you, Harley. You really are more beautiful than ever."

He saw doubt in her expression. Fine, if she didn't trust his words, he'd have to show her. He slid his arms around her and drew her flush against him. He dropped kisses along her shoulder, nuzzling, nibbling, enjoying the faint salty taste of her skin, the smooth texture of her flesh. The scent of the jasmine perfume he'd given her on their wedding night clung lightly to her. With one hand, he caressed her side, then moved to cup her breast.

Harley moaned and arched her back.

He leaned over and took the hardened nipple into his mouth.

Her hands sought the buttons on his shirt and began

pulling on them. He straightened, then assisted her in the task, shrugging off his shirt.

Flesh met flesh, and Harley sighed with delight, fingertips tracing his washboard abs, hand darting lower to stroke him through the material of his slacks. He groaned, sending a heady feeling of power through her. The button over his fly popped open easily for her eager fingers. The zipper rasped as she tugged it downward with tantalizing slowness. Then she placed her hands against his chest and pushed gently. "Peel off those pants and lie down."

Quickly obeying, he stretched out on the area rug in front of the tree. Mercy, the man was magnificent. And for tonight, she could once again pretend he was hers.

She crossed to his side, then straddled him, lowering herself to her knees. Pure, undisguised longing flashed across his face as she settled against his erection.

She swiveled her hips over him and her fingers played in the traces of dusky hair on his chest, sometimes touching with feather-light caresses, sometimes massaging with firm, broad strokes.

When she could stand it no longer, she reached down, guiding him inside her.

He filled the physical emptiness within her—and filled a lifelong emptiness in her soul.

Jake grasped her hips and struggled not to move. The desire to hold her tight and thrust into her hard nearly overcame him, but he bit his lip and lay as motionless as he could, letting her establish the pace.

They still fit together, the way they had that first time. Their wedding night…

Two months away from her and five months' worth of obvious pregnancy had done nothing to quench his thirst for this remarkable woman.

He was in damn big trouble.

And right now, he really didn't care.

The lights from the tree glistened off the sweat on their bodies and the Christmas carols masked their moans of passion as they hurtled toward completion.

She sat astride him for another minute before she lowered herself to his chest and slipped off, lying against his side. He automatically circled her with his arm and held her close. "Now, that's what I call a present. Merry Christmas, Harley."

She lifted her head, and for once, the emerald eyes were a complete mystery to him. She offered him a tentative smile. "Yeah. Maybe it will be."

She rested her cheek on his shoulder as he stroked her hair. "It will be. I'll cure your Scrooge complex once and for all."

"You're off to a good start."

"Thank you. I pride myself on being the spirit of Christmas personified."

She traced abstract patterns on his chest. "Do you pride yourself on anything else?"

"Like what?"

"Like, um, how quickly you recover?"

"Recover?"

Her hand breezed lower, circling his navel. "Yeah, recover."

He chuckled. "You're insatiable."

"So, what are you going to do about it?"

The husky purr in her voice and the teasing actions of her fingers stirred new life in his groin. "I'm going to make love to you until you *are* sated," he murmured. "How's that?"

"Empty promises. Prove it."

So Jake rolled onto his side and proceeded to prove it.

CHAPTER TWELVE

MUTED LIGHT FROM THE STREET filtered through the master bedroom's blinds, casting a faint glow across Jake's face. His low, even breathing assured Harley he slept as she reached out to lightly caress his cheek.

His return had been far different from what she'd anticipated. Not that she was complaining.

Her stomach growled, and the baby fluttered within her. Harley smiled and caressed the mound of her stomach. All that exercise had depleted her energy. She was ravenous. She slipped from the bed, swiping his black robe from the footboard and belting it over her nightshirt.

She padded barefoot into the kitchen, pausing to rub her belly again. "Well, Peanut, what'll it be? Turkey? Ham? PB&J?" The baby shifted beneath her hand and Harley chuckled. "Peanut butter and jelly it is. Excellent choice." She flicked on the light, then made herself a sandwich and poured a glass of milk. The cat jumped onto the opposite counter. Lifting his paw to his mouth, he began bathing.

"Irving, get off the counter. If Jake catches you up there, you're in trouble. Go on." She whisked her hand in the cat's direction. He sent her a baleful look, then leapt from the counter to circle her ankles. She nudged him with her foot. "Get lost. I'm not feeding anyone but myself tonight."

She gathered up her plate and glass, carrying them into the living room and setting them on an end table. She glanced at the tree in front of the window. "Why not?" Squatting down, she plugged in the wire, lighting the room with multicolored winking. Sighing contentedly, she settled on the sofa with her snack.

A small smile played on her lips as she ate. She'd never again look at a Christmas tree in quite the same way, not after the experience she'd had beside it tonight. She just wished she understood exactly what it meant. Simple chemistry? Lust? But he'd been so tender, so considerate.

That's how he always is. It's his nature. Mr. Nice Guy, remember? She surveyed the decorations he'd put up in one afternoon: the robotic Santa doll standing on the far end table, the snowman face on the wall, the Nativity scene on the top of the entertainment center, well away from Grace and Hope's eager hands. Oh, and the mistletoe, which hung in the archway between the living and dining rooms. Jake's holiday spirit was infectious. Maybe that had something to do with it. Maybe the lovemaking had simply been a gift to her.... Maybe Jake was just showing his festive mood.

Harley sighed again, popped the last bite of sandwich into her mouth, then washed it down with the remainder of the milk. Having learned the hard way not to go back to bed immediately after eating, she leaned upright against the sofa's arm.

Why was it that she felt lonelier and more lost now that he was home? Now that he'd made love to her again?

Because you know it's only temporary. Temporary, like most things in her life. Like all the foster homes she'd passed through. Like the jobs.

The digital clock on the VCR read 12:08. Harley scrambled from the sofa and yanked open the drawer on the end table. She retrieved a prepaid calling card. Snatching up the portable phone, she returned to the couch, this time sitting near the arm closest to the tree. Using the colored lights to read the access code, she punched it in, then dialed the number long committed to memory.

"This better be good."

She smiled at his gruff act. "Who are you kidding? You're always up at this hour."

"And you're the only one who'd be calling me at this hour. You're interrupting Letterman. So, it better be good." The volume of the television in the background was reduced dramatically.

"Charlie, I just couldn't sleep so I thought I'd give you a holler and see how you're doing."

"Can't sleep? I'd have thought with that husband of yours back today, you'd be plenty busy tonight."

She was silent for a moment. "How did you know Jake was home today?"

Charlie had learned about her marriage after receiving the Erie paper with the marriage license listing that included her name. He'd given her hell for not telling him during their next phone call. Much as she'd hated doing it, she'd lied to her old friend. He was under the same impression Jake's family was—it was a loving marriage, based on a sudden and overwhelming attraction.

Her hand splayed across the lump of her belly. Somehow, there had to be a way of keeping the baby's birth out of the paper so he never found out. She could only imagine his disappointment if he ever learned what she'd done to get her degree.

"I called you earlier today, but you weren't there. I told your husband he had a lot of nerve, taking off like that for two months."

"Oh, I'm sure that went over well. He must've forgotten to tell me you called."

Charlie's deep laugh sounded through the phone line. "I'm not surprised. If you want the truth, kid, your husband sounded a little jealous to me."

"Jealous? No way." *Jealous? Of Charlie?* That certainly was an interesting tidbit.

"Yeah. I know jealousy when I hear it. Maybe if he'd stayed home instead of leaving you alone, he wouldn't be feeling insecure."

Her mind whirled as she tried to piece this new information together with his behavior. She plucked a needle off the end of a branch. Were Christmas miracles really possible? Did she dare even think it?

"Kid?"

"Yeah, Charlie?"

"I know how you feel about Christmas, but Harley,

you've got a new life started there as a married woman.''

Her hand covered the swell of her stomach. Thankfully, he didn't know the half of it. And she wanted to keep it that way.

"Try to enjoy it this year, kid. Have a merry one.''

"I'll…try. You do the same, okay?''

"Oh, I will. Actually, uh, there's this lady who lives a few doors down from me, and she invited me to her place, and you know, I, uh, I think I might go.''

Well, I'll be. The old scoundrel had finally found a girlfriend. His wife of many years had died shortly before Harley had met him, and he'd never shown any interest in hooking up with another woman. "Good for you, Charlie. That sounds nice.'' So, why did it make her feel even hollower inside? Charlie deserved some happiness.

And what about you? a soft voice whispered in her head. *Don't you deserve some happiness, too?*

"I'm not sure I'm going yet,'' he growled. "So don't start with me. Tell me, you having a white Christmas?''

"Sure are.''

He chuckled. "I don't miss that.''

"I miss *you,* you old goat.'' Moisture welled up in her eyes, and she blinked hard as the lights from the tree blurred.

"Yeah.'' His voice lowered. "Me, too.''

"You take care of yourself, Charlie. I gotta run. I'll talk to you before the New Year, okay?''

"Okay. Night."

With a click, the connection was severed. Harley jabbed the off button on the phone and dropped it on the end table.

"Who's Charlie?"

She jumped. Jake stood framed in the arch of the hallway. "Jeez, you scared the life out of me! What are you doing up?"

Clad in a pair of dark sweatpants, he crossed the living room. "I woke up and you were gone. I wanted to check and make sure you were okay." He flopped onto the sofa and folded his arms across his chest.

"I'm fine. The baby was hungry." She gave him a slight smile, uncertain of his mood.

"You haven't answered my question. Who's Charlie?"

Have mercy, the man *was* jealous. What exactly did that mean for them? She mirrored his posture, crossing her arms. "Why didn't you tell me he'd called today?"

"It slipped my mind."

"Well, I'm glad it wasn't anything important, like him calling to say he'd been admitted to the hospital or anything!"

Jake shook his head. "I'd gladly have passed that on."

"What a horrible thing to say!" She yanked a pillow from behind her back and threw it at him. "Charlie is my friend."

He caught the cushion and deftly tossed it to the floor. "How good a friend?"

"Oh, for crying out loud! For your information, Charlie is sixty-two years old. He's my only friend. And...my former parole officer."

"No."

"No, what?"

"No, he's not your only friend." He shifted toward her on the sofa.

She inched back. "How would you know?"

"Because I'm your friend, too, Harley. At least, I thought I was." He edged closer.

"You're—you're my...business partner." She ran her hand over her belly. "Here's the proof."

"Business partner? Do they usually do this?" His fingers curled around the back of her head and he pulled her in, kissing her hard, a kiss of possession.

It left her gasping for breath. "O-okay, you're my lover, too."

"Oh, I'm more than that, Harley." He nuzzled her earlobe. "I'm your husband."

"You're my temporary husband." His warm breath against her ear scrambled her brain cells, and she struggled to remain rational. He was her husband in name only, and only because *she'd* insisted. He licked the curve of her ear and she shuddered. Okay, maybe he was her husband in body as well, but it still wasn't real. *It's not real. It's not real.*

"I'm your husband now, and now is all that matters. Wasn't it you who told me to enjoy the little things?"

She nodded.

"Do you know what I'm going to do?"

She shook her head.

"I'm going to carry my wife back to bed and enjoy making love to her again." He lifted her from the sofa cushions, cradling her against his chest.

Harley wasn't sure exactly what was going on; she was afraid to even contemplate it. Maybe she'd finally lost her mind and had begun to live in a fantasy world.

Or maybe Christmas really was a time for miracles.

She allowed herself a tiny sliver of hope as he carried her back to his bedroom.

JAKE HADN'T ANTICIPATED Christmas morning this eagerly since he'd been a kid. Outside the kitchen window, fluffy snowflakes swirled in the wind—not too much, just enough to add to the holiday cheer. He positioned the mug of coffee on the tray, then added a small plate with one of Harley's other favorite foods. Holding the tray in both hands, he headed down the hall. He used his toe to nudge open the door to the master bedroom.

Harley lay on her left side, back to him, still asleep. He set her breakfast on the floor and shook a warning finger at the dogs. Face stern, he pointed at the door. Benji and Pepper slunk from the room to lie just over the threshold in the hallway.

Jake perched on the edge of the bed. Leaning over, he brushed back her hair, tucking it behind her ear and easing closer. "Hey, Sleeping Beauty. Wake up, it's Christmas."

She shifted onto her back with a low groan. "G'way. It's still night."

"I bet I have something that'll make you open up those eyes." He retrieved the coffee from the tray. Steam wafted from the cup as he passed it near her nose.

"Mmm." One eye opened to peer at him. "That smells great. Why are you tormenting me with it?"

"Because this is for you. I brought you breakfast in bed."

The second eye popped open and she stared at him. "You're kidding, right?"

"I'm a stick-in-the-mud. I never kid." He rose, replaced the mug on the tray, then picked up the whole thing. "Your breakfast."

She propped herself up on her elbows to examine it. "Is that real coffee? It smells real."

"Of course."

"To what do I owe this unexpected pleasure?"

He smiled broadly. "It's Christmas, Harley."

She eyed him warily and picked up the cup. Inhaling deeply, she took a small sip. "Mmm. Oh, that is heaven."

"And, there's this." He flicked a paper napkin off the small plate with a flourish. "Ta-da."

"Chocolate cake? All right, this is serious. Who are you and where is Jake Manning? Oh, I know what happened. The pod people have invaded Virginia Beach, and you're not the real Jake Manning. He's gone, and now you're here to take over Erie. There's a pod in the basement waiting for me."

"The only pod growing around here is this one." Jake fondled her belly through the comforter.

"Oh, that's funny, thank you very much. You ply me with coffee and cake, and then make fat jokes." Her eyes glinted. "Besides, I'll bet I can find another growing pod right in this room."

He swatted her hand as she reached for his lap. If she touched him, he was done for. "Cut that out. You start that and we'll still be in this bed when the family shows up expecting dinner." He dipped a fork into the cake and lifted a small piece toward her mouth. "Now, be quiet and eat so we can get to the good stuff."

"What's the good stuff?" she mumbled, mouth full.

"Why, presents, of course."

He fed her the cake bite by bite, then returned the tray to the kitchen while she got dressed. The turkey was already in the oven and, luckily, that was his only responsibility for the family meal. Kate and Mel would bring the stuffing, the mashed potatoes and gravy, the vegetables and desserts.

Jake counted out dinner plates, taking them from the cupboard and placing them on the counter. An even number. How nice not to be the odd man out this year.

Harley cleared her throat in the doorway, and Jake turned to face her. The white sweater with blue snowflakes made him smile. "I remember that sweater. That was Mel's favorite while she was pregnant with the twins."

Harley gave him a half smile in return, her hands hidden behind her back.

"What are you hiding?"

"These." She showed him two gift-wrapped boxes.

"Oh great, presents. Are those for me?"

She nodded.

"Well, come on out by the tree, because that's where yours are. And ladies go first."

"No, Jake. I'm not very good at this sort of thing, so I want you to go first." She tentatively held the packages out to him.

The uncertainty in her eyes undid him, as always. He leaned against the kitchen counter. "Okay, you twisted my arm. I'll go first." He accepted the gifts, setting the smaller package on the counter.

"No, open the little one, then the bigger one."

"No problem." He exchanged the two boxes and eagerly tore into the gold wrapping paper. Crumpling it in a ball, he shot it into the garbage can on the other side of the kitchen. He held up the gift. "Refills for my day planner. You shouldn't have." He grinned at her.

She smiled back. "I know, but I figured you'd love it."

The second set of wrapping paper peeled away to reveal a shoebox. Harley chewed on her lower lip while he held the gift to his ear and shook it, then set it on the counter to remove the lid. A model replica of his Mustang lay nestled in white tissue paper. Jake lifted the little car from the box, turning it this way and that, examining it carefully. "Harley, this is wonderful! Thank you."

Her eyes shone with excitement. "Do you really like it?"

"Yes, I do. I think I'll take it to my downtown office and put it on my desk there."

She sighed deeply. "Good." She smiled again. "There's one more thing, but it's out in the garage, and you have to give me a few minutes to get it ready, okay?"

"That sounds interesting. All right, you call me when you're done."

"Okay." She crossed the kitchen, avoiding a few pieces of kibble Benji had dumped from his bowl. Opening the door to the garage, she glanced once more over her shoulder before disappearing to prepare her surprise.

"Very curious," he murmured. He busied himself counting out silverware for the holiday table. Then he searched the cupboards until he found the glass Christmas plate with the candles etched into it. Mel had brought it home during the yard-sale summer—the summer after Bud's death, during which Mel alternately baby-sat and spent her money at yard sales, dragging home piles of stuff that ended up in the basement, the shed, just about anywhere she could find space. That was her way of dealing with the whole thing. Jake hadn't paid a lot of attention to it. Dusty had been the bigger problem, suddenly getting into fights in the neighborhood. Yard-sale junk-collecting had seemed harmless by comparison. Most of the stuff had gone by the wayside, but the Christmas plate became a special family tradition. And Mel would have his head if it wasn't ready for her homemade cookies when she arrived.

"Jake, come out now!" Harley called from the garage. He eased the cookie platter into a sink full of sudsy water and hurried to the doorway.

She'd removed the cover from the Mustang and stood next to it, back ramrod-straight, hands gesturing toward his old car like a model on *The Price Is Right*. The car glistened beneath the glare from the overhead lights.

"Wow." He hustled down the stairs and began to study the hood closely. "I can see myself." He reached out to touch the polished finish, but Harley grabbed his wrist.

"Don't touch it! Are you crazy?"

He laughed at her. "At times, I do believe I am. The car looks great. What did you do to it?"

"I compounded it out and gave it a wax job. You really neglect this poor car, you know."

"I know." Wrapping an arm around her waist, he drew her close. "Thank you, Harley. They're wonderful presents." He dropped a quick kiss on her lips and caressed her belly with one hand. "And this, this is the most incredible gift anyone could ever give me."

Pink stained her cheeks and she stared at the floor.

"Now, come on. It's time for your presents." He grabbed her by the fingers to tug her toward the door. "I hope you'll like them."

He pulled her through the kitchen and dining room, then into the living room, guiding her to the sofa. With a quick grin, he retrieved two packages from beneath the tree. Santa Claus paper covered the large gift, a box he needed both hands to manage. A smaller box wrapped in silver paper with a sparkling bow was balanced on top of the large one. "We're going to do mine backward. I want you to open the big one first." He set it on her knees and scooped up the smaller one, then stepped back for a more complete view.

She glanced up at him. "This big thing is for me?"

He nodded. "Go on."

With painstaking precision, she slit the tape with a fingernail and gingerly removed the paper.

Jake rocked on his feet. "Hurry up!"

She looked at him from the corner of her eye but continued her process. When the blue-and-red box became visible, her mouth dropped open. A second later, she began to laugh, sending warmth surging through his chest. "Oh, Jake. This is… I don't know what to say, except thank you." She raised it for a better look. "I always wanted one of these. Can we play with it?"

"Of course we can. That's what it's for. I thought we'd set it up on the pool table downstairs." He took the electric racecar set from her and placed it on the floor. "But I get to be Jeff Gordon."

"Ha! Be my guest. I'll blow your doors off no matter who you are."

"We'll see, won't we?" He lowered himself to the

sofa and held out the little silver package. He watched anxiously as she fumbled with the paper.

Harley looked down at the jeweler's box resting in her palm. She'd never received jewelry from a man before. The plain gold wedding band he'd given her didn't count. That was part of their charade. Besides, it didn't fit anymore.

She snapped the lid open. Her name, in graceful gold script, twinkled against a red velvet background. She extended one fingertip to lightly brush over it, then caressed the fine gold chain attached to either end. "Jake, it's lovely."

He stroked her cheek, then lightly tapped her nose with his finger. "Just like you. Can I help you put it on?"

"Yes, please." She handed him the velvet box, then turned her back toward him. Gathering her hair into her hands, she lifted it off her neck.

He reached around her, fumbling with the clasp. "There." He followed through with a quick kiss along her spine, and she dropped her hair, allowing it to cascade over him. "Hey!"

She shifted position again, turning to face him. The necklace flashed reflections from the tree lights. "Thank you. This is the nicest Christmas present I've gotten…in a very long time."

He leaned forward to kiss her. "You're welcome. Merry Christmas, Harley."

She clutched the necklace in her hand. "Yes, I believe it is. Merry Christmas, Jake."

CHAPTER THIRTEEN

THE CLINK OF SILVERWARE against plates gave way to weary, contented sighs, and the diners pushed their chairs back from the table. Harley stole a peek at Jake as she slipped a few more chocolate chip cookies off the glass platter in the center of the table. He winked at her.

The twins, decked out in red velvet dresses and white tights, ran around the dining room, chattering happily, new stuffed kittens clutched in their chubby little hands. Dusty paced the floor and jiggled Matthew in his arms, the baby alternating between fussy periods of relative quiet and outright screaming. "Kate, I really think you need to handle this." The young father leaned over his wife's shoulder and lowered the baby into her arms.

"It's about that time, anyway," Mel announced, dropping her fork to her plate, then tossing a balled-up napkin at her husband. Peter grinned in response.

"What time?" Harley asked.

"Time for the men to have KP duty. We cooked, they clean."

Harley licked a smudge of chocolate from her finger. "I didn't cook. Does that mean I have KP, too?"

Kate pushed her chair back from the table, gently jostling the fussing baby. "Nope, you're pregnant, you're excused. You can come with the rest of us and put your feet up."

Jake gathered several serving dishes into a pile. "You know, I'm not quite sure how this particular tradition evolved," he complained.

Mel swatted him on the shoulder. "You want to go back to cooking the entire meal?"

"No, thanks."

"All right, then be quiet and clean up."

As Harley rose, a large gas bubble rolled across the top of her stomach and she belched loudly. Cheeks hot, she covered her mouth and mumbled an apology. The rest of the room broke into good-natured laughter.

Mel reached out to rub her tummy. "Baby's fault."

"I shouldn't have had that many cookies, especially after Kate's yummy brownie," Harley admitted. Jake smiled at her and she pointed her finger at him. "No comments from you. It's Christmas," she added smugly.

"Indeed it is."

Mel took her by the arm. "Come on. Let's go into the living room and enjoy the tree. It'll be time for presents soon."

"Presents! Come on!" Grace shrieked. Her shiny new Mary Janes clattered against the wooden floor as she ran into the living room.

"Not yet, Grace!" Mel took off after her daughter.

Harley laughed and followed at a more sedate pace,

not wanting to risk upsetting her overfilled stomach. She really had eaten too much. But she'd never experienced a holiday like this and figured overindulgence was part of it.

A small hand tugged on her sweater. "Har-we, Har-we, me want up."

Harley smiled down at Hope. While she liked both little girls, the smaller twin had claimed a special place in her affections. To Harley, Hope was the underdog, and she always rooted for the underdog. "Come here, squirt." She grasped the child under the arms and lifted her, carrying her into the living room.

Mel wrestled a bright red-and-green package from Grace. "I said not yet, young lady." She glanced at the box. "This one's not even yours."

Grace stuck out her bottom lip and her big blue eyes filled with tears. "My present. For me."

"Where's the kitty Santa brought you? How about you play with him?" Mel looked up at Harley from the floor. "Why are you carrying her? Hope, you can walk perfectly fine. Aunt Harley doesn't need to carry you."

Hope stuck her fingers in her mouth and rested her head against Harley's shoulder. The sweet scent of baby shampoo drifted upward. The child in her womb shifted again, and her heart turned over. She stroked Hope's fine blond hair. "It's okay, Mel, I don't mind."

"Let her practice now, Mel," Kate suggested, settling onto the couch with Matthew. "In another few months, she'll have one of her own, and then she'll understand.'' Kate opened the buttons of her blouse, pulled down the flap on her bra and put the baby to her breast.

Harley watched in fascination as the baby latched on immediately and started nursing. ''He looks like he's starving. Doesn't that hurt?''

Kate laughed. ''As long he remembers not to use his new tooth, it doesn't.''

''Ow.''

''Seriously, Harley, it's wonderful.'' Kate touched the downy fuzz on Matthew's head. ''Aren't you going to breast-feed?''

Grace tossed wooden blocks out of the small toy box Jake kept in the corner of the living room and Hope squirmed in her arms. ''Down. Me want down.''

Grateful for the interruption, she set the little girl on her feet. Hope immediately darted toward the blocks and her sister. Harley strolled to the far end of the sofa and lowered herself into the cushions with a sigh. For several minutes the only sounds in the living room were those of the playing toddlers.

''Are you, Harley?'' Mel asked, finally breaking the lull in the conversation, picking up right where they'd left off, much to Harley's dismay. ''You really should. It's best for the baby, it's a wonderful bonding experience, and—''

''And it's always ready,'' Kate added, slipping a finger into the baby's mouth and removing him from her breast. She raised him to her shoulder despite his protests and thumped him on the back.

"What's always ready?" Jake asked as the men came into the living room.

Peter dropped to the floor next to Mel, and Dusty perched on the arm of the sofa beside Kate. Jake leaned against the wall near the entryway.

"Breast milk," Mel informed him. "We were wondering if Harley was going to nurse your baby."

This time it wasn't a gas bubble that caused the weird sensation somewhere between Harley's stomach and her chest. She stared pointedly at the tree, unable to meet Jake's eyes. There wouldn't be a chance for her to nurse the baby. The child cradled within her body would be a bottle-baby out of necessity.

"We don't know yet," Jake said softly.

A hand closed around her knee and Harley looked down into Mel's eyes.

"You don't have to decide now. You've got four months before the baby's born. And you don't have to do it if you're not comfortable with the idea."

Harley nodded. "Thanks, Mel. I guess I'll have to think about it." She didn't *want* to think about it. She just wanted to forget what would happen when the baby was born and enjoy the rest of her first real Christmas celebration.

"Don't let Jake push you into it, either." Dusty leaned over Kate, who was now nursing Matthew on the opposite breast. He stroked his son's head. "It's a pretty personal thing. I think it's the most beautiful thing in the world, but I'm not the one who has to nurse him."

So there *was* a soft side to the overzealous cop. Harley hadn't been sure there was anything that marked him as Jake's brother besides the blue eyes.

"You just like it because it means you don't have to do two o'clock feedings when you're not on third shift," Kate pointed out.

Dusty grinned. "There is that."

Kate slapped him on the thigh. The baby released his hold on her breast and stared up at his mother. "Had enough?" She passed him to Dusty. "You can burp and change him. The diaper bag's in the foyer."

"Yes, ma'am. You know, you're beautiful when you're bossy." Dusty bent over to kiss his wife firmly on the lips.

Kate's cheeks glowed a pretty pink when Dusty released her. "I have to go and pump."

"Pump?" Harley groaned. "I don't think I want to know about that."

Kate laughed, buttoning her blouse. "You're going to get over your body squeamishness real soon, Harley. Don't worry—I'll pump in private. But my husband and I have a big date in a few days, and I need to have enough milk to leave with the sitter."

Husband and wife exchanged a heated glance. For all his bluster, Harley could tell that Dusty was a marshmallow when it came to his wife—or his son.

Mel clapped her hands as Kate left the room. "Hurry back, Kate. Who's ready for presents?"

The twins scampered from the corner, shouting and squealing, and the room dissolved into barely controlled chaos as the little girls shredded wrapping paper and emptied boxes.

Delighted giggles merged with low chuckles and murmurs. The scent of turkey, sage and pine filled the room. Harley lost herself in the sensations. Closing her eyes, she let her head fall back against the sofa.

So this was what it felt like to be part of a family at Christmas. Thanksgiving had been low-key by comparison; this was all-out celebrating. Warmth infused her whole body. She belonged here. She was comfortable here. She finally understood what home meant, what family meant, and how it felt to actually be on the inside, instead of on the outer edge, looking in, like a kid with her nose pressed against a toy-store window. This cozy feeling—this was family.

A full stomach and the sense of warmth lulled her into contentedness, and she dozed off.

Sometime later, a light but insistent pat on her knee demanded her attention. She opened her eyes and raised her head, glancing down to find Hope standing beside her. Harley stifled a yawn and hoped no one had noticed her lapse.

The little girl had her arms around a box almost as big as she was. "Har-we, this for you." Hope dropped the gift on Harley's lap and clambered up onto the sofa to sit beside her.

Grace dragged a similar box across the room to Kate, who now sat nestled on the love seat, Matthew sleeping in her arms, Dusty cradling her protectively.

"You have to open them at the same time," Mel

announced. "I'm afraid I'm not terribly creative. You both got the same thing."

"It's a cow, isn't it?" Harley asked.

"That would be appropriate," Dusty joked.

Jake pushed from his post against the wall to slap him on the back of the head. "Watch it."

Kate paused in the act of handing the sleeping baby to her husband. "Thank you, Jake. You'll pay for that when we get home, mister. On behalf of both of us." She passed Matthew to him, then accepted the box from Grace. "Ready, Harley?"

Harley nodded and smiled down at the little girl beside her. "Will you help me, Hope?"

The blond head nodded assent and the small hands grabbed onto the paper. Harley had already learned that any task done with toddler assistance took twice as long, but she didn't mind.

Once all the green-and-red paper lay piled on the floor in front of them, Harley opened the lid of the white box. Lifting the tissue paper, she pulled out a sweatshirt. She unfolded it, then held it up to inspect the design.

A lump filled her throat. *World's Greatest Aunt* curved boldly in green letters across the top. Two sets of small red handprints decorated the rest of the shirt, Grace's labeled on the left, Hope's on the right.

Harley's nose tingled, and the lights on the tree blurred. A sudden vision of the little pizza-stained handprints on the dining-room wall obscured her vision. *World's Greatest Aunt.*

She realized they were all watching her expectantly, Jake more so than the others. His face was carefully composed, no clue to his emotions apparent. He nodded his head slightly and eyed the child beside her.

She set the sweatshirt back down on her lap and forced a response past the enormous ball bearing lodged in her throat. "It's beautiful, Hope. Thank you so much." She dropped a quick kiss on the girl's head and rose from the sofa, unable to sit still.

The World's Greatest Aunt was a complete fraud.

Her stomach lurched and she fought the rising nausea. Tossing her cookies suddenly seemed a real possibility.

She held up the shirt in front of herself again, and glanced at Kate's similar one, struggling to maintain her composure. "I just have one question. How come mine's so much bigger than hers?"

Mel laughed and jumped to her feet, enfolding Harley in a hug. "Because you're going to get bigger before you get smaller, sister dear."

Harley stiffened in Mel's arms at the endearment. Christmas wishes made in the past flooded her memory, wishes made as a "lonely only" before she'd lost her father, and wishes made as a lonely foster child.

Wishes for a sister. Wishes for a family. Wishes for a loving home.

Mel released her but slid an arm around her shoulder, turning to face the room at large. "Just think, you guys. Next year, this will be even better. Matthew will be walking by then—"

Kate groaned.

"And Jake and Harley's baby will be even older than Matthew is right now."

The room tilted beneath Harley's feet and the grand illusion she'd tried to create and indulge for the day came crashing down around her.

There'd be no next year for her.

Her baby would be here with this loving family.

Harley would be somewhere else.

Kate would be the only greatest aunt.

Clutching the sweatshirt to her chest with one hand, she covered her mouth with the other but the sob escaped anyhow. Mel stopped her chatter about next year to stare at her.

Harley backed away, gaze darting around the room. Jake's poker face slipped. Concern and fear showed in his eyes. What was he afraid of? He wasn't the one who'd be alone come next year.

Her bottom lip trembled. "I...I can't do this." A low-pitched moan crawled from her throat. "I'm sorry."

She whirled and bolted down the hallway, racing for the solitude of her room, hoping to reach it before she completely fell to pieces.

CHAPTER FOURTEEN

STUNNED SILENCE DESCENDED on the living room in the wake of Harley's unexpected outburst and disappearance. Jake stared in the direction she'd vanished. Cold fear pulsed through his veins. She couldn't do *what?* And what the hell was she sorry for?

"What did I say?" Mel asked.

He pasted what he hoped would pass for an apologetic expression onto his face and glanced at his family. "Hormones." He shrugged. His brother and brother-in-law nodded in understanding, while the women pierced him with expressions sharp enough to cut.

"Why is Har-we sad, Mommy?" Hope asked.

Mel bent over and picked up her daughter. "I think maybe Harley's a little tired, sweetie."

"She don't wike my present?"

"I think she loved your present, honey."

Jake edged toward the hallway.

"Go to her, Jake. We'll finish cleaning up and get out of here." Mel offered him a shaky smile.

"She's not used to having family." Jake shrugged again. He didn't want to make a major issue in front of them, but he needed to go to her. Now. He had to know exactly what Harley felt she couldn't do.

"God knows we take some getting used to," Dusty said. "Go on, Jake. See to your wife." He jerked his head at the hallway. "Get going."

"Thanks." Without a second thought, he turned his back on the now-somber group in the living room and hurried down the hallway.

The closed door muffled but couldn't conceal her heartbreaking sobs. He slipped into the room and shut the door gently behind him.

Dim winter light filtered in through the window that faced the side yard. Jake allowed his eyes to adjust to the dark room before turning toward the bed shoved against the far wall.

She gave no indication that she'd even heard him come in. He'd never seen her shed so much as a single tear, not when she'd admitted to being beaten at the hands of a foster father, nor when she'd spoken of her mother's abandonment or father's death. Now she lay on the small bed sobbing as though her world had ended.

Compassion overcame his selfish fear. Jake sat on the edge of the bed and reached for her. "Harley—"

She shook her head, entire body trembling. "No. No." Tears spilled from her eyes and trickled down her cheeks.

Jake eased himself onto his side and snuggled up behind her. He propped his left elbow on the mattress; with his right hand he stroked her arm. "No *what*, Harley?"

"No. Don't—don't touch me."

"All right." He placed his hand on his hip, but

stayed next to her. "You want to tell me what's going on?"

She sniffed loudly. "It's not real. It's not real."

"What's not real?"

"All of it. Us. Them. Oh, God! I can't..." She shook harder, body racked with sobs.

"Shh. Take it easy." He grasped her shoulder and rolled her over until she faced him, then he gathered her into his arms.

She pressed her face into his shirt. "I want it to be real!"

Such a state of near-hysteria couldn't be good for her or the baby. He stroked her hair and back, murmuring softly into her ear. Tender words of comfort flowed from his tongue with little thought or care for the actual meaning. What in the world was she thinking?

"I—I can't," she hiccupped into his chest. Her hand slipped to the mound of her belly and she rubbed it protectively. "Peanut...I can't, Jake."

Damn it, she was going to renege on their arrangement. He was going to lose this child, like he'd lost Austin. Well, not without a fight. This one belonged to him.

"And what about her?" a demanding voice asked from the back of his mind.

He shoved the fear aside, deciding to focus solely on calming the trembling woman in his arms. Only when she could talk coherently could he get any real information out of her, and there was absolutely no point in panicking before that. "Shh. Try to relax."

She inhaled in short, jerking gasps, and he worried she'd hyperventilate. "Breathe slowly. It'll be okay." He continued to caress her hair, murmuring commands to help her regulate the harsh breathing. "Everything's going to be fine."

He wasn't sure Harley was the one he needed to convince.

Gradually, she relaxed in his arms, muscles losing their tension little by little. She no longer twitched or sobbed, and her breathing evened out to a smooth tempo only occasionally broken by a small hiccup.

It took him a few minutes to realize she'd fallen asleep. Harley the invincible, Harley the stoic, had cried herself to sleep in his arms. Without providing the answers he sought.

He sighed and rested his chin against the top of her head. The warmth of her body in his arms had an innate rightness about it, a perfect fit—something he was loath to give up. The absurdity of the situation wasn't lost on him. He'd planned their relationship carefully, logically, all contingencies considered in advance. Except for one. He'd never expected to fall in love with her. And looking backward, he could see he'd lost control of the situation early on.

What did he do about it?

He needed a new plan. One that wouldn't involve losing her. Or their child. He wasn't certain he'd survive such a loss.

How exactly did one go about keeping a woman? He'd never really thought about it before. When Stacy left—once he'd gotten over the initial shock and pain—he'd simply said good riddance and turned away from women in general. Come to think of it, his stepfather had acted the same way when Jake's mother had walked out.

What made a woman stay?

Give her what she wants.

Great. Now, if he just knew what Harley wanted. But he had the nagging suspicion that even she didn't know.

The shadows in the room deepened as he lay with his arms around her, pondering his future and designing plans that would persuade the mother of his child to stay with him.

HER LEG TWITCHED AGAINST his, then her arm, jolting Jake back from his nap. She stirred restlessly in his arms, murmuring under her breath.

"Harley?"

She stilled again, body relaxing back into the comfort of untroubled sleep. He brushed his fingertips along her cheek, gliding over the soft lines of her features. Moving closer, he placed a gentle kiss just above her eyebrow. "I love you," he whispered. "What am I supposed to do about that?"

He reached down and lifted the hem of her sweater, letting his hand sneak underneath. He slipped it beneath the waist of her pants to caress the warm, firm flesh of her pregnant belly.

The baby bumped lightly against his palm. Single-minded and determined, plan carefully worked out, he'd achieved what he'd set out to do. A child of his own, one he had legal rights to, lay cradled in the warmth below his hand. "I just wanted to protect you," he whispered. He wanted to spare his child the pain he'd known, the pain he'd watched Mel and Dusty suffer, hell, even the pain Harley herself had suffered. But in doing so, he'd managed to plan himself into a situation fraught with even greater pain for everyone involved. And he'd only come up with one clear solution—Harley had to be persuaded to stay. Forever. No revolving door for her.

"Will you help me, baby?" He wasn't certain she actually wanted the child, or to be a mother. Her incoherent ramblings had left him with more questions than answers.

Her body twitched again, and Jake slid his palm along her belly, soothing, caressing. She moaned in her sleep and pushed at his hand. "No."

"Easy, Harley. It's okay."

She thrashed her head. "No, don't."

"Don't what, sweetheart?"

She whimpered softly and her legs jerked, obvious indications of a nightmare. He removed his hand from her stomach and put his arms around again, drawing her close. "Shh. It's going to be okay."

"Don't!"

The single word held a heartfelt plea that struck to the core of his soul. "Don't what? What are you afraid of?" He rubbed small circles on her back.

"Don't take my baby."

Funny, he knew exactly how she felt. She shifted in his arms, hands instinctively seeking the mound beneath her sweater. "Peanut, Peanut..." She dissolved into soft whimpers again.

"No one's taking the baby, Harley. Everything's

fine.'' Or it would be. He'd see to it. ''Shh. You just sleep now.''

WARMTH. BLESSED WARMTH and a sense of security enveloped her as she rose toward wakefulness. The spicy, sharp scent of a man, the texture of a firm chest beneath her cheek, stimulated her reviving senses. She stirred gently, not wanting to disturb him.

''You awake now?'' he whispered.

She opened her eyes. The bedroom was dark, making sight damn near impossible. ''Yeah.''

''You okay?''

The memories of what she'd done—Hope's gift, making a scene, bolting from the room—came flooding back. ''Oh, God, Jake. I'm sorry.''

''There's no need to apologize.''

''What must they think?'' She sighed.

He cupped her cheek in his palm, thumb caressing her skin. ''They think you're a tired, hormonal, pregnant woman who isn't used to holidays with family.''

''Then I didn't blow it? I didn't say anything to give us away?''

''No, not really.''

''What does that mean?''

''It means you and I need to have a little talk. I want to know exactly what was going through your mind when you lost it. You scared the hell out of me.'' He unwrapped his arms from around her and sat up.

Panic grabbed her. ''What are you doing?''

''I'm just going to turn on the light. I want to see you when we talk.''

"No!" She groped around until she found his hand. "Please, leave it dark."

"Why?"

Because she'd always found the darkness soothing. She could hide in it. If he turned on the lights, she was done for. "Please, Jake."

"Are you going to give me straight answers?"

"The best I can."

"All right, I suppose I'll have to settle for that." He turned back toward her and stretched out on the bed again. "Why don't you start with what scared you so badly?"

Her tentative fingers sought his face, traveling lightly across his features, pausing at his lips. She leaned forward to brush her own over them. His mouth was unyielding beneath her kiss. She increased the pressure.

He grabbed her upper arm and pushed her back. "Harley, no. You're not going to play those kinds of games with me. The question of whether we have incredible chemistry has been answered with a resounding yes. There are a lot of other questions that need to be answered now. Starting with what upset you."

She pressed her forehead against his chest. "I'm not big on spilling my guts."

"I've noticed. I also noticed that keeping things bottled up inside you seems to lead to a big explosion." He toyed with her hair. "Talk to me, Harley. I really am your friend, you know." His large, soft hand stroked her head. "I care about you."

She snorted lightly. "Then besides Charlie, that makes you a first."

"I can't help the fact that the world is crazy, sweet-heart," he said into her ear. "Tell me."

"Jake, what would you do if I gave you a shirt for Christmas, and it didn't fit right?"

"I guess I'd take it back."

"And if it was the wrong color? Or was defective? Or you simply decided you didn't like it?"

"I'd take it back. But what does that have to do with anything? Or is this just another of your change-the-subject-to-avoid-the-hard-stuff conversations?"

She shook her head against his chest. "No." She fought against the rising tide of her emotions. "I'm tired of being returned, Jake," she whispered. It had happened to her too many times.

"Aw, Harley."

The compassion in his voice nearly sent her into another fishtail. She struggled for control, inhaling deeply.

He cradled her in his arms, then placed a kiss on her head. "What if I told you I didn't want to return you?"

The small hairs on the back of her neck bristled. "What?"

He cleared his throat. "I love you, Harley. I have no intention of returning you. I want to keep you."

"No. That's the holiday talking."

"It most certainly is not. That's my heart talking." He slipped his hand to her waist. "I've been doing some thinking. It's totally unfair of me to bring a child into the world without a mother. I mean, I know it can be done, that a single man can raise a child by himself. But I look at Dusty and Kate, and Mel and Peter, and I want what they have."

So did she. The dream of a family, a dream she'd buried deep in a tiny corner of her heart many years ago, had been awakened by these people. By him. By the movement of his child within her belly. The problem was, she knew it couldn't come true. Dreams *didn't* come true for people like her. That was a truth she'd learned over and over. Besides, he deserved better. And so did their baby. "You say that now, and I hope you get what you want, Jake. But it's not going to happen with me." Why did the truth have to hurt so much?

He stiffened against her. "What do you mean, it's not going to happen with you?"

"I'm not wife and mother material. You knew that when you picked me as the biological mother of your child. Hell, if we're being honest, that's one of the biggest reasons you picked me."

"Why no longer matters. What matters is that I love you. You want this baby, Harley. I can see it in the way you act. And don't tell me you're not happy here, in this house, with me."

"We can't always have what we want, Jake. Trust me on that. Just because I'm bonding with Peanut doesn't mean I'm the best thing for her. Or you, for that matter."

He moved away from her, sliding farther down the bed. "I don't understand."

"Like I said, I'm not wife and mother material. What's not to understand? I don't know how to take care of a child. And when you married me, it wasn't for real. What man in his right mind would marry a female mechanic with a criminal record?"

"I did."

"But it wasn't *real,* Jake. You didn't really choose *me.* You married me because you thought I could give you what you wanted, a baby, no strings attached. You figured a woman with a past like mine, growing up without a mother, not planning on being a mother, would be perfect." Her voice quavered. "I agreed because I thought maybe giving one child in the world a terrific home would balance things out. A terrific home with *you,* Jake. Not with me. I don't know a damn thing about raising a child or being a wife. Or even being a woman, for that matter."

"Sweetheart, you are definitely all woman, don't kid yourself."

"I'm not what you need, Jake."

Jake suddenly reached over and snapped on the light.

Harley closed her eyes against the brightness. Damn him, why couldn't he leave well enough alone? If he pressed her, if she had to look into those blue eyes and see his compassion, or even worse, if she actually saw love, she'd never be able to follow through with their arrangement. She steeled herself to present a calm facade.

"You have no idea what you're talking about," he insisted. "You have plenty to offer—"

"I have nothing to offer. Nothing. I'm a poor choice to bet your future on, Jake. I'm my mother's daughter. I'll leave you and the baby eventually. It's in my blood."

"I don't believe that, and neither do you. I've watched you with the twins. You're great with them—"

"Oh, yeah, the world's greatest aunt. Aunts don't

have to take care of kids, Jake. They don't have to do the hard things. Being an aunt is not the same as being a mother.''

''No, it's not, but you *can* be a mother. I believe in you.''

''Well, then you're a bigger damn fool than I thought!'' Harley clutched her pillow to her chest, hoping to muffle the pain in her heart. Half of her longed to throw herself into his arms and swallow every word he said; the other half realized the most wonderful man in the world, a real live Mr. Nice Guy, deserved far better than an ex-con with a sordid past and less-than-sterling social graces.

Jake jumped to his feet. ''I don't understand you at all. You say you're tired of being returned, but when I want you to stay, you say you'll leave eventually, regardless. What the hell is wrong with you?''

''There's nothing wrong with me. I am who I am.''

''You don't have a clue who the hell you are! And that's your problem, Harley. Maybe when you figure it out, you'll know what you want.'' He stalked to the doorway, then turned to stare at her. ''The offer is on the table. I want you to stay. I love you.''

''Pretty words,'' she mumbled.

''I'll always love you, no matter what you decide to do.''

''Empty promises.'' She picked at a loose thread in the bedspread's side seam.

A low rumble issued from his throat. ''When my mother left him, my stepfather begged her to stay. It didn't change her mind. I won't beg, Harley. And here's one promise I intend to keep—I won't let you take the baby from me. That's my child, and I have as many legal rights to him as you do. So you'd better decide what you want. I already know what I want. And you know where to find me when you make up your mind.'' He slapped his hand over the light switch, plunging the room into darkness again as he marched off.

Harley blinked back tears and lowered herself onto the bed, still clutching the pillow. ''Oh, Peanut. I wish I could believe him. But he doesn't really want me. His head's buzzing from the holiday and he's scared I'm going to try to take you away from him. It's you he wants, baby, not me.''

What if it's real? What if he does love you?

She wished she had as much faith in herself as he seemed to. He was offering the dream of her lifetime—a real family. If only she could measure up and be what he and their child deserved....

CHAPTER FIFTEEN

HARLEY LEANED OVER the Toyota's engine. Her mechanical tinkering contradicted her new desire to measure up to the standards of a typical wife and mother. But if Jake wanted reality, she'd give him the real Harley, the grease monkey from the wrong side of the tracks. *That's who I am, and I'm not ashamed of it.*

Hell, she didn't know *what* she wanted anymore.

The doorbell rang. The dogs leapt to their feet and raced up the steps, waiting by the kitchen door to be let into the house. Benji yapped, while Pepper's deeper bark bounced off the garage walls. The wrench slipped from Harley's grasp to clatter to the concrete floor and she banged her head on the truck's raised hood. "Damn it." She rubbed her skull just over her right ear.

"Harley, would you get that?" Jake's voice came from the basement stairs. "I've got my hands full down here!"

She glanced at her grease-stained fingers. Like she didn't? She yanked an old red handkerchief from the back pocket of her denim overalls and began removing some of the grime while she trudged up the steps. The second she opened the screen door, the dogs were off and charging through the house. "Sure, no problem," she called down to the cellar, hoping he caught the sarcastic edge.

In the four days since Christmas, they'd been prickly with each other. Jake acted extremely attentive toward her yet distant at the same time, as though trying to provide her with reasons to stay but not wanting to get his hopes up. Harley wanted to believe his pretty words, wanted to believe the two of them could make it work, but fear prevented that.

She hurried through the kitchen and headed for the front door, still wiping grease from her fingers. The doorbell chimed again, twice in quick succession. "Don't get your valves stuck, I'm coming," she muttered, tucking the rag back in her pocket.

Her greasy hand slipped on the door handle and the dogs jostled her. "Get back, you beasts." She nudged them with her foot, tightened her grasp on the gold handle and flung open the door. "Can I..." The greeting died in her throat.

An elegant blond woman in a full-length gray fur and a man with salt-and-pepper hair, wearing a long navy-blue wool coat, stood on the front porch. She held a large wicker basket. The gentleman removed his hat, inclining his head in greeting. "We're looking for Jake Manning."

The dogs shot out the door, nuzzling the couple's feet, snuffling and wagging a welcome. The woman glanced scornfully down at them, then leveled an icy stare at Harley from beneath well-plucked, perfectly arched brows.

"Sorry about them." Harley snapped her fingers. "You guys get back in here *now*." She stepped onto the porch and grabbed Pepper by the collar, hauling the dog inside. Benji scampered into the house without further encouragement. "Come on in." Harley held the door open and ushered the elegant couple into the foyer, closing the door behind them.

"Jake's working down in the basement. Who shall I tell him is here?"

The man inclined his head again, offering her his hand. "I'm Theodore Spandler. And you are?"

"Harley. I'm…Jake's wife." She pumped the man's hand enthusiastically, pleased with his firm grip. "It's nice to meet you."

"This is my wife, Daphene."

The woman shifted the basket into her left arm and extended her fingertips, giving her an up-and-down glance. As they brushed fingers, Harley realized what she must look like through this woman's eyes, wearing a pair of denim maternity overalls with only one shoulder fastened, a tight, long-sleeved T-shirt underneath it, and the greasy rag hanging out of her pocket.

Grease. Harley snatched her hand back from Daphene's, but it was too late. The woman held her hand disdainfully in the air as though she'd been infected with some kind of plague.

"Oh, I'm sorry about that. I was working on my truck—"

Daphene sniffed and thrust the basket into her husband's arms. "How…quaint. If you would be so kind as to direct me to the powder room, I'll just tidy up."

"The *bathroom*—" Harley emphasized the word "—is through the living room, then turn left into the hallway. First door on your right. Can't miss it."

The hard heels of Mrs. Spandler's elegant, fur-trimmed boots beat a rhythm against the wooden floor as she walked across the living room. Harley returned her attention to Mr. Spandler, who tactfully shoved his white handkerchief back into his pocket at her glance. "I'll go get Jake," she informed him.

"Thank you very much."

Cheeks hot with embarrassment, she snapped her fingers again and quickly retreated, the dogs at her heels. The Spandlers. Of all people to appear in front of looking like a grease monkey, it had to be the Spandlers? Poor Jake. He was going to be furious when he found out.

This was exactly the kind of thing she'd been afraid of. He deserved a wife who wouldn't humiliate him with his clients. Damn it, why did she have to pick today to fool around with the truck?

On her way through the kitchen, Harley grabbed a couple of treats for the dogs. She opened the screen door to the garage and tossed the biscuits onto the cement floor, then closed the door behind Benji and Pepper. Bad enough she'd smeared grease on the Spandlers; at least now the dogs wouldn't shed or slobber on them. She stood at the top of the basement steps. "Jake, you need to come upstairs. There are some people here to see you. The Spandlers."

"Did you say Spandlers?" His voice echoed up the stairs.

"Yes, that's what I said."

He clattered upstairs and rushed past her. "What the hell are they doing here?"

"I don't know, but Jake, there's something I need to tell you...." She trailed along behind him.

"Not now, Harley," he murmured over his shoulder.

"But Jake..."

Too late. He'd already reached the foyer where Mr. Spandler still stood, hat in his hands.

"Mr. Spandler, how nice to see you again." Jake thrust out his hand, and the hotel mogul grasped it. "What brings you to Erie?" The men disengaged hands. Jake gazed down at his palm, then looked at Mr. Spandler, who shrugged apologetically and smiled in Harley's direction.

Please, let the floor open up and swallow me now. Harley grinned weakly at Jake, who turned back to Mr. Spandler.

"The hotel is involved in First Night Erie, so we wanted to come to town for the celebration. We decided to get here a few nights early to take care of some other business."

"Please, won't you come in? Have a seat." Jake gestured toward the living room. "Can I take your coat?"

Harley almost groaned. Good grief, Mr. Spandler must think her a totally inept social moron. She hadn't even thought to offer him a seat.

"Thank you." Mr. Spandler handed Jake the expensive-looking coat and followed him to the living room. He sank gracefully to the sofa cushions.

"Jake, darling, there you are." Daphene Spandler glided past Harley in a cloud of sickeningly sweet perfume. The woman extended her hand to Jake, who accepted it with a pleased smile Harley longed to wipe off his face. Daphene air-kissed his cheek. "Aren't you surprised?"

"I certainly am."

Harley hesitantly cleared her throat. "Can I get anyone something to drink? Coffee, tea?"

Mr. Spandler waved a hand. "Oh, no, dear, thank you very much." He glanced down at his gold watch. "In fact, we can't stay too long. We have dinner reservations in an hour." He looked pointedly at Jake. "In fact, we made reservations for three, hoping you'd join us. We had some business we wanted to discuss with you." He glanced back at Harley. "You didn't tell us about your beautiful wife, Jake. Now I understand your hesitancy to leave town for two months. Especially with her expecting."

He hadn't spoken about her while he was gone. This man, who now professed to love her, hadn't even told these snobs about her or the baby. He'd worked with them for two whole months, and he hadn't even mentioned her. Harley's heart ached. Maybe the other night *had* only been pretty words and empty promises.

"I'd like some sparkling water with lemon." Mrs. Spandler didn't even look in Harley's direction. She leaned over to snatch the wicker basket from her husband's arm. "Honey, you didn't give this to Jake yet?" Saccharine smile plastered on her face, she presented the gift to him with a flourish. "A little Christmas cheer, darling. There's some pâté and caviar, along with a bottle of superb champagne."

Harley's stomach heaved at the thought of liver paste and fish eggs. How in the world did rich people eat such horrible things?

"Thank you, Mrs. Spandler." Jake brought the so-called "goodies" to Harley. "Will you take this into the kitchen, sweetheart?" He turned back to Mr. Spandler. "I'm sorry. Dinner sounds very nice, although I wouldn't dream of going without my wife. However, I certainly look forward to doing more business with you." He turned to stare at Harley. "Provided it doesn't mean leaving home again…"

Maybe he *did* care? Damn, she couldn't make up her mind whether she wanted him to love her or not. No matter what, she had to leave in the end. Because he deserved more. Better that he didn't love her, she decided.

"In any event, I already have plans for the evening." Jake nodded at the clock on the wall. "As a matter of fact, my sister will be dropping off her twin daughters any minute."

Mrs. Spandler's vibrant red lips twisted into a pout. "Surely your wife could take care of the children? Darling, this really is critical."

Maybe she wants a little cheese with that whine? Harley stifled a snort at the woman's behavior. The last time she'd seen that expression had been on the face of a three-year-old. Grace, to be exact.

"I don't think so..."

"But Theo and I have been talking about building a new house, and we wanted to see if you had some ideas. We're considering having you do the design. You know we'll pay you very well."

Harley couldn't come between him and the opportunity of continued work with such an important man. The baby would need a lot of things, and Jake could use the Spandlers' money to provide them. "Jake, could I see you for a minute in the kitchen?"

"Yes, see if you can talk some sense into him, dear," Mrs. Spandler said. She glanced around the living room. "It looks like you could use the commission."

"Daphene..." Theodore Spandler censured his wife with one even-toned word and a pinched expression that signaled his unhappiness with her.

Harley's fingers dug into the palm of her empty hand while the other tightened its grip on the basket. How dare this bitch condemn the wonderful home Jake had created? It might not measure up to her mansion or penthouse or whatever the hell she lived in, but Harley would've bet just about anything that Jake's home had more joy in it.

Clamping her teeth shut, she turned on her heel and stormed to the kitchen, not waiting to see if Jake followed or not. She curbed her initial impulse to hurl Daphene's basket of Christmas cheer—liver and fish eggs, some cheer—into the garbage can. Instead, she plunked it down on the countertop, shoving it behind the toaster.

After scrubbing the remaining grease from her hands, Harley flung open a bottom cabinet and rummaged in it, searching for a bottle of club soda. She slammed it down on the counter, then reached for a glass. Her fingers lingered near one of the cups Jake kept in the house for the girls—a cup with a sippy lid. Imagining the precious, elegant Daphene Spandler drinking from a sippy cup was just what Harley needed. She stifled a giggle and pulled a regular glass from the shelf.

Jake entered the kitchen to find Harley splashing soda water into an ice-filled glass. She turned to him, face immediately somber. "Jake, I'm so sorry. I didn't mean to get the Spandlers' hands dirty, and—"

"Don't worry about it." Jake spoke softly. "I've always thought Daphene was kind of slimy. A little grease could only improve her as far as I'm concerned." *That's the understatement of the year.* He'd never warmed up to Daphene Spandler. Though she'd certainly made a play at warming him up—especially when her husband wasn't around. Fortunately, Jake had managed to avoid her most of the time in Virginia, and fortunately, her husband wasn't cut from the same cloth as she was. What did Theo see in her?

"Really?"

"Yup." Jake grabbed her hand, then kissed her fingers. "Real women aren't afraid of a little grease."

"Why don't you go with them, Jake? I can watch

the twins for Mel. You know how important this account could be to your future.''

Jake studied Harley carefully. "*Our* future." It was too good an opportunity to pass up—and he wasn't thinking just about the Spandler account. He was thinking about Harley alone with the twins, taking care of them by herself. Maybe she'd realize she could make a good mother, after all. "Are you sure about that? Those two can be quite a handful.''

"Two sweet little girls, Jake. They're not babies like Matthew. They're even potty-trained. How hard can it be?''

Jake skimmed a finger across her cheek. "If you're sure?''

She smiled at him. "I am.'' She ducked away from him to open the refrigerator, pulling out a green plastic bottle of lemon juice. "We don't have any fresh lemons,'' she whispered theatrically. "Don't tell Daphene, will you, darling?''

Jake laughed. "You're bad.''

"I am not. I'm innocent. I was framed.''

"There's something to be said for a little bit of bad in a woman.'' Jake grabbed her by the hand and wrapped his arms around her. He lowered his head, seizing possession of her lips with his own. Demanding and certain, the kiss left no room for doubt.

Her face flushed pink and her eyes were wide when he released her. "Wow. Bad *is* good. I'll have to give that one a nine.''

He drew his fingers over her kiss-swollen lips. "If you let me, I'll try harder.''

Harley swatted at him. "Go and get changed, Jake."

"I haven't changed my mind, Harley," he whispered in her ear. "I still want you to stay. I still want you, period." He licked the rim of her ear, delighting in her little shiver of response. "I love you, Harley."

She stepped away from him, face lined with tension.

Would she ever believe he wasn't just handing her "pretty words," as she called them? How would he ever convince her his love was true?

"Go change." She retrieved the glass of water from the counter. "Give this to Mrs. Spandler on your way through."

Jake accepted the beverage. "You keep them company while I get dressed, okay?"

"You've got to be joking! Look at me. I should be locked in the garage with the dogs. I need to change to be anywhere near the Spandlers."

"You don't need to change a thing."

Her stunned expression was priceless. But he didn't think she quite believed him.

HARLEY HEAVED A SIGH and leaned against the door. She'd never been so happy in her life to see people leave. Jake was right; Daphene Spandler left a definite slimy feeling, like the trail behind a slug. Though in Daphene's case, perhaps that would be an escargot.

Harley stifled a slightly evil chuckle. Grace had managed to unwittingly pay back Mrs. Spandler with a well-timed sneeze after the woman had scooped her up, slanting Jake a look to make sure he was watching. Apparently Grace hadn't liked the woman's overpowering perfume, either. Theodore Spandler had been genuinely enthralled with Hope when she'd given him an endearing pat on the cheek. He'd fussed over her like a proud grandpa while Daphene had thrust Grace into Harley's arms and wiped her fur coat with a lace hanky.

After a quick kiss and some whispered assurances that she'd do a great job with the twins, Jake had grinned at Harley as he ushered the Spandlers out the door.

She traversed the living room to perch on the arm of the sofa near the girls' toy box. "Well, ladies, it's just you and me now. What are we going to do tonight?"

"Buiwd!" Hope announced, holding up a square wooden block.

"Cowor!" demanded Grace, jumping to her feet. "Where my crayons? Where my book?"

"I was thinking more along the lines of watching a video. What do you say?"

"Me want to cowor!" Grace shouted.

Harley held up her hand. "All right, we'll color. I'll get the stuff, you guys go and sit at the table."

She retrieved the fat crayons and coloring books from the bottom drawer in the kitchen and laid them on the dining room table. The girls knelt on chairs at either end. "Okay, here you go." She handed each child a book and a box of crayons. "Make a pretty picture for your mommy."

She'd just lowered herself into a chair and propped her chin on her palm when the front door opened again. "Oh, great, now what?" She moaned, levering herself from the chair. "You girls sit here and color nicely. I'll be right back."

"Jake?" Dusty's voice carried from the foyer into the living room.

Harley trudged through the room to find Jake's brother, snowsuited baby in arms, setting a bulging diaper bag on the tiled floor. "Jake's not here, Dusty. He went out with the Spandlers."

"The Spandler Hotel Spandlers?" Dusty paused in the process of opening Matthew's zippers.

"That'd be them."

Dusty cursed under his breath. "I thought Jake was watching the twins tonight."

"I'm watching the twins tonight."

Dusty raised an eyebrow, then narrowed his eyes.

Something in his expression irritated the hell out of her. "What, you don't think I can manage them?" Like everyone else, with the exception of Jake, his judgment of her was based on her past, and she was sick to death of his condescending attitude. She folded her arms across her chest. "The girls and I are having a wonderful evening."

Something gave way in Dusty's eyes. "Glad somebody is. Poor Kate." He started to rezip the baby's snowsuit.

"What? Poor Kate, what?"

"We had dinner reservations at the Stone Inn tonight. It's the anniversary of our first date."

"Oh, that's so sweet."

Dusty sighed. "She's been looking forward to it for weeks. Then our baby-sitter called at the last minute, saying she's sick." He transferred the baby to his other arm. "She'd better be sick. If she ditched us tonight to go on a date herself, I'll make her wish she *was* sick."

How romantic, taking his wife out on the anniversary of their first date. Again she realized there was more to Dusty than the ex-con-hating, brother-protecting ogre he seemed to be in her presence.

An insane idea occurred to her. Maybe she *could* be mother material. This would be a good test to find out, to prove the smug Dusty and everyone else—including herself—wrong. She'd certainly failed as wife material earlier in the evening, but maybe that wasn't her fault. Jake didn't normally socialize with such rich, snobbish people. If she could prove to herself that she wouldn't be a complete disaster as a mother, maybe she could accept his offer. Maybe they could be a real family, despite her past.

"I'll watch Matthew for you, Dusty." She held out her arms for the baby.

Dusty eyed her warily. "You?"

She made a big show of glancing around the foyer. "I don't see anyone else. I'd hate it if *Kate* was disappointed."

The twinkle in his blue eyes reminded her of Jake for a second before it was replaced with skepticism. "I don't know. You'll have your hands full as it is."

"I need to learn sometime, Dusty."

"So learn on someone else's kid, not mine."

Harley shrugged. "Okay, whatever. Tell Kate I'm sorry you guys didn't get to go to dinner. I have to go and see to the twins. 'Night." She began to walk away.

"Wait!" He sighed again. "All right. There's a bottle of breast milk in the diaper bag. Put it in the fridge till later. Clean clothes, diapers and wipes in the bag. Here's his favorite pacifier." Dusty handed her a blue-and-white ring. "My cell number is in there, and I've already told you where we'll be."

"The Stone Inn." Harley nodded and held out her arms once more. This time Dusty reluctantly passed his son into her care.

"We shouldn't be more than two hours or so." He narrowed his eyes again. "Are you sure you'll be okay?"

"Hey, one baby and two little girls. It's nighttime. They should be falling asleep. How hard can it be?"

An hour and a half later, as she bounced a screaming infant and tried to ride herd on two over-active little girls who seemed to believe sleep was a dirty word, Harley had an all-new appreciation for exactly how hard it could be.

The baby cried, tucking his head into her chest as she tried to get him to take the bottle. "I know, I know, Matthew. But there's nothing there, pal. You're going to have to make do with the bottle." Harley paced a circuit across the living room.

Matthew finally latched onto the latex nipple and began to suck.

She sighed in relief. "That's a good boy."

With the baby silent, she realized just how quiet it was in the house. The hair on the back of her neck tingled. Too quiet. "Girls, where are you?" Maybe they'd finally fallen asleep? Yeah, right, and maybe they'd decided to tear apart the transmission in her truck and rebuild it.

A smattering of giggles came from the direction of the dining room.

"That does *not* sound good." Doing her best to feed Matthew and race across the living room at the same time, Harley skidded to a stop in the dining room archway. "What do you think you're doing?" she shrieked.

Purple crayon in hand, Hope turned away from the wall to smile at her. "Cowaring. Make pretty picture for Unka Jake."

"Oh, yeah, I'm sure he's just gonna love it." Harley crossed the room, setting the bottle on the dining room table. She snatched the crayon from the chubby hand, carefully balancing the baby in her left arm. "Hope, you can't color on the wall. You have to color on paper or in coloring books. That's it"

A trail of red intersected the purple lines running across Jake's chair-high wood paneling. "Where's your sister?" she asked the little girl.

"Under da table." Hope pointed.

Matthew began to cry. Harley repositioned him on her shoulder and bent over. Sitting directly in the middle of the space, Grace was peeling the covers off crayons. A small mound of paper littered the floor in front of her.

"Grace, come out of there." A muscle twinged in Harley's back and Peanut kicked her solidly in the stomach. "Hey, you're getting in on the act, too, Peanut? Thanks a lot."

She straightened, pressing one hand to her spine. "That wasn't a very smart move." Jostling Matthew against her shoulder, Harley pulled a chair away from the table and sat down. "Grace, I mean it. Come out from under there."

"No."

Hope got down on the floor and crawled under a chair.

"Hope, don't you dare. Your sister is being very naughty. I want you to go in the living room and play with the blocks, okay?"

Hope stared at her for a minute.

"Please, Hope?"

The child stuck two fingers in her mouth and nodded her head, then crawled out from under the chair and scampered toward the other room. The textured bottoms of the pink flannel foot-sleeper she wore whisked against the floor as she scooted away.

One down, one to go. "Grace, I'm warning you. I'm going to count to three, and if you're not out, then I'll…"

What? What the heck would she do if the kid refused to come out? Drag her out kicking and screaming? That would mean she'd have to get down there herself.

Why didn't kids come with instruction books? She'd rather drop an entire new engine in a car than deal with this. She'd rather deal with an insurance adjuster. She'd rather have a root canal. Performed by an insurance adjuster.

See? You're not mother material.

Had it been this kind of thing that had caused her own mother to flee? Had she simply been overwhelmed by the demands of caring for a child?

Matthew clenched his hands into fists, tightened his body and let out a wail loud enough to be heard clear across the lake in Canada. Harley shot out of the chair, jiggling him. "Shh, shh, Matthew. It's okay. What's the matter, huh?" She patted him on the back, rubbing circles and gently thumping him. A loud burp preceded the sensation of oozing wetness on her neck, running under the collar of her shirt. "Never mind. I get the picture."

Still bouncing the baby lightly, Harley walked into the kitchen, retrieving a dishtowel. She mopped up the mess he'd created. Irving circled her ankles, mewing plaintively. "Forget it, cat. I've got enough going on right now. You'll have to wait to eat."

Whining and scratching came from the other side of the door to the garage. The dogs. She'd forgotten all about them. "Sorry, boys. You can just stay out there. I'll let you in later." Like after Jake came home.

Neck cleaned as much as she could manage one-handed, Harley strode back into the dining room. Grace now sat on top of the table, unwrapped crayons scattered around her.

Grateful she didn't have to crawl underneath to haul the child out, Harley opted to ignore the fact that Grace was sitting on the table. "Give me those crayons, young lady. You do not color on walls, do you hear me?"

Grace helpfully held out a green crayon.

Harley grabbed it and placed it in the box. "Let's put the rest in the box, Grace." She sighed in relief as the little girl did as she asked.

They came up two crayons short.

"Grace, where are the red ones?" Harley glanced around at the floor, but didn't see the MIA colors. "Did you leave them under the table?" She dreaded the idea of bending over like that again.

"No. Red crayons aw gone," Grace sang.

"All gone? What did you do with them? Did you throw them in the garbage?"

The little head shook, bouncing the freshly washed blond hair.

Suddenly exhausted, Harley was no longer in the mood for games. "Then where are they?"

Grace opened her mouth and pointed to her tongue.

"In your mouth? I don't see anything—ohmigod, you ate them?" She leaned closer. Telltale shards of red wax clung to the little molars. "Grace, you don't eat crayons!"

Stay calm, stay calm. Harley snatched up the box, turning it until she found the words she sought.

"Nontoxic. That means if you eat them, nothing will happen, right?"

Matthew chose that moment to begin crying again.

Oh, yes, she made a fine mother figure.

Harley bolted for the kitchen and grabbed the phone. Cradling the receiver against her shoulder and juggling the infant in her arms, she flipped open the phone book on the counter. A quick call to poison control set her mind at ease, reassuring her that Grace had not been poisoned, that nontoxic meant exactly what she'd thought. She didn't need to do anything, the nurse told her, nature would take care of the crayon in the toddler's tummy. Though if for some reason nature *didn't* take care of it, the child needed to be observed for signs of severe stomach pain in the next day or so.

That meant she had to tell Mel she'd let her kid eat a crayon. What a night this had become. First she'd made a fool of herself in front of Jake's most important client, and now she was realizing just how much work actually went into being a mother.

What else could go wrong?

As if in answer, Matthew tensed his body in her arms. Harley peered down at his face, all scrunched up again and turning red. A rather large stench emanated from the tiny body. "Oh, Matthew. Thanks a lot. You couldn't save that for your father?"

Harley carried him into the living room. She passed the twins playing happily with the blocks, then went to the foyer to collect Matthew's diaper bag.

Laying the baby on a blanket on the sofa, she began

the task of changing him. The sleeper outfit he wore posed few problems. The snaps along his legs opened easily, and she lifted his feet from the clothing. She tried to recall all the times she'd watched Jake change a diaper. "Okay, you have to help me," she whispered. "I'm new at this, so be gentle with me."

The baby kicked his legs.

"Yeah, right." She unfastened the tabs at his waist, and peeled the diaper down. "Oh, man! This qualifies as toxic cleanup. Call the EPA." Harley grabbed a wipe in one hand and the baby's ankles in the other. Once she had him completely clean, she tossed the dirty wipes inside the messy diaper and rolled it up. She maneuvered a clean diaper under the baby. "Hey, that wasn't too bad." As she lifted the front flap, a yellow stream caught her right in the chest. Quickly lowering the flap over the baby's stomach, she managed to catch the last of the urine in the diaper. "Puked on and peed on. Thanks again, Matthew."

She pulled out another clean diaper. "Are you all finished now? Can I put this one on and be safe?"

The baby cooed in delight, wriggling and waving his hands. Harley fastened the sticky tabs around his waist, then tucked his feet back into the sleeper. She began to fasten the endless row of tiny snaps.

A scream of pure pain ripped through the air. Harley swung around.

Hope clutched her face, screaming at the top of her lungs.

Harley jumped up, racing to the child. She scooped

her off the floor and into her arms. "Hope, what happened? What's wrong?"

Toddler tears flooded Harley's shirt.

She carried the little girl into the kitchen and sat her on the counter. Gently grasping the tiny hand, she peeled the fingers away from Hope's cheek. "Let me see what happened."

Just below her eye, right across the cheekbone, the skin appeared puffy and red.

"We can fix that, Hope. No problem." Harley wrapped an ice cube in the corner of a clean kitchen towel and pressed it against the swollen cheek. "How did this happen?"

"Grace hit me."

"What did she hit you with?"

"A bwock."

"Aah." Harley turned to glance at the doorway, where another little blond head peeked around the corner. "Grace, you have been very naughty tonight. I want you to go and sit on the sofa. You hurt your sister." Harley gathered Hope into her arms again, holding the ice on her face.

A thump sounded in the living room.

Harley's heart stopped.

Matthew's piercing scream demanded immediate attention.

"Damn, oh damn!" Harley set Hope down just inside the living room and raced to the sofa. The baby lay facedown on the floor between the couch and the coffee table, still hollering loudly.

"Ohmigod, Matthew!" Harley knelt beside the

baby, hands trembling. She gently rolled him onto his back. Already a discolored lump the size of a small egg protruded from his forehead. He waved his arms and legs, hands tightly fisted. Harley picked him up and cradled him against her chest. "Easy, easy, shh, it's going to be all right."

Behind her, both twins cried and yelled.

Harley wished she could cry and yell, too.

How could she have left the baby on the couch like that? What the hell was wrong with her?

She raced into the kitchen with him for more ice, which she wrapped in a paper towel. Matthew howled even more loudly when she gingerly placed the ice against his goose egg.

"Har-we, Har-we!"

Back to the living room. Screaming baby in her arms. Two whining and crying toddlers bouncing on opposite ends of the sofa.

Matthew wouldn't settle down.

Hope wouldn't keep the ice on her cheek.

Harley's stomach churned in response to all the crying and the overwhelming guilt rushing through her. She tried patting Matthew's back, rocking him, singing to him.

Oh, yes, she'd make a perfect mother. A few hours caring for children, and two of them were hurt, while one had eaten something not meant to be eaten.

Jake heard the screaming before he even opened the front door. Chaos swirled around him as he entered the house. Hope flung herself off the sofa, throwing her arms around his legs. He picked her up.

Harley hurried across the room with Matthew in her arms. "Oh, Jake, thank goodness you're home! I can't get him to stop crying."

A gust of cold air blasted Jake from the foyer. "I didn't know you were watching Matthew tonight. What's he doing here?"

"Never mind that! He fell off the sofa and hit his head on the coffee table. He's got a bump on his forehead—"

"What?" Dusty roared from behind him. "How the hell does a baby fall off a sofa?" He shoved Jake aside and snatched his son from Harley's arms.

"I don't know. I'm sorry!" Harley followed Dusty to the couch. He laid the baby down and began examining him.

"You don't know? Weren't you watching him?"

Harley twisted her hands together. Jake knew that if there'd been any paper within reach, her fingers would've been shredding it. He jostled Hope in his arms, trying to settle at least one of the kids. "Dusty, calm down and let Harley explain."

"Explain? What's to explain? I left my son in her care and she's so damned incompetent that he got hurt."

"I was changing his diaper and then I had to get some ice for Hope and—"

"Hope got hurt, too? What were you doing, sleeping on the job?" Dusty unfastened the baby's clothes, checking him from top to bottom.

Harley shook her head.

Jake lifted the cold, wet towel from Hope's face and examined her injury. "What happened, squirt?"

"Grace hit me wif a bwock."

"He's got a bruise on his arm, too!" Dusty scooped Matthew back up and whirled on Harley. "Teenage baby-sitters can manage better than you. What the hell kind of a mother are you going to make? That baby doesn't stand a chance!"

All the color drained from Harley's face and her eyes widened. Her lower lip quivered. She backed away from Dusty, hands covering her abdomen. "You're absolutely right," she choked out, then turned sharply and vanished down the hall.

"Damn it, Dusty, that was a lousy thing to say! Who the hell do you think you are?" Jake stormed across the room to his side, Hope still in his arms—luckily for his brother. Dusty was doubly lucky he held Matthew, as well. Or else Jake would've let him have it this time. This time he'd gone too far.

"I'm the father of the baby she neglected tonight." Dusty cuddled his son closer. "Your wife needs some parenting classes, Jake, and she'd better take them now, before your child's born. I'm taking my son to the hospital to have him looked over!"

Dusty brushed past Jake.

Another gust of cold air entered the house, and Mel and Peter appeared.

"Check your kids over carefully," Dusty snapped at them. "Our incompetent baby-sitter did one hell of a job." He gathered the baby's snowsuit and diaper bag.

"Wook at Grace!" Hope shouted.

Jake turned his attention to the twin still on the sofa. A puddle of vomit oozed across one of the beige cushions.

Mel sighed and moved toward her daughter. "Poor Grace. Is your tummy upset?"

"I'll go get some paper towels," Peter offered, heading for the kitchen.

"Jake?" Mel glanced up at him. "What did she eat? It looks like…I'm not sure what it looks like."

"Red cwayons," Hope supplied.

Jake groaned. Harley had obviously endured the worst night of baby-sitting possible. Add that to Dusty's insults, and his plan for making her feel comfortable as a mother had certainly blown up in his face.

Jake helped Mel get the twins cleaned up and into their coats. He thanked his lucky stars for his understanding sister when she easily forgave the night's disasters, confessing Grace had eaten crayons before and no ill had ever resulted from it, and the block in Hope's face wasn't exactly an unprecedented incident, either.

After his sister's family had left and he'd released the whining dogs from the garage, Jake hurried to Harley's room. He turned on the light in the hallway and opened her door. "Harley?"

She lay with her back against the wall, the pillow clutched to her chest.

Jake eased himself onto the bed. He reached out

and skimmed her cheek with his fingertips. Sticky tear tracks crossed her face. ''Harley?'' he whispered.

A slight hitch in breathing was her only response.

A full night's sleep would do her good. He untied her sneakers, removing them and dropped them alongside the bed. He grabbed the afghan from the bottom of the bed. Unfolding it, he draped it over her, then leaned down and kissed her forehead. ''All accidents, Harley. Definitely not your fault.'' He caressed her cheek with the back of his index finger. ''I love you. You're going to make a fine mother.''

But tonight definitely qualified as a setback in his plan to get her to realize that.

CHAPTER SIXTEEN

IMAGES FLASHED. A gala ball. Crystal chandeliers. Daphene Spandler looked down her finely sculpted nose and wagged a finger. A chorus of crying babies wailed in the background. Dusty appeared, head shaking. "You're not good enough for my brother or his child."

Daphene tsked. "Look at those clothes. She simply won't do."

Judge Ephraim took Daphene's elbow, twitching a finger in Harley's face. "I told you to walk the straight and narrow."

"But, I haven't done anything!" Harley protested.

Jake emerged from the crowd, carrying a delicate little girl with big blue eyes and light brown hair. A large bruise discolored her forehead and a plaster cast encased her left arm.

Harley recognized her instinctively. "Peanut. What...what happened?" She reached for the baby.

Jake turned to the side, shielding the child from her grasp. "You happened. You weren't watching her!"

Two uniformed cops flanked her. "Ma'am, we're placing you under arrest for endangering the welfare of a child. You have the right to..."

Harley heard no more as handcuffs bit into her wrists. *"No, no! I didn't do anything!"*

She awakened in a cold sweat, heart hammering in her ears, breathing ragged. She threw off the blanket and launched herself upright. A menace. She was an absolute menace.

They'd all be better off without her around.

Staying had ceased to be an option. She endangered his career with her crass manners and lack of social graces. She endangered all the children. Her fingers slipped to her belly. Peanut especially didn't need a mother like her. Better to have none at all. After all, Harley had survived without a mother. And Jake would make an even better father than her own had been.

Rising quickly in the predawn darkness, she changed her clothes, then pulled her duffel from the closet. She rummaged in the drawers and stuffed as much into the bag as she could. For the first time in her life, she owned more than she could possibly carry.

The white satin nightgown whispered across her fingertips, and she snatched it from the drawer, rolling it into a tight ball and cramming it into a corner of her bag. Her hand hovered over the glass perfume bottle on the dresser. *Endless Possibilities.* No. Not that. Her endless possibilities all revolved around this house, this home, and they'd cease to exist the minute she walked out.

She left the World's Greatest Aunt sweatshirt on her pillow.

The bedroom door creaked as she opened it, and Harley winced. Freezing in place, she waited for any reaction, but the house continued its quiet slumber.

In the garage, she gathered her tools and returned them to the chest in the back of her truck. The hood still gaped open from her explorations yesterday. Luckily there hadn't been anything wrong with the engine. She'd just had the overwhelming urge to tinker. Fat lot of good that impulse had brought.

She eased the hood down softly, satisfied by the click that it was properly shut. Only one more task to complete. She tiptoed back into the house, heading for his office.

Words flowed onto paper in spurts. Explaining her actions without hurting him was difficult. She had to make sure he understood that the failing was in her and not in him. How could she tell him he was the most wonderful man she'd ever had the good fortune to come across and in the next line rationalize walking out the door?

She could hear her father telling her, "This is for your own good," and "This is going to hurt me a lot more than it will you" when he disciplined Harley by sending her to her room—or worse, by banning her temporarily from the garage. She hadn't understood that as a child. But now she did. Sometimes you had to do something really hard in the name of love. She was doing this for Jake. And she knew from the huge ache in her chest that it hurt her a lot more than it would him.

She folded the paper and put it in an envelope, then turned off the lamp on his desk.

The crayoned scribbles on the wall of the dining room brought back horrible memories of her baby-sitting fiasco. Yet as she laid the letter on the table, she also saw Grace and Hope, stained with pizza, sitting in their booster chairs.

A tear slipped down her cheek, and she dashed it away with the back of her hand. She paused in the archway to the living room. Outside, the sky was just beginning to lighten. The Christmas tree cast a faint silhouette in front of the window.

There were too many memories, she couldn't linger here.

The need to see him one last time warred with the need to turn tail and run, to put as much distance between them as possible. To begin to salvage her shattered heart.

He won.

She tiptoed across the room and down the hallway, cautiously avoiding floorboards that creaked. His bedroom door stood ajar, and she quietly swung it open.

Pepper and Benji lifted their heads to look at her curiously. She waved a hand at them, and they shifted but stayed put.

She could make out his form on the bed. The covers had fallen aside, exposing his muscular back. Her fingers knew every inch of that back. She drank him in, resisting the overwhelming desire to move closer, to touch him. To kiss him farewell.

"I love you, Jake Manning." She mouthed the

words, then caught her lower lip between her teeth to quiet its trembling. She fingered the necklace he'd given her for Christmas. If nothing else, she'd always carry a new appreciation for her name. He'd taught her what it meant to love.

And sacrifice was part of it.

Time to go. Before she lost the courage to do the right thing.

She turned away from his door, bolting for the kitchen. Her stomach rumbled, and she could feel the baby move. "Not now, Peanut. I'll get us something to eat later." She grabbed the bottle of prenatal vitamins from the counter and stuffed them in her shirt pocket.

Toenails clicked on the linoleum behind her. She whirled to find the two dogs staring up at her. "You guys go back to bed," she hissed at them.

They both sat instead.

"Obedience never was your strong point," she whispered, reaching for the box of Milk-Bones. She took a handful and squatted down, dropping them on the floor. The dogs each grabbed one, chomping and crunching. Harley ran her hands over Benji's wiry fur and Pepper's sleek head. "You guys take care of him for me, okay?" She patted them again. "I'm still afraid of dogs, you know. Just not you two. Don't tell anybody."

Harley rose to her feet and slipped out the door while they were still occupied with their snack.

By the time she'd backed the truck from the garage, closed the door and pulled into the street, the sky had lightened and a gray Erie winter dawn had commenced. She allowed herself the luxury of a final, lingering examination. The little white house where her child would be raised glistened cozily, frosted with snow.

She stepped on the clutch and put the truck in gear, driving away without another backward glance.

A COLD, WET SENSATION in the middle of his back jolted Jake from sound sleep to totally awake in one rude leap. He groaned and swatted blindly at the offending dog nose. "Pepper, cut it out."

The dog whined.

Jake rolled over and opened his eyes.

The Labrador danced in place next to the bed and whined again.

"I take it you have to go out?"

Pepper woofed in response.

"All right, hold on." As Jake slid out of bed, cool air caressed him. He moved to his dresser, pulling out a pair of sweats and a T-shirt. Harley had taken his robe several days ago and hadn't returned it yet. Not that he minded. There was something powerful about the sight of her in his clothes, something that brought out his possessive instincts.

How would she feel this morning? Last night's nightmare would surely remain in her mind. Dusty's harsh words rang out in his memory and Jake clenched his hands. His brother was begging for a kick in the ass, and if he didn't straighten out with regard to Harley, he was going to get it.

Pepper whined from the doorway.

"I'm coming." He strode from his room. Benji lounged on the living room sofa. Jake snapped his fingers. "Come on, Benji, let's go out." The little dog scampered down and both animals ran for his office.

Jake followed more sedately, still clearing the remnants of sleep from his body and his brain. He let the dogs out via the back deck. The frigid winter air rushed in, and he slammed the door behind them.

He laced his fingers together and stretched out his arms, first in front of him, then up over his head. That done, he rotated his head to get the kinks out of his neck and shoulders. He ran through a quick series of additional stretches, finishing just as Pepper scratched at the door.

The dogs back in the house, he wandered into the kitchen. "Morning, Irving." He ran his hands over the cat's sleek black fur, then patted his rump. "Now, get off the counter." The cat jumped to the floor. Jake set a pot of decaf to brew and filled the animals' food and water bowls, then glanced at the clock. Normally Harley was up by now.

He walked rapidly through the house, then knocked on her door. "Harley?"

No response. Maybe the night's horrors had worn her out more than he'd thought. He pushed the door open.

She wasn't in bed. The afghan had been folded and replaced at the bottom, the comforter carefully smoothed out. The sweatshirt lay across the pillow.

Her clothes from the previous day were heaped on the floor in front of the dresser.

A cold chill ran down Jake's spine. The urge to yank open her drawers and check for her clothes spread through him, but he squashed it quickly.

He headed for the bathroom. "Harley?"

No running water—not a sound—but he entered, anyway. "Harley?"

He already knew she wasn't in his office, the living room or the kitchen, and that didn't leave very many options. He raced for the garage and threw open the door.

For several minutes he stared at the empty spot beside the Mustang where her truck had stood. "She's gone out, that's all."

Eventually he forced himself to descend the stairs and examine the garage more carefully, knowing from previous experience that he could confirm his worst fears by seeking out her most prized possessions. With his first wife it had been her jewelry and the stereo. With Harley, it would be…her tools. And they were gone.

Which meant she was gone.

It could not, could *not*, be possible.

Jake's body went numb. He forced his feet to carry him back into the kitchen. Mindlessly, he dumped the fresh pot of decaf down the sink and unplugged the coffee machine. He slogged into the dining room, where a white envelope with his name on it caught his attention.

At least this one left a note.

Jake pulled out the paper, ripping it in his haste to unfold it. He could hear the words as clearly as if she spoke them aloud in that sultry voice of hers.

"Damn it to hell." He crumpled the letter and tossed it onto the table. "Fine time to tell me you love me, Harley!" He stalked to her bedroom. "Very nice!" He poked through her closet. She'd left her prematernity clothes behind. He yanked her black jeans from the hanger and hurled them to the floor. "You use love as an excuse to walk out on me?"

Jake wrenched open a dresser drawer so hard it fell out, landing beside his foot. He kicked it, and grabbed the next one. "You're all the same, damn it! None of you ever stay." Shirts and sweaters flew into the air, some landing on the bed, some on the dresser, others in heaps on the floor.

The dogs poked their heads in the doorway. Jake stamped his foot. "Get out of here! Next thing I know, you'll be leaving me, too."

He turned his rage on the dresser, sweeping a pile of her textbooks onto the floor with his arm. He latched onto the bottle of perfume, cocked back his arm and hurled it against the wall. The resultant shattering mirrored the breaking of his heart. The room filled with the fragrance of jasmine—her scent. He blinked back tears. "Damn you, Harley," he whispered. "How could you do this to me?"

THE FRONT DOOR OPENED, then slammed shut. Jake quelled the small hope that rose within him. She wasn't coming back. Her note made that clear.

"Go away!" he snarled. He reached for the beer bottle on the end table and slugged back the last swallow. Placing the bottle on its side, he sent it into a lazy spin with a flick of his finger.

"Hey, Jake, I forgot…" Dusty's voice trailed off into a string of muttered curses. "What the hell happened here?"

"Christmas is over. I was taking down the tree."

"Looks more like you were mutilating the tree."

"Why are you here?"

"I forgot Matthew's pacifier in the confusion last night." His brother's expression grew sheepish. "He's fine, by the way. And I think I overreacted. I owe your wife another apology."

"Good luck delivering it."

"What?"

Jake's fingers sought out the balled-up note lying beside him on the sofa. He tossed it at Dusty, catching his brother in the chest. "Read it and rejoice, little brother. You certainly got your wish."

Dusty stooped to retrieve the paper from the floor near his feet, then uncrumpled it and read aloud.

"Dear Jake,
First, let me tell you I love you. I know I never said it to you. I couldn't. I hope you'll understand when I say I'm truly sorry for all the mess I've caused. You've got a big heart, and you're the most wonderful man I've ever met."

Dusty glanced at him over the paper. "I'm not sure I like where this is going."

"Keep reading—it gets better."

"I embarrassed and humiliated you in front of the Spandlers. I'm sorry. I hope everything works out with them.

"You and the baby deserve far better than me. Your brother was right about that. An ex-con who can't ensure the safety of three small children is not someone you need in your life.

"I love you and Peanut with all my heart, but I know you'll both be better off without me. I'll let you know when it's time, and you can come and get the baby.

"Whatever you tell her about me, please leave out the part about my record. Don't let Dusty tell her, either."

His brother coughed, then continued reading.

"And don't tell her I was willing to have her in exchange for a piece of paper. Tell her I loved her—and her father—more than anything. That much won't be a lie. Protect her from this cruel world with everything you can, and love her enough for both of us.

"Take care of yourself.

Love always, Harley."

Dusty cleared his throat. "Exactly what does she mean by 'have her in exchange for a piece of paper'?"

"What the hell difference does it make?"

"Plenty. I don't know exactly what's going on here, but if she offered to have your baby for money, that's illegal and—"

With a roar of outrage, Jake launched himself off the couch and tackled his brother. They thudded to the wooden floor. Jake reared back and slammed his fist into Dusty's face. "Enough!"

Dusty squirmed beneath him, wrapping one leg around Jake's and rolling to the top. Panting, he leaned all his weight onto one arm pressed across Jake's shoulders. "What the hell is wrong with you?"

"Wrong with *me?* You hammered the final nails into my coffin with your words last night, little brother!" Jake drove his fist into Dusty's side. "Thanks to you, she's gone!" His hand slammed into his brother again.

Dusty winced and loosened his grip. Jake seized the advantage, tossing his brother back onto the hard floor, then staggered to his feet.

Dusty lurched to his knees. He dragged his sleeve across the corner of his mouth, wiping away a trickle of blood. "Come on, is that all you got?" He curled his fingers into his palms repeatedly, egging him on. "Take another shot. Maybe it'll make you feel better."

Jake cocked back his fist, glaring down into his brother's face. No anger or malice shone in Dusty's blue eyes; he made no move to defend himself.

Jake let his hand fall to his side. "No. Punching you again isn't going to make me feel better." He stumbled to the couch and collapsed into the cushions. "Nothing will."

Dusty scrambled to his feet. He lowered himself to the opposite end of the sofa. "Maybe you'd better start at the beginning and tell me the whole story."

"Maybe." Jake raked his hand through his hair and sighed. "I guess." He launched into the complete story of his relationship with Harley.

When he'd finished, Dusty stared at him for several minutes, shaking his head. "Did she take anything when she left?"

"Yeah."

"What?"

"My heart." Indeed, he felt as though a huge hole had been torn in his chest. Funny how he'd thought he felt pain when Stacy took off. But this was much worse. Now it seemed as though all the light had gone out of the world.

"So now what? You have a plan?"

"Hell, no. It was a damn plan that got me into this in the first place."

Dusty nodded. "What exactly does she mean to you?"

"I love her! I didn't set out to love her, but I do."

"You know what your problem is, Jake?"

Jake shook his head. "Enlighten me."

"You give up way too easily. Did it ever occur to you that if Dad had gone after Mom, he might have brought her back?"

Why he'd have even wanted to was beyond Jake. He'd heard the fighting that night, heard his stepfather beg her to stay. Heard their mother tell him that her new lover didn't like kids, so she was leaving them all with Bud. "We were better off without her, Dusty. You don't remember because you were so little, but she ignored you and the rest of us when she was here."

"So, are you better off without Harley?"

"That's what she thinks."

"But what do you think?" Dusty prodded.

"No," he whispered.

"Then go after her."

Jake sucked in his breath sharply. Simple as that. *Go after her.*

Of course he should go after her. And drag her back home if necessary. He wasn't about to let this one get away; this one was for keeps. "Right. I'll go after her." He smacked his fist into his palm. "I even have a damned good idea of where she's gone." He jumped to his feet and raced to the kitchen, to the caller ID box on the counter next to the phone. He began scrolling backward through the latest calls.

Dusty skidded to a stop right behind him. "What are you doing?"

"I'm going to call Harley's only friend in the world."

"Who's that?"

"Her old parole officer." Jake scribbled the number on a pad beside the phone.

"Her old parole officer is her only friend in the world?" Dusty's eyes widened.

Jake picked up the receiver and dialed. "So she thinks. Why?"

"If a parole officer believed in her enough to befriend her, then I owe your wife another apology. Those guys see and hear it all. She must be innocent of those charges."

"No kidding. God, you're quick on the uptake." Jake mock-slugged Dusty on the chin while he waited for Charlie to answer.

CHAPTER SEVENTEEN

JAKE PACED A THIRD CIRCUIT around the white living room, silently counting the steps it took to make one complete trip.

"Boy, you're wearing a hole in my floor. Why don't you just sit down?" Charlie said.

Jake stopped to stare at the man sprawled in the recliner. Gray hair fringed a mostly bald crown. Charlie's weathered, wrinkled face matched his unpressed shirt and spoke of a harsh life, a man with many miles beneath his belt. Amazing to think he'd once been jealous of the mysterious Charlie. "I can't. If I sit down, I'll jump out of my skin. Where is she? It's been four days." He resumed his pacing. "Four days. I flew in so I could beat her here, but four days? She should've made it in two. Three at most."

He grabbed the newspaper off the back of the rattan sofa on his journey past and shook it in the air. "January 2. She should've been here New Year's Eve. We should've started the New Year off right, with this whole mess cleared up and put behind us." He tossed the *Herald* onto the glass-topped coffee table. "God, Charlie, what if she had a wreck? What if some drunk ran her off the road on New Year's Eve and she's lying in a ditch somewhere?'' *Or a hospital. Or, oh God, a morgue.*

Charlie yanked the handle on the leather recliner and put down the footrest. ''I know you're worried. So am I. But Harley's used to looking out for herself.''

''I know, but I like looking out for her. She's my wife, I love her, and besides, she's—''

The phone jangled. Jake swung his gaze toward it, hoping the caller would bring news of his runaway wife.

Charlie reached over the end table, shoving the television remote out of the way to grab the receiver. ''Hello? Harley! Where the hell are you, kid?''

Jake sank down onto the sofa, relief flooding his entire body. If she could talk on the phone, she was okay.

''What? Of course I'll come for you.''

Jake's muscles tensed again, his relief short-lived. Why did she need someone to come for her? Had her truck broken down beyond her repair abilities or what? That scenario was a little hard to believe, but he preferred it to some of the others his imagination had created.

''Let me talk to him. Yes, this is Charlie Rafferty. No, I'm just a good friend. Yes, I can come and get her. Where exactly are you? That's a few hours from here. Be there as soon as possible. She's okay, right? What happened?'' He cocked his head and listened intently for several minutes. ''What? Damn. All right. Thank you, Sheriff.''

Jake shot back to his feet. "*Sheriff?* My God, is she okay? What's going on?"

The older man slowly hung up the phone. Fire blazed in his eyes as he glared at Jake. "You didn't tell me she was pregnant. Neither did she. What exactly is going on between the two of you?"

"It's a very long story, Charlie."

"Well, we'll have plenty of time because we've got a very long ride ahead of us. I want all the details."

"Is she okay?"

"No, she's not okay. If she was okay, she wouldn't need us to come and get her."

The blood rushed from Jake's head and his heart thumped against his ribs. "She's hurt?"

"I didn't say that."

"Where is she?"

"Across the state line in Georgia. In jail."

Jake's knees buckled and he sank down into the overstuffed cushions of the rattan sofa. "Would you mind repeating that?"

The old man rose from his chair and pulled his keys from the pocket of his faded jeans. "What's the matter, boy, you got a hearing problem? I said she's in jail. Now, let's go and claim her." He arched a bushy white eyebrow. "Unless you got a problem with that?"

Jake shook his head. "No. I don't care where she is. I just want her back."

"You wanna know what the charges are?"

"No."

"You wanna know if she actually did it?"

"No."

Harley's ex-parole officer rubbed his whiskery chin and nodded. "You'll do, boy, you'll do. Let's go get her."

THE STORY ABOUT HIS DESIRE for a child, the failed adoption attempts, his arrangement with Harley and their marriage at her insistence had nearly gotten him tossed out of Charlie's old Lincoln somewhere in northern Florida. Only Jake's revelation about how he'd fallen in love with Harley and wanted her by his side for the rest of his life had saved his ass from one hell of a long hike.

"There's Harley's truck." Jake pointed to the silver Toyota parked beside the small backwater sheriff's office. Two patrol cars flanked the front entrance.

How was she holding up? How would she react to seeing him? Jake yanked on the door handle as Charlie pulled to a stop in the gravel parking lot.

"Easy now, boy. Don't go rushing in half cocked. You'll get yourself and Harley into worse trouble that way." Charlie laid a restraining hand on Jake's arm. "She needs you to be calm."

Jake took a deep breath, feeling anything but calm. "You're right." With that, he jumped from the car and slammed the door.

The cement on the corner of the building had crumbled; the weathered paint was peeling. Charlie was one step behind him as they entered the sheriff's office.

A large wooden desk loaded with papers and a computer sat in the middle of the room; two other similarly laden desks lined the far right wall. A private office was off to the left, Sheriff embossed in gold lettering on the frosted glass. Jake guessed that the metal door just behind the main desk led to the cells—and to Harley.

If not for the computers, he'd have sworn they were in Andy Griffith's station.

A young deputy pushed back from behind the far desk and rose to his feet. "Can I help you folks?" A nasty black-and-blue bruise covered the young man's cheekbone.

"I'm Jake Manning. You're holding my wife, Harley Emerson."

The deputy's tanned face lost its color. "I'll get the sheriff for you."

Short with an ample stomach that spilled over the belt of his khaki uniform, the sheriff ambled from his office a moment later. Jake wanted to grab the man and hurry him up.

"Sheriff, this here's Mr. Manning. It's his wife we're holding." The deputy gave Jake a strange look, then glanced away.

"And I'm Charlie Rafferty. I'm the one Harley called." Charlie extended his hand to the sheriff.

"Mr. Manning? Well, now, that explains why we didn't find a phone listing for Emerson in Erie. Shoulda been looking for Manning. Pleased to meet you both." The sheriff shook their hands. "I'm Sheriff Cyrus McKenna."

The slow pace of Southern hospitality grated on Jake's nerves. Next, the man would be offering them lemonade on the veranda. "Can I see my wife now?"

"Well, I'd like to explain things afore you go back and see her." McKenna scowled at the deputy. "Jimmy Ray, you need to go on patrol."

"Uh, yes, sir…Sheriff." The young man edged past Charlie, but stopped, turning his hat in his hands just as he got to Jake. "Sir, I'm right sorry for what hap—"

"Now, Jimmy Ray!"

Jimmy Ray jumped, crammed his brown felt hat on his head, then darted out of the building with one final glance over his shoulder.

The sheriff sighed as the door clattered shut. "He's a good kid, but he's got a lot to learn."

Charlie snorted. "I know what you mean."

"Gentlemen, let's have a seat in my office." McKenna gestured toward the frosted window.

"I don't suppose I could convince you to let me see my wife first?" Jake asked plaintively. A strange sense of despondency had fallen over him once they'd walked into the jail. He could only imagine how Harley was feeling.

"Nope."

"Didn't think so." Jake settled onto the edge of a chair in front of the sheriff's oversize oak desk. "All right, what are the charges, Sheriff?"

The sheriff's wooden chair creaked as the portly man lowered himself into it, reminding Jake of Ned and the day he'd met Harley. How far they'd come since then.

"I'm willing to drop the charges, son, provided your wife will sign a paper indicating she won't press any charges of her own, or file any lawsuits."

"What?" Jake leaned forward. "I'm sure she'd be happy to do that. So, why didn't you just have her sign the damn paper and let her go?"

Charlie again placed a calming hand against Jake's forearm. "Remember what I told you in the car." He shifted in his chair. "Sheriff, why don't you tell us exactly what happened."

"I've been out of town for the holidays—else you woulda got a call afore today. I only just got back this morning. That's when I found out what happened."

Jake's fingers beat a quick cadence on the arm of his chair.

"You got to remember Jimmy Ray's just an eager young buck. Seems he pulled your lady over for doing sixty-nine in a sixty-five."

"Sheriff, most of the time that wouldn't even be good for a ticket, let alone a trip to the slammer."

McKenna nodded. "I know, but this was New Year's Eve. Gotta be watchful, you know."

"The fact that she had northern plates didn't help, either, did it?" Jake murmured.

Charlie glared at him.

The sheriff ignored his comment. "Jimmy Ray, being the overeager pup he is, checked her out using that damn new-fangled computer he carts around in his car, and he found out she had a record.''

Jake stopped tapping his fingers. The court's mistake seemed destined to plague her forever. He didn't give a damn about it, but this was going to be yet another setback.

"He ordered her out of the vehicle and conducted a search—with her permission, of course. Now, while your wife weren't real pleased with that, it weren't until Jimmy Ray decided to frisk her that things got ugly.''

Jake's blood ran cold, then fired with indignation as he imagined the young deputy's hands on Harley's body. Her pregnant body. "What happened?''

"Your wife took affront to something Jimmy Ray said or did, and she hauled off and popped him one. He surely weren't expecting a pregnant woman to do something like that. Anyway, he was damn mad at that point, and he arrested her for assaulting an officer of the law.''

"Harley isn't prone to fits of violence, Sheriff,'' Charlie insisted. "I've known her for years, and I worked with a lot of cons before and after her. She's the only one I still have contact with, the only one I consider a friend. That ought to tell you something. In the scenario you've described, I can think of only one thing that might have set her off. We both know there can be a fine line between frisking and groping. Does your deputy generally have a problem when he's got his hands on detained females?''

McKenna's bulbous nose and cheeks flushed.

Jake's hands curled into fists and he jumped from his chair. The SOB had molested her on the pretense of doing his job. "I want to see my wife *now!*"

"Listen, son, I do not have to drop these charges. They're valid. Jimmy Ray's wearing the bruise to prove 'em. So, if you want to get hot under the collar with me, you just go ahead."

Shaking his head, Charlie grabbed Jake's arm. "Sit down."

Teeth gritted tightly, Jake sank back into the chair, glaring at McKenna. He struggled to regain enough control to talk without getting himself—and Harley— into a deeper hole. "All right," he muttered. "So your deputy got too familiar with my wife's body, she clocked him, he arrested her. I still don't understand why you didn't just ask Harley to sign whatever you wanted this morning and send her on her way. Why did we have to come up here and get her?"

McKenna leaned back and folded his hands over his belly. "Well, now, that's where things get a little sticky. The second Jimmy Ray fastened the handcuffs on her, your wife just kinda shut down on us. Took her right to remain silent a little too seriously. She didn't say nary a word until this morning, and I think that's only 'cause I told her we were fixin' to send her over to the hospital in the next county for a psychological test if she didn't perk up a bit.

"Truly, son, and I'm sorry to say it, but your wife ain't in no condition to drive herself any distance. Now, I did have Doc Freidly come round and examine her, just to be sure everything was fine. He said physically she's all right, it's just emotional.''

Jake eased forward in his chair again, his heart in a whirlwind. "She's pregnant, we're having problems, your deputy assaulted her and she's locked up in jail! I'd say that entitles her to being emotional, wouldn't you?"

"You got to admit, shutting down ain't a usual response. She called her friend here, and then she wouldn't say another word. All she's done since Jimmy Ray brought her in is hum."

"Hum?" Charlie asked. "I don't think I've ever heard Harley hum. What's she hum?"

"'I'll Be Home for Christmas.' Over and over again. Real soft-like, but that's the only thing she did. Didn't even cry."

Jake's heart seized. *I'll Be Home for Christmas.* The very song he'd hummed repeatedly during their holiday. *Hang on, sweetheart, you'll be home before you know it.* He stood. "Please, Sheriff, let me see her now. We'll sign whatever papers you want, just let me take her out of here."

Charlie nodded. "I'll go over the papers, Jake. You tend to Harley."

The sheriff shoved his chair back. "Come on." He unlocked the outer solid-metal door, then handed Jake a key. "This will open the cell. The main door's still gonna be locked. Bang when you're ready to come out."

Jake accepted the key and entered the holding area. A faint locker-room scent permeated the air. The steel door clanged shut behind him. Four cells lined the wall. Harley lay on a cot in the first one. The rest were empty.

She hadn't stirred at the sound of the door. Jake moved quickly, fumbling with the key. "Harley?"

Still no response. She lay on her side with her knees drawn up as far as she could manage. Her hair hung loose, some of it cascading over her face as though sheltering her from the bleak reality of the cell. She wore her own clothes, including the green plaid flannel shirt she'd worn the night they'd made love near the tree. Only socks covered her feet, her sneakers neatly placed on the floor beside the cot. The shoelaces were missing.

Missing shoelaces. Loose hair.

They'd been afraid she'd harm herself.

Obviously they didn't know Harley Emerson very well. She was a survivor.

But she looked so forlorn, so alone. He wanted her never to feel alone again.

Jake jiggled the key in the lock. Still no results. "Harley? Wake up, sweetheart, it's time to get the hell out of here and go home."

Somewhere in the foggy realm between sleep and waking, Harley heard Jake's voice calling her name. She wrapped her arms tighter around herself and tried to drift back into the dream. Dreams were the only thing she had left of him....

"Harley! Wake up!"

The scrape of a key in the lock reached her ears,

followed by a string of muttered curses the likes of which she'd never heard from his mouth.

No, no, no! It couldn't be.

Harley's Law. Just when you think your life is the worst it can possibly be, fasten your seat belt.

She opened her eyes and peered through the curtain of hair to see Jake struggling with the key to her cell door. Her heart sank. Of all the things she never wanted him to see, this ranked at the top of the list.

Where was Charlie? And how the hell had Jake found her?

Maybe if she ignored him, he'd go away.

She felt an itch on the bottom of her left foot and scratched it with the toes of her right.

"Ah, good. At least now I know you're alive in there."

She rolled onto her other side, presenting him with her back.

He laughed. The man actually had the audacity to laugh. "Don't think that's going to work. That's just a silent version of your talking-in-circles trick, and it doesn't work on me anymore."

"Go away, Jake. I don't want you here. In fact, I don't want you anywhere near me, or didn't you get that message?"

"Oh, I got the message, all right. The one where you said you loved me—"

"I lied."

"And how wonderful I am."

"Go away!"

The key noises stopped. "I'm not going anywhere without you, Harley."

Her chest tightened and her nose tingled. Finally a white knight had ridden to her rescue, and she couldn't have him. Why didn't he understand she wasn't any good for him? Well, if this didn't convince him, nothing would. She rolled back over, sat up on the cot and flipped her hair over her shoulder. "Did you come to see the animal in the cage, Jake? Take a good, long look at the mother of your child. Here she is, behind bars. Imagine what the Spandlers would have to say about this."

"The hell with the Spandlers! I don't give a damn what they think, or anyone else, for that matter. As far as I'm concerned, you had every right to clock that guy, and I'm damned proud you did."

"You're crazy!" She kicked her sneaker across the cell.

"Crazy about you."

Harley clambered to her feet. "I'm a menace to you! And to our baby! I have nothing to offer either of you!"

Jake grabbed the cell bars in his hands. "You could offer us yourself, your love. That's more than enough."

"I'm...I'm not good enough for you, Jake."

"Ah, Harley." He shook his head. "I think you're the one who has the problem with forgiving and forgetting your past."

"I'm branded by it for life, Jake, even though I didn't do it. I didn't commit that crime. But Ned fired me because of it. I'll never get a decent business job, not even with the most outstanding college degree. And that damn deputy made up his mind about me based on my conviction." She shuddered.

"Harley, look at me," he commanded.

She lifted her gaze from the floor to meet his.

"I'm here for you. I've flown a thousand miles and spent hours riding in a car with a cranky old man grilling me about my intentions toward you. I love you. I love you exactly the way you are."

"Why? Nobody, not even Charlie, has ever loved me the way I am."

"You're wrong about that. He does." Jake leaned closer to the bars and spoke softly. "And I love you because you've got guts and spunk and a wonderful sense of humor. You've taught me to slow down and enjoy things. I love that underneath your tough exterior is a tender heart."

Harley's nose started to drip, and she snuffled.

"Sweetheart, I asked you this question once before. I want you to really think before you answer me this time. What's your dream? I mean your absolute have-it-all dream."

A tear slid down her cheek. "To be part of a real family. To have a place where I belong, a place for always, where no one will ever make me leave."

"I can give you that, Harley. I didn't make you leave, sweetheart. I didn't return you."

"It's only a matter of time. I won't measure up. I'm not good enough."

His face became harder, more stern. "I'll be the

judge of who's good enough for me.'' The lines around his eyes softened again. ''Harley, you are a unique woman. The most special woman I've ever known. I said I wouldn't beg, but I lied. If that's what it takes, I'll beg.'' He sank to his knees, still clutching the bars. ''I'm begging. I love you. Come home with me and let's make a real family.''

The sight of him on his knees almost convinced her. Surely a man who would travel all this way and grovel like that had to be sincere, not merely offering pretty words and empty promises. A man who professed his love on his knees to a woman in a jail cell was truly a special man. ''You really love me?''

''Yes!''

''Even if I'm a mechanic?''

Jake laughed. ''It was never *me* that had a problem with your being a mechanic, it was *you*.''

''But the day we made the agreement, you said a garage was no environment for an expectant woman....''

''Right, an *expectant* woman. I just didn't think it would be good for the baby if you were in that tiny oil-change shop all day with those chemicals and the exhaust. It had nothing to do with you being a mechanic. Why waste good talent?''

A tentative smile tugged at her lips. ''You just want someone to keep the Mustang in shape.'' He loved her. The real Harley.

''Absolutely. Imagine all the money I can save with my own in-house mechanic. Actually, I've been thinking...maybe you should put this new business degree you'll be getting to work running your own shop. Harley's Hot Rods.'' He winked at her. ''Has a nice ring, don't you think?''

''It does.'' A tiny bit of uncertainty still nagged at her. ''You *sure* you want me?''

''Yes!'' He grinned at her. ''Can I tempt you with chocolate cake?''

''Only if it has a file in it.''

His laughter washed over her, warming her, comforting her. ''I've got better than that, I've got the key.'' He rose to his feet and dangled the metal key by its ring. ''I just can't get it to work.''

Harley retrieved her sneakers and slipped them on her feet, then moved over to the bars. She reached through to grab for him.

The key clattered to the floor. Passing his hands through the bars at different levels, he wrapped one around her waist and caressed her cheek with the other. ''God, Harley, I thought I'd never touch you again.'' He released her and sank to one knee this time. ''Harley Emerson, will you be my real wife and the mother of my child?''

Her lower lip quivered. ''But...but I might hurt her.''

''Don't be ridiculous. Mel told me it's not the first time Grace ate crayons or the first time she's hit Hope. And you're not the only one to have a baby fall while in your care.''

''Really?''

''Do you think Mel's a good mother?''

''Yes.''

"When Grace was seven months old, she fell off the changing table. Mel felt guilty as hell for weeks. Harley, kids don't come with instruction manuals like cars do."

"I noticed."

"It's a learn-as-you-go deal. I thought you mechanics were good at hands-on work?"

Harley stared down at him. *Grab it, grab the dream, and don't ever let go!* "We are. Wanna see?"

Jake shot to his feet, the key in his fingers. "I sure do."

She took it from him. Inserting it into the lock, she lifted the door upward while turning it. The click as the bolt released satisfied her more than any other thing she'd ever heard—except her husband's avowal of love. She stepped out of the cell and into his arms.

Clasping her hands behind his back, she pressed her face into his chest. This was love, being there for someone at the worst of times. This was the home she'd sought for so long—in his strong, loving arms.

Jake drew her as close as possible. He stroked her back, ran his fingers through her hair.

She looked up at him, green eyes sparkling. "I love you, Jake."

He closed his eyes for a moment. A lump swelled in his throat, but he swallowed it. He looked down at her, tracing her chin with his fingertips. "I love you, too, Harley. I didn't think I'd ever hear you say that to me."

She nuzzled his palm with her lips. "I mean it. They're not just pretty words."

"I know that." He brushed his mouth across her forehead, then leaned down to crush her lips in a powerful, soul-baring kiss. Her warm, receptive response stoked the flames within him. Reluctantly, he broke away from her. "You ready to go home?"

"Actually, I was hoping to visit with Charlie first."

"Your wish is my command." He kissed the tip of her nose. "Just promise me one thing, Harley."

"What's that?"

"Promise you'll never leave me again."

She held his face between her hands. "Promise you'll never ask me to?"

He nodded. "I promise."

"So do I." She touched her mouth to his. "Sealed with a kiss. There's just one more thing...."

"What's that?"

"Can I...I want to be a Manning, too."

"Ah, Harley." She'd probably never know how much that statement meant to him, perhaps even more than her declaration of love. She wanted his name. "Of course you can be a Manning. I'd be proud if you were a Manning."

Jake felt a nudge against his belly and he glanced down at Harley's stomach. He reached between them and caressed the place where his child—their child—moved. "I think the baby agrees."

Harley removed her hands from his face and joined them with his. "What can I say? Peanut's already a smart kid."

"I hope she's a girl," he whispered. "A girl who's just like her mom."

Her eyes glistened. ''Oh, Jake...''

He placed his arm around her shoulder and guided her to the metal door, hammering against it with his fist. ''Let us out! We're ready to go home!''

''Home.'' Harley sighed.

Jake tightened his grip on her. ''You won't just be home for Christmas next year, sweetheart. You're going to be home forever.''

EPILOGUE

"AAAAGH." SWEAT BEADED on Harley's forehead and trickled down her face.

"Nine, ten." Jake lowered her to the birthing-room bed. "Relax, Harley. You're doing great." He'd be doing better if she'd release the death grip she had on his left hand. He wiped a damp cloth across her forehead with his free hand, then stroked her arm. "Relax everything, Harley. Relax your fingers."

She let go of his hand and opened her eyes. "You get in this bed and try to relax, mister."

Jake smiled at her while he wiggled his fingers in a covert attempt to restore circulation. "The bed looks fairly comfortable."

"Then get in it, let me fold you up in a position that would make a gymnast cry, and while you're at it, you can drive a Volkswagen through your—"

"Harley!" Jake's face grew hot.

The nurses laughed.

"That's a perfect way of putting it, honey," quipped the red-haired nurse assisting the doctor.

Harley's eyes widened, then her nostrils flared as she dragged in a deep breath.

Jake knew that expression and what it meant. He

pulled on her arms, bracing her in an upright position. "All right, push, Harley!" He started counting.

She struggled in his arms. "I can't, I can't!" she wailed. "I can't do it anymore! I changed my mind, you can have your own baby!"

Dr. Hansen's chuckle was muffled by his mask. "It's a little late now to change your mind, Harley. You can do this. Come on, push."

Jake lowered his mouth to her ear. "You can do it. Come on, don't you want to find out if you're right about Peanut? I think he's going to shock you and turn out to be a boy."

Harley grabbed for his hand and squeezed as she bore down, laboring to bring their baby into the world. Jake winced at the pressure but knew better than to say a word.

"That's it, good! The baby's crowning, Harley!" Dr. Hansen reported.

A few more contractions and intensive effort on Harley's part, and the doctor announced that the baby's head was born.

"Forget the head, get the rest of her out here!" Harley gasped.

The birthing room erupted in laughter.

"Almost, Harley. Just a little more," the doctor soothed. "I've got the shoulders. Now, just one more push."

"Aaaaagh." The sound, wrenched from Harley, ended on a note of relief.

Jake glanced down to watch their child enter the world.

"It's a girl!" Dr. Hansen said. "You were right all along, Mom." He placed the wriggling, crying baby on Harley's stomach.

Jake's heart kicked against his ribs. Life would never be the same from this moment on. They had a daughter. He was a daddy. The thin, piercing wail of his child was the sweetest sound he'd ever heard.

"Peanut." Harley sighed and reached out a tentative finger toward the infant. "Happy birthday."

The nurses swooped in to claim the baby for cleaning, weighing and all the other necessary medical steps, promising a speedy return to the new mother.

Harley slumped back in the bed. Jake brushed a sweat-soaked tendril of hair from her forehead, then leaned over to kiss her.

She smacked him. "Get away from me with those lips. Those lips are nothing but trouble."

He ignored her, placing another kiss on her forehead. "Thank you, Harley, for giving me the most wonderful gift in the world."

Her face softened. "No, thank *you*. I can't believe it's true. I'm part of a family now."

"Daddy and baby, and Mommy makes three."

She smiled at him. "I guess that's not the order most people would do it, but then, we're not most people, are we?"

"Definitely not."

Harley rested as much as possible while the doctor took care of the final procedures, including a few stitches. Jake averted his gaze for that, grimacing empathetically. The nurse came back with their daughter swaddled in a pink blanket. "Here you go, Mom. Eight pounds, two ounces, and twenty inches long." She carefully placed the bundle in Harley's arms.

The panicked look returned to Harley's face.

"It's okay, Harley. You're not going to break her."

"You want to put her to the breast now, honey?" the nurse asked. "It's a good time to start."

Harley nodded. The nurse helped her pull down the shoulder of the gown she wore and then position the baby. After a few false starts, the baby latched on and began to suckle.

Harley turned wide eyes to Jake. "Amazing."

He bent closer to gently stroke the silky skin of his newborn daughter's cheek. The tiny muscles moved beneath his finger as she nursed. "It sure is. She's smart and beautiful, just like her mom."

"Do you have a name picked out for her, or do I need to haul out the name book from the nurse's station?" The red-haired nurse looked quizzically from Jake to Harley.

They hadn't been able to agree on one yet. "Well, I think Mercedes is the perfect name."

Harley shot daggers at him. "That's not funny, Jake."

"Why not? Why can't a mom named Harley have a baby named Mercedes? It's pretty."

"Because Harleys and Mercedes don't go together. Trust me. You wanna name her Toyota? Maybe Mustang would be good?"

"Okay, Harley, I get the point." Jake couldn't tear

his eyes from the sight of his wife, nursing their newborn.

"I want her to have a feminine name. Something pretty, but not too unusual." Harley ran a fingertip over the baby's downy hair, a light strawberry-blond fuzz. "Peanut, what's your name? Can't call you Peanut all the time." The baby waved a tiny fist in the air. "I know! Jennifer. When I was a kid, I always wanted to be Jennifer. And we'll call her Jenni. J-e-n-n-i. It's pretty, and it's different, but not too different."

"Jenni." Jake smiled. "Jenni Manning. I like it." He gingerly touched his daughter's head. "Now I have to go and tell the rest of our family. They've probably taken over the waiting room."

"Our family." Harley sighed and smiled, tears welling in her eyes. "Yes, go tell our family. And call Charlie. Then, while you're at it, tell Dusty he owes me twenty."

"Twenty? Did he bet Peanut was going to be a boy?"

"No, he bet you'd end up face-first on the floor. I told him that would never happen, that you'd be at my side, taking care of me."

Jake planted another kiss on Harley's forehead. "You know it. Always."

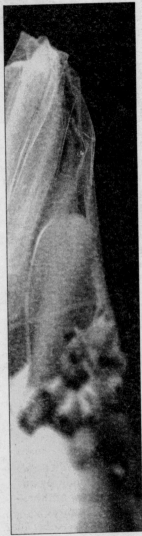

HARLEQUIN Super ROMANCE®

The Healer
by Jean Brashear

Diego Montalvo's life changed forever after the
Special Forces mission that nearly killed him.
Now a *curandero*—healer—whose healing tradition
calls into question everything that cardiac surgeon
Caroline Malone believes, he may be her key to
regaining the career that's her life. Except,
success in healing means losing each other.
Because he can't leave his home in West Texas…
and she can't stay.

*Look for more
Deep in the Heart
Superromance titles
in the months to come!*

**Heartwarming stories with
a sense of humor,
genuine charm and emotion
and lots of family!**

*On sale starting
January 2003 from
Harlequin Superromance.*

*Available wherever
Harlequin books are sold.*

HARLEQUIN®
Makes any time special ®